A DOSE OF BRIMSTONE

Van Helsing Organization Book 2

NOREE COSPER

Copyright © 2015 by Noree Cosper
All rights reserved.
No part of this book may be reproduced in any form or by any electronic or
mechanical means, including information storage and retrieval systems,
without written permission from the author, except for the use of brief
quotations in a book review.

Book cover design by Rebecca Frank.
http://rebeccafrank.design/

Editing services by Pauline Nolet. Proofreading services by Wayne Scace,
Amanda Kuzma, and Cassie Hess-Dean.

Visit Noree Cosper's Website

As Oulixes sat on the bench, he crossed the ankles of the man he possessed and leaned against the wall. Bits of the crumbling brick ground away into his hair. The humans had abandoned this part of the Subway tunnels decades ago, but that didn't mean the place was empty.

An immaterial woman in a long coat passed by him and stopped on the edge of the platform. One foot dangled over the edge before she completely disappeared. In a few moments, she would be back to repeat the process all over again. The woman, like the other apparitions on this platform, were just imprints, mere memories of what had tainted this railway station. Mostly harmless, and useless, unlike a real soul.

He raised a hand. His true hand, dark blue and clawed, was semi-imposed over the mortal flesh. It held a spiked chrome chain that extended through the wall and beyond his sight. The chain, like his true form, existed beyond the material world, and it connected to a human soul; one that he had a claim on. He smiled, relishing the memory of how he had gained this particular contract. It hadn't been easy, or legal, but Oulixes didn't have to deal in legal. The mother had been desperate to stop her daughter's abuse at the hands of her husband. She never even thought about the deal she made. A drunken woman was all but useless to him. The daughter, however, a soul of innocence, that was a prize that many demons dreamed of obtaining. Only he could. Well, he and his other selves.

Light filled the arched tunnels, causing Oulixes to blink. Booted feet clacked on the steps to his right. He straightened and watched the man descend. Highlights reflected in his white-blond hair from the lamps in the ceiling. He looked a little thin in the long black coat he wore. His red lips twitched to one side in a smirk as he crossed his arms and looked Oulixes up and down.

"Are you the broody one of us?" The man's smooth voice echoed through the forsaken halls. "Sitting here in the dark?"

Oulixes stood so that he towered over the thin man. "I'm the one who will strip the flesh from the bones of that body you ride."

The incubus smirked. "I doubt Faust would allow that. Not when you have a package to deliver to me."

Oulixes gritted his teeth. The seed at the core of his essence kept him from ripping that arrogant face apart. He had a mission. "Let's get this over with."

The incubus held out his hand, and Oulixes slid the chain into it. The chrome color shimmered and lightened, taking on a purple tint. The incubus ran a tongue over the chain and sucked in the breath.

"Succulent," he said. "Such anger. I bet she's wild in bed."

"All yours to test out now," Oulixes muttered.

He narrowed his eyes. Now that the exchange was over, he could rip into this little weasel and claim the power for his own. The pressure within him thrummed, sending jolts through his essence like the lash of a whip. No. That wasn't part of the plan. He gritted his teeth, pushed past the incubus, and headed up the stairs. In just a few feet, he would be above ground and on his way to claim other souls. He didn't need the jaded, angry girl's contract. Her soul had become bitter with the realization of her fate. The incubus was welcome to her for whatever plans Faust had. He could find someone else pure and spend his time breaking them.

At the top of the stairs, instead of an exit, a decaying brick tunnel stretched out before him. He stopped and blinked. What in the Seven Thrones? He spun around and let out a guttural curse. The stairs had been replaced with the tunnel as well. His steps echoed off the stone surrounding him as he quickened his pace. He must have gotten confused. Human architecture was mind boggling to him with its materialistic laws and strange angles, but there had to be another turn or a door somewhere. If not, he could always abandon this body and find another not trapped in this underground pit. He sighed loudly, relieved to see another turn ahead. But as he rounded the corner, he realized this new tunnel stretched out beyond both the range of the body's eyes and his own perception.

Oulixes growled and slammed his fist into the bricks. The walls shook with the force of his blow and the stone beneath his fist crumbled into bits of rubble as dust sprayed into the air. Once the air cleared of the particles, a hole the size of his head revealed a passageway identical to the one he was currently in, including a hole on the opposite wall. He took a step back as his mouth went dry, and he scanned the tunnel. Someone was playing games with him. He felt their eyes on him, and he shuddered. He'd been in this body for too long.

A sharp pain burst in his abdomen, spreading past the physicality of his body to his own essence, and his hold on the human he rode slipped.

Iron.

The tunnel broke away into little bits of dust and darkness before it dissolved. Oulixes stood in the subway station with its vaulted ceilings and ghosts. In front of him stood the incubus with his hand on the iron dagger buried deep in Oulixes.

"I think any value you had is gone," the incubus said. "I can find a better use for that piece of Faust you carry."

Oulixes dropped his control on the body and let his essence pour out of it in a dark red light. The incubus flashed in a pale purple light and caught Oulixes. He inhaled, and Oulixes felt himself being drawn in. He tried to fight, but the iron had already weakened him. He couldn't escape. Soon, he knew nothing.

On a normal night I would have been chasing a demon down with my sword in hand, not standing in line outside of a club with the bass of the music pounding into the bricks against my back. My definition of normal was skewed from most people.

I shivered and hugged my arms to my body as a gust of wind pummeled me, forcing me to spread my legs to keep my balance. My knee high white boots did little to warm me. I'd bought them on a whim weeks ago, even though I would have very few occasions to wear them. Tonight was such a night. I was here to do a little business and have a lot of enjoyment. Besides, they went well with the white, V-neck mini dress that accented my black hair.

Esais stepped in front of me, and I breathed a sigh of relief as the blustery assault abated by the wall that was his tall, broad-shouldered frame. He grinned at me with a boyish smile and brushed a lock of his cinnamon hair out of his face. Tres winked at the three girls standing in front of us. They burst into giggles and whispered amongst themselves as their gazes drank him in. It was no surprise. Michelangelo himself could have sculpted the boy's face with those high cheekbones and smooth skin. Many girls had found his full lips kissable in the last three months. Adrian stood in the rear of our group with his back to us, his ponytail, the same color as his brothers', brushed against the back of his long black coat as he scanned the line behind us. Marge stood beside me, tapping her foot out of time with the beat that pounded through the door of the club. She shoved her hands in the pockets of her maroon leather jacket and the tips of her blonde hair blew into her face as she turned to glare at me.

"Why here?" Marge's voice cracked the cold night air like a whip.

"Lucy's idea." I wrapped my arms around myself. "She wanted to celebrate her reunion with the boys."

Esais adjusted his square glasses. "We're not boys, Gabby."

"Lucy still thinks so," I said.

"Who gives a damn about them," Marge said. "Why am I here?"

"Well, do you have any new leads about your contract?"

She snorted. "Not since I found out that Oulixes died."

"Lucy can find the new demon that has your contract."

Marge let out a low growl and stared ahead. I didn't blame her. She only had a few more years until a demon claimed her body and soul for a contract she didn't make. Such a thing shouldn't have happened since the person who owned the soul was the only one who could sell it, but here we were. Marge's mother had tried to protect her in some misguided way, but it had just made Marge's predicament worse.

"Just have some fun, Marge," Tres said. "Even Adrian came."

Adrian glanced at his brother with his good eye. What was left of his other eye was covered by a black leather patch. He stood six feet tall—shorter than his brothers but still enough to tower over me—and a reddish beard ran along his jawline and connected with a thin mustache.

"If I didn't, Lucy would pout," he said.

Tres pulled down the sleeves of his grey suit jacket and smirked. "She probably just wants to have a few drinks, and then the night is ours."

The bouncer's muscles bulged underneath his black t-shirt as he waved us forward. I swaggered in. The blue and purple search lights flashed throughout the club. A glass dance floor hovered over a pool of water, lit so it gave a wave effect off the walls. Fast music pounded as a sea of bodies gyrated. One long bar lined the walls around the dance floor. Metal stairs led to the second floor.

Marge scowled and rubbed her ear. "How long do we have to be here?" she yelled.

I scanned the crowd. Dancing on top of one of the raised platforms in the middle of the dance floor was a girl with black pigtails. She wore a white shirt cut to her midriff that closed by only one button. The purple bra was visible through the shirt even in this light. She wore a short, black skirt with ripped purple tights underneath. Knee-high black combat boots completed her ensemble. Her arms were raised above her head as she bounced up and down to the music. I pointed her out to Marge.

"Her," I said.

Marge did a double take. "You've got to be shitting me."

"She's not," Tres said. "Lucy's always been a party girl. I bet she's wild under the covers."

I shuddered. "That's disturbing on many levels."

"What?" Tres asked. "I can't enjoy the beauty of a woman?"

"She's like our big sister," Esais said.

"She probably changed your diapers," I said.

Adrian raised a brow. "She would have been a child then."

Esais frowned, his eyes going distant as if he was trying to catch hold of a memory eluding him. They didn't know about Lucy. Interesting that she and Jonah had kept their secrets despite being almost family to the Van Helsings. With everyone meeting in New York, and given Esais's unique abilities, I doubted it would stay a secret for long.

Lucy glanced in our direction, and our gazes met. A grin spread across her face. She hopped off of the platform and pushed her way through the dancers. She bounded up the stairs and practically threw herself into Esais. Her arms wrapped around his shoulders, and she laughed.

"It's so good to see you," she said.

He grinned, hugging her tight. "Hey, Lu."

She pulled away and turned to Tres. "Hey there. Look at you all grown up and sexy."

Tres gave me a look as if to say *"you see?"* before spreading his arms out for a hug. She pulled him close before turning to Adrian.

"You look better outside your cage," she said. "I'm glad you broke free."

He chuckled, giving her a kiss on the cheek. "I was only waiting for the right time. Ms. Di Luca provided the right reason."

She glanced at me with a smile. "Hello, dearie. Good to see you again."

I smiled but remained where I was. I didn't want to intrude upon the brothers' reunion with her. "You as well. It's been a few years, hasn't it?"

She nodded. "I think it was that demon in Germany."

"Hmm, that was fun." I pulled Marge forward. "This is Marge Devereux."

"Ah, yes, the one searching for her own demon," Lucy said. "A pleasure to meet you, dearie."

"Yeah, whatever. Where is it?"

Lucy took a step back with a frown. "No need to rush things. How about we enjoy the night and start tomorrow?"

"Not interested. Can you find it or is this another waste of my time?"

"Most likely, I can. However, it would be easier with my cards, which I don't have."

I touched Marge's shoulder. "You can wait one more night. Why don't we visit Lucy tomorrow for a reading?"

Lucy studied Marge for a few moments. "I'll think about it."

"That's it? You'll think about it?" Marge mumbled. "Why the hell am I here at all?"

"I wanted to meet you and get a feel for you before I did a reading," Lucy said.

"So I had to pass some sort of test?"

Lucy winked at her. "Maybe I just wanted to see if you were hot."

Marge scowled and muttered, "Fuck this shit."

Lucy laughed and turned to the brothers as Marge stalked toward the exit. "Let's get a drink. I'm parched."

I stared after Marge. I could try to drag her back, but it would make her angrier. Besides, why should I ruin my night? I would find her later when she calmed down and then try to convince her. I followed behind Lucy as she led us to the closest bartender to order drinks.

He approached and leaned down, his blue-dyed hair fading so that brown roots peeked through. "What can I get you?"

Esais did a double take as Lucy ordered the drinks. His eyes narrowed as he focused on the bartender. Lucy turned and handed me a frozen peach-colored beverage. She waved to the row of shots that sat on the bar for the brothers. She raised a matching drink to mine and downed it. I sipped, wincing at the ache the cold brought to my head but enjoying the peach flavor that mixed with the warm bite of alcohol.

"So tell me all the juicy tidbits," Lucy shouted over the music. "We have a lot to catch up on."

Tres shrugged. "Nothing much, just enjoying the city."

She waggled her eyebrows. "And the girls in it?"

He laughed. "Maybe."

"You need to show me around. You probably know the best clubs, unlike your brother here." She waved her drink in Adrian's direction. "What have you been up to?"

Adrian tapped his fingers on the bar and gave her a smile. "I've been busy with the security system for the new office."

"New office?"

Adrian nodded to Esais. "He decided to take Jonah's words about building our father's dream of a hunter organization seriously. So, we have an office."

Lucy grinned and poked Esais in the side. "Look at you, trying to be all responsible. Please don't say you'll be as boring as Dad."

Esais glanced at her and chuckled. "No one can be as boring as your dad. I just thought we need some place to settle, and New York is a hub—is that the right American word?"

"I get what you're trying to say," Lucy said.

"And they decided to start paying Marge," I said. "Mostly because she didn't want to do anything that didn't concern her demon anyway. So, now they have an employee."

"You're not getting paid then?"

"And be on the same level as Marge?" I threw my head back and laughed. "I have enough of a nest egg."

Mostly from antiques I'd liberated from demons and sold over five centuries, but it ensured I didn't have to find work.

Lucy finished her second drink and grabbed Tres's arm. "Let's dance."

Tres merely laughed as she led him to the dance floor. Adrian stood up with the shake of his head and disappeared into the crowd toward the bathroom. Esais held his full shot glass, still watching the boy behind the bar who had served us our drinks. The boy appeared to be in his mid-twenties and thin, as if he hadn't had a good meal in a month. He leaned against the bar, watching the dancers. The holes in the elbows of his shirt didn't match the artful slashes in the upper sleeves.

"That's your type?" I asked with a raised eyebrow.

He blinked at me. "What?"

"If you're interested, you should go talk to him."

"I, no . . ." He shook his head and laughed. His gaze traveled back to the boy. "There's something different about him. I can sense it."

I narrowed my eyes and studied the boy through my second sight. The world shifted to gray and the landscape was outshone by the rainbow of colors drifting from the dancers. I focused on the boy, blinking at the torrent of colors swirling about him. The aura was a representation of the human soul, and his was a state of desolation. The inky black of despair, livid blue of fear, and a muddy red anger mixed with the azure of loneliness and the burnt sienna of hunger. He didn't have anyone in the world looking out for him. I swallowed the ache in my throat. I'd had several times in my life where I'd been in the same position, lost and alone. Only my need to destroy Allegra had kept me on my path. His aura formed a halo that swirled around his head like gold dust caught in sunlight.

Hmm, I hadn't seen something like that in quite a while. I let my gaze pass over the blur of drunken auras until it came to rest on Lucy as she swayed with the music. She burned bright and blazing with pleasure. Her aura peaked into two spikes at her crown with a red sparkle.

"Well?" Esais asked.

I turned back to him and kept from wincing at the bright golden white light that surrounded his aura. It almost obscured the winged figure that stood behind him. The angel seemed to have grown since the last time I checked, almost as if it had gotten closer. I couldn't stand it any longer. I let my vision return to normal and rubbed my eyes.

"You should talk to him," I said. "He's not tainted or anything, but he's special. And he could use a friend."

"Are you trying to play matchmaker?" he asked, crossing his arms.

I chuckled. "Not anymore. He's in need, and you have a way with people."

He flushed and ran a hand through his hair. I pushed him in the direction of the boy. He glanced back at me with a smile before approaching. I turned back to find myself alone in a sea of strangers. Tres was back at the bar, several seats away, chatting with a young redheaded woman. She batted her eyelashes at him and laughed. He would be lost for the night. Lucy and Adrian were on the dance floor, moving to the music. I chuckled at how Adrian's stiff movements contrasted to Lucy's wild gyrations. She was all head shaking and flinging hair. I frowned. I really needed to talk to her about the bartender, but she would brush me off if I interrupted her. I would have to find a chance tomorrow when she was in a serious mood.

The music beckoned me to the dance floor. Everyone was occupied, and it was time I had some fun of my own. The tense muscles in my shoulders relaxed as I undulated my hips to the quick tempo and let my mind wander.

An angel had gifted Esais with power of telepathy, the same as a spirit had granted me the ability to see souls and other entities. Mine was useful in hunting demons. Actually, all three of the brothers had gifts from different spirits. Lucy and the young bartender were something else. Nephilim. My son might have been one if he had survived long enough. I scrunched my eyes closed and swallowed hard.

"No point in dwelling on what could have been. There's only what is."

The music filled my ears, my pulse pounding in rhythm with it. Fingertips brushed my upper arm, and I spun around. Adrian caught my swinging arm at the wrist. We stared at each other, frozen for a few seconds before he raised our arms. The people around us blurred as he twirled me. We stopped as he pulled me against him. His fingers slid down my arm and over my hips as we began to move to the song. I rested my arm on his shoulder and my gaze locked on his with my heart racing a mile a minute. One corner of his lip lifted.

"What about John?"

There went my head again, acting the voice of reason. The beat shifted as the song changed, and I pulled away from him. He gave me a mock bow, and I curtseyed with a smirk. I slipped through the crowd and grabbed my coat on the way out. I had enjoyed myself enough tonight. Marge's time grew shorter and someone needed to kick her out of her stubbornness. One of us would be going to sleep tonight with a few more bruises.

❧ 2 ❧

The keys jangled in my hand as I opened the door to our office and slipped in. Adrian had complained how easily the keys could be lost. He claimed his new system would eliminate the need for any kind of key access. His project was still unfinished. So, for now, we used the keys.

Adrian. My heart sped up at the thought of his name. What had that been about tonight? Sure, he had stopped resenting me for living while his family died, and had been less antagonistic in the past three months, but I had proven myself against Ose in Texas. I had risked my sanity to rescue Adrian and his brothers from that devil. Over the last few months, Adrian had come to accept me, even found me useful, but I doubted it went any further than that. And what about John? Despite my misgivings, I'd slept with him. Would this change our long friendship? Was he expecting more? I really didn't know since we hadn't seen one another since we parted ways in Texas. I shook my head. I needed to stop mulling over this. A good workout would distract me and help me think with a clearer mind.

I knelt in the corner of the entry hall and ran my finger over the spiral of writing carved into the floor. The angular symbols started tiny in the center and grew larger until the edge of the spiral was the size of a sunflower seed. Each corner of every room held a similar symbol. I chuckled softly. Jonah had blanched at the amount of quicksilver I'd use to paint these devil's traps. He's always had a thing for money and rare alchemical ingredients, and quicksilver was one of the rarest. Most people thought it was another word for mercury, but it wasn't. It held tremendous magical potency. This would make damn sure that no demon or devil stepped foot here.

I passed by the glass doors and walls on either side of me that led into two large rooms. When this building thrived, the left had been a diner. We'd kept the kitchen and added a few tables. We never knew when we would have to work through several days, and to have food onsite was just brilliant. The right had been some sort of store. Tres had gutted the place and turned it into an infirmary with Adrian's help. I walked past the elevator to the stairwell. I wasn't in the mood to deal with that tiny deathtrap, even on the best of days.

When I opened the door to the fourth floor, the thudding of a foot hitting leather and a woman's grunt greeted me. Marge had become predictable in the past month. If she wasn't out roaming the streets in search of her demon, she came here. I slipped into the office we were using as a makeshift changing room and dressed in a pair of shorts and a tank top. The main room had been cleared of the cubicles of the previous occupants and navy blue mats spread over the carpet. Marge worked over one of the three punching bags that hung from the ceiling in the left corner of the room. Along the wall were weight benches and other contraptions that looked as if they belonged in a torture chamber. I grabbed the bag and steadied it as Marge landed a solid kick.

The impact vibrated up my arms. She hopped back, her hands held in a defensive position and her mouth open as she panted. Her eyes narrowed as she leveled a "Go to Hell" glare at me.

"What the fuck was that?" Marge asked. "She made me go to that shithole, just to say no?"

"She said maybe," I said.

"So, this was all some game to her."

"You were being a bitch. Do you expect everyone to take your abuse?"

Marge sneered and slammed her foot into the side of the bag. "Fuck it. I'll do it on my own."

"How long do you have left?" I asked. "Five years?"

A hard kick thudded against the bag.

"When your contract is up, the demons don't kill you. They use your body for whatever they want; they ride you, and there's no way to stop them. Banish them, and your soul goes to Hell with them."

A shock reverberated through my hands and to the rest of my body.

"That is if you manage to live that long. If you die before your contract is up, your soul is claimed."

"I'll figure something out."

I ground my teeth together. Marge constantly grated on me, but I didn't want to see her lost. Unfortunately, it seemed that all she understood was violence. I shoved the bag forward. It caught Marge in the side, and she stumbled back with a grunt.

"Fine," I said. "Reason doesn't work on you. Let's talk in a language you do speak."

I leapt forward, aiming a punch to her gut. She side-stepped and brought her arms up, spreading her legs. "You wanna fight?"

"If you win, you can go and do whatever it is you want with your last years. If I win, we go to Lucy tomorrow."

She smirked. "Let's do this."

"Prepare to have . . . what is the term? 'To have your ass kicked?'" I said.

Marge snorted. "Whatever, Old Lady. Just make sure you don't hurt your back or anything."

Marge walked to the corner of the closest mat. She bounced slightly on the balls of her feet as she brought her fists up. I took my place at the opposite corner and pulled my arms up. I felt more comfortable with a weapon in my hand, but this was just a sparring match. Luckily, Eskrima taught a variety of methods, including barehanded. Marge specialized in Tae Kwon Do, focusing mainly on kicks. I had to watch out for her deadly feet.

We stared at each other across the empty space between us, waiting to see who would break and make the first attack. Marge let out a breath of air with a small kiai and charged me. She leapt into the air and thrust her foot at my chest. I stepped to the side and lowered my shoulder a little. My arm wrapped around the thigh of her extended leg, and I pushed forward. She flipped backwards and landed on the ground.

Without wasting a breath, she rolled up to one knee. Her other leg swung around and caught me in the weak point in the back of my knee. Her momentum knocked my feet out from under me, and I landed flat on my back. She stood up, with her fists raised and a grin on her face.

"Getting slow in your old age," she said.

I rolled away and rose to a crouching position. I lunged at her, staying low, with my elbow pointed out. I connected with her abdomen, and she doubled over with an oomph.

"You waste time gloating," I said. "It makes you slower than these old bones."

She straightened, and we circled each other, scanning for the slightest muscle twitch or twist of foot. Now was my chance. I could take her down if I was fast enough. She wouldn't expect an offensive strike from me. I hopped in, hooked my foot around her left ankle, and jerked. She tumbled backwards, her shoulder slamming into the mat as she hit the ground. I was on her before she could recover, jamming my knee into her throat.

"Dead," I said.

She glared at me but laid her hand flat on the mat in our symbol for submission. I stood up and held my hand out. She pushed herself up and stood, her eyes never meeting mine.

"I'll see you tomorrow," I said as I headed to the door. "Around the bright and early time of noon."

A few moments after I knocked, Lucy flung the door of her hotel room inward. Her hair was a mess with one large tangle lifting the left side several inches away from her face. The eyeliner from the previous night had smudged, giving her two rings like a raccoon. She blinked at us with bleary eyes.

"Oh, hey." She stepped back to let us in. "Welcome."

I whistled as I stepped into the living room. Clothes draped across the back of the peach couch, a blanket lay in a pile on the Persian rug that covered the wood floor, and her leather jacket was tossed over one of the chairs. A movie blared from the television.

"Star Wars?" Marge raised an eyebrow.

"I like it, and I needed something to play while I took a nap." Lucy smiled and rubbed her hands together. "Let's start with some coffee and breakfast."

"We're here for a reading," Marge said.

"Oh, I know, dearie, but I need a bit of a pick me up," Lucy said in her crisp English accent that enunciated the consonants.

I sat on the couch, pushing some of the clothes to the side. "Coffee would be wonderful. Cappuccino if they have it."

"You think they have one to your standards?" Lucy asked.

"It's a five star hotel. What else would your money go to?"

She smirked as she walked to the telephone. "Silk sheets and a maid service."

I waved for Marge to sit down. Her eyes narrowed, traveling from me to Lucy. I tilted my head, raising an eyebrow, and mouthed the word "patience". She sighed, crossed her arms, and began tapping her foot again.

"Well, that's done," Lucy said. "They should be prompt."

"Let's hope so," Marge said.

Lucy sat, turned the volume of the television up, and grabbed a small wooden pipe and lighter. Her crossed feet rested on a stack of magazines on the coffee table as she leaned back, grinning as she watched the movie. She lit the substance in the pipe and inhaled deeply. She blew out a puff of white smoke, and the room filled with a pungent smell, like burning sage.

"Seriously, pot?" Marge crossed her arms.

Lucy held the pipe out. "Want some?"

Marge glared at me. "What the hell?"

Lucy smirked. "It helps me focus."

"If you start babbling in tongues, I'm leaving."

I sighed. Lucy was always a wild one who preferred the baser pleasures of life. Even all the years I had known her, she still hadn't matured. There was a knock on the door. Lucy sprang up and let the bellhop push in a small cart with a coffee pot and two cups. My cappuccino was set separately. I picked it up and took a sip. The warm liquid filled my mouth, and the heady aroma erased the lingering smell of burnt herb.

"Now, let's get down to business," she said once she had a cup of coffee in her hand. "Gabby, can you clear the table?"

I scooped up the magazines and set them on an end table near the wet bar. I threw the empty beer bottles in the small trash bin. Lucy pushed the coffee table to the center of the floor and sat on the floor facing the couch, pulling out her tarot deck. She motioned Marge to sit across from her as she began to shuffle.

The backs of the cards had two rows of symbols. The ones on the left gleamed in white and consisted mostly of connections of lines, triangles, and circles. The row on the right was red and looked more like tribal scrawling. The edges were rounded but held circles. I recognized four of the white symbols from the Hermetic spells I sometimes performed. They were four of the archangels: Michael, Gabriel, Rafael, and Uriel. I stared at the red symbols, especially the one that stuck out the most to me. It looked like a backwards C that had been pressed inward and leaned against a triangle with the point down. In the center of the top curve of the C was a large dot. I knew the symbol for the Throne of Lust well. I'd done almost everything in my power to learn about that particular part of Hell since the demon who cursed me was from there.

"New deck?" I asked.

"Mmmhmm, I drew them myself." Lucy glanced up at Marge. "You need to shuffle. Keep your thoughts on the question you want to ask the cards."

Marge cut the deck in half and flicked her thumb on the edges so that both stacks of cards mixed together. She repeated this a few more times and pushed the cards to the middle of the table. Lucy took the deck and dealt out ten cards face down. The first and second formed a cross in the center of the table. The third was placed below them, the fourth to the left, the fifth above, and the sixth to the right. Cards seven through ten were placed in a vertical line to the right with the seventh on the bottom.

"This is the Celtic Cross," Lucy said. "It's one of the most popular spreads. I like to use this for first timers because it gives me an overall view of the situation at hand."

"So get on with it," Marge said.

Lucy gave a half snort, half sigh and flipped over the first card. It depicted a dark-haired woman in a red Grecian style robe. In her right hand, she held a sword, pointing up, and in her left, she held a set of scales. The card was upside down, facing Lucy.

"Justice," Lucy said. "This card's position represents what is currently influencing you. I'm getting a sense of the injustice that you feel."

Marge snorted. "No shit. My mom sold my soul to a demon."

"This doesn't only imply what happened to you. This is the whole situation. The reverse of Justice could also mean vengeance. You have to be careful not to lose yourself; it's what they want."

Marge glared at her. "Right, because the contract on my soul is nothing. How about you just find my demon so I don't end up as one of Hell's bitches."

"You don't need a contract to end up in Hell. People have been doing that all on their own for centuries." Lucy flipped over the next card. "This represents the obstacles you face."

Her gaze met mine with a deep frown before looking back down at the card. This one I knew personally, though the picture was unique. A woman with hair blacker than a starless night and goat legs perched on a pillar. Her breasts were bare and bat-like wings spread out behind her. In her hand, she held two chains connected to a man and a woman. I shivered at the purple flames in her eyes as she stared up at me with pouty, sensual lips. The Devil. Lucy had drawn this card on the first reading she ever gave me. It spooked her enough that she refused to do another.

"A lot of fortune tellers say this represents the baser desires we must break away from," Lucy said.

"But?" Marge asked.

"But we are all hunters here. I think we all know that real evil affects our lives. I'm getting a feeling that this represents that more than anything else."

"Right, so what does that mean?"

"This demon is going to do everything in its power to stop you."

The next card was a picture of a skyscraper with a cloudy night sky behind it. Flames leapt up from the base of the building and lightning struck the top.

"We are still dealing with your past. This time it's the distant past," Lucy said. "The Tower represents a time of turmoil. Your father's abuse and what your mother did puts us in this situation."

Marge's eyes narrowed at her. "How the hell do you know that?"

"It's my job to know such things."

"Bullshit. You're just some party bimbo who thinks she can see the future."

Lucy chuckled and raised her hands. "You're still sitting here. Where else do you have to go?"

Marge clamped her mouth shut and glared down at the table. Lucy turned over the fourth card. A young man with red brown hair held a wooden staff. His face held a youthful mischievousness.

"The Page of Wands," Lucy said. "This is what is in your recent past and how it influences you now. I would say that meeting the Van Helsing brothers and Gabby will bring you closer to your goal. It already has, right?"

"This isn't shit I don't know," Marge snapped.

"Listen, the first of these cards set up your question.

Besides, I get the feeling that your demon is deeply connected to Gabby and the boys."

Connected to me? How was that even possible? It wasn't like I knew every demon in Hell. The only one I knew that would be connected to me and the Van Helsings was Ose, but he was dead. As far as I knew, the few lackeys he had were with him in Texas, and they had perished by the edge of my sword.

"Let's continue," Lucy said, cutting me off as I opened my mouth.

Marge rolled her eyes, but this time she kept control of her tongue. Lucy flipped the next card. A female angel wearing a golden helmet held a trumpet to her lips.

"Judgment," Lucy said. "Which is apt because that is what you want, freedom from not only the bonds holding you but from your past. The problem is we can never be truly rid of our past. It shapes us."

The sixth card was of five people: a woman with dark hair, a woman with strawberry blonde hair, and three men with cinnamon colored hair. They held staves which crossed in the middle of the picture.

"This card is what the future holds in store for you. The Five of Wands shows there's going to be a lot of conflict. I see several different entities in competition with one another."

"Like others after my demon?" Marge said.

"Or other demons that want you."

"I'm getting tired of all the possibilities."

Lucy shook her head and moved to the next card. It depicted a woman in a chariot driven by two lions. Her blonde hair whipped out behind her. A crazed look filled her face.

"The Chariot. You want this badly, but you need to be careful your ambition doesn't impede you."

"My ambition is to kill this demon. How the hell am I going to fuck that up?"

"You're so busy thinking about killing, you will miss the clues around you. Like this reading."

"I haven't seen any useful shit in this."

Lucy folded her hands in her lap. "If you're going to act like this, we might as well stop now."

"You have three cards left," I said. "What could it hurt to finish it? Less time than wandering the streets."

Marge grumbled. "Fine."

The eighth card was a man with a reddish brown beard and an eye patch over one eye. He wore a dark, hooded robe. Goose-bumps rose over my arms as I stared at the card.

"Lucy, what were you thinking when you drew these?" I asked.

She smiled mysteriously and turned back to Marge. "The Hermit. You also try to keep yourself apart from those who can help you. Remember your cause is their cause."

She turned over the next card and stared at it intently. It was of a wheel divided into quarters. Ringed around it in two circles were the same angelic and demonic symbols as on the backs of the cards. It was reversed.

"There are situations in your life that are coming to a close. I see major changes coming, and not all of them in your favor. Remember that you have weathered other storms, you can weather this one," she said.

"What events?" Marge asked.

Lucy just shook her head. "I'm uncertain exactly what, dearie, but they are major."

The last card was of a tall figure in a black cloak holding a scythe. On the scythe was one of the angelic symbols. It looked like an hourglass with two sickles extended from the middle on each side. One skeletal wing extended from the figure while a white, feathered wing curled behind him.

"Death," Lucy whispered. "Whether you fail or succeed, you're in for a transformation, and it's going to be a difficult one."

Marge stood up. "What kind of bullshit was that? How was that supposed to help?"

"It's supposed to give you insight on what you are up against and what you have aiding you," I said. This was turning out to be a mistake.

"How about giving me a straight answer?"

"Fortune telling is rarely straightforward," Lucy said. "From what I've read, your best bet to getting your demon is connected with Gabby and possibly the Van Helsings. From what Gabby has told me, it probably has something to do with how you met."

"Ose?" Marge frowned. "He didn't have anything to do with my contract."

"But you were still there."

"I was chasing down a lead from that biker gang. A lot of good it did," Marge muttered. "They didn't give me shit useful."

"But you met Gabby and the Van Helsings. Even though you were chasing different demons, or a devil in Gabby's case, you still ended in the same town." Lucy looked at me. "Why don't I do a reading for you to see if we can get a clearer picture?"

My eyebrows rose. This was a change. "You're sure?"

"It's been years. I think I'm better. Besides, these are my special cards."

I took Marge's place as Lucy shifted the cards. Marge paced behind us, muttering to herself. This time, Lucy laid out the cards in a horseshoe pattern from left to right. She flipped over the first card, and a shiver ran through me. The Devil. The image forever haunted me. She frowned at the picture and shook her head.

"Your past. Brought upon by evil," Lucy said.

"Allegra," I said.

"Maybe, there are a lot of others. You've led a life of bloodshed. It still drives you."

"How much of that is from the card."

She chuckled. "I know you. Part of my job is reading the people as well as the cards."

She flipped the next card. It depicted a sword surrounded by rays of light. It was reversed.

"This is your present. The Ace of Swords," she said. "There are a lot of illusions surrounding those around you. You're being played."

The next card depicted a dark-haired man on a throne with a sword in his hand. His face was blurred so that I couldn't quite see the features.

"King of Swords," Lucy said. "There appears to be a strong forceful man in your life. The two of you may be at odds, but he could be a foundation for you."

An image of John came as did, strangely, Adrian. "Great. Which one?"

Lucy laughed as she turned over the next card. A werewolf in a half-man, half-wolf form howled at the giant moon in the sky.

"The Moon," she said. "Your situation is steeped in deception. This is the second card that has talked about trickery in this reading. You need to be careful. Nothing is as simple as it seems."

The fifth card was of a dark-haired woman crowned with stars and seated on a throne, holding a scepter.

"The Empress," Lucy said. "Others are going to look to you for guidance on this."

She flipped the next card. A holy woman in robes sat holding a scroll. A pair of ghostly white wings floated behind her.

"The High Priestess." Lucy's hand hovered over the card. "Have you had any dreams recently? Different from usual?"

I bit my lip as my child's screams and Allegra's laugh echoed in my head. My dreams never really changed. Almost every night, I saw my husband's and child's death at the hands of the demon who cursed me. I shook my head.

"Well, you may start. Pay attention to them. They are going to reveal something necessary."

The last card was Death.

"Again," Lucy whispered.

"So, I'm going to die again," I said.

Lucy shook her head. "No, maybe. Death represents a major change. The status quo is about to break."

I rested my hand on my chin, frowning down at the card. "What is that symbol?"

She peered at it. "That's a representation of Sariel, the Archangel of Death."

Marge turned back to us with her arms crossed. "Great, but what did any of that have to do with my reading?"

I stood and stretched. "I think we're going to have to figure that out ourselves."

"Again. What was the point?"

"Insight," I said. "We have a few more clues."

"No, we have a whole bunch of vague bullshit." Marge threw her hands up. "How did this get us any closer to finding out the name of the demon or where it is?"

"It was more preliminary," Lucy said. "However, with your attitude, I'm not sure I want to go ahead with the ritual I'd planned."

A shiver ran up my spine. There was only one ritual that I knew of that Lucy would use. "That's highly dangerous. Lucy, it could hurt even you."

"Which is why I'm not going to risk it if all she's going to do is rant like a spoiled brat."

Marge's fist clenched. "You're one to talk. I don't even know what the hell you're talking about."

"The Ritual of Delphi will allow Lucy to be an Oracle for a brief time. She can answer three questions you have. But you can only have the ritual performed for you once. Ever."

I knew from experience. I'd had my own moment in front of the Oracle. With her help, Dimitri and I had found Allegra. Unfortunately, I'd failed to kill her, and Dimitri had been injured. I sighed.

"So, I can ask anything, and I won't get this vague bullshit?" Marge asked.

"It won't be like the Tarot cards. Though some of the other things she says might be a little weird," I said.

"This is what I came here for."

Lucy crossed her arms and sucked the inside of her cheek. "All right, but after this I don't want to hear anymore bitching."

"If I get the name of my demon, sure."

Lucy turned toward the bedroom. "I need to get the supplies. Move the tables and couches. We need all the room we can get. And someone turn off the smoke detectors."

Now was the first and probably only chance I had to talk to Lucy alone. I followed her into the bedroom and shut the door behind me. I turned the volume up on the television. She glanced at me as she dug through her suitcase and pulled out a small plastic bag filled with black rocks.

"You need to tell the van Helsing brothers you're a nephilim."

❧ 4 ❧

Lucy scrunched her nose; her eyes filled with confusion. "Why would I need to, dearie?"

"Esais came across a nephilim last night. It's only a matter of time until he knows," I said.

Lucy pulled a large black bag on the bed and took out a stack of bronze braziers. "I don't see how that has anything to do with me."

"Your power isn't the most inconspicuous. If you get injured once, they will know."

She shrugged and set a large plastic bag filled with herbs on the bed. "So, I won't get hurt."

I raised an eyebrow. "Look, you really need to tell them. If they find out on their own, there will be conflict. I see a lot of arguing and pointing fingers. Adrian especially won't like it."

"It'll be fine. You shouldn't worry so much. I've known the boys their whole lives. We're pretty much family."

And I wasn't. I was just a stranger who barged into their lives a few months ago. A relic from their family legacy. Still, I got to see the fallout from the brothers keeping secrets from one another. Adrian hadn't known about Esais's telepathy or

Tres's power to heal. To say he'd been a little upset when he did find out was an understatement. I sighed. Perhaps Lucy knew better, though. It was more her business than mine.

"Let's concentrate on getting this ritual to work," Lucy said.

"How many times have you been successful?" I asked.

"Including yours, once. I'm hoping for my second success tonight."

I blinked at her. "Let's not tell Marge we're pinning all her hopes on a mostly untested ritual."

She grinned at me. "Understood."

"What can I do to help?"

"Take the braziers and set them up in a circle around the center of the room. Pour the herbs in each one."

I carried the braziers into the living room. Marge crouched on the floor, gathering the stack tarot cards that must have fallen while I was in the room with Lucy. Her mouth was pressed in a thin line and she held one of them up. The front was white with a gray symbol painted on the background. A stick figure stood in the center holding a scepter. Long strands stream from under a crown on its head.

"Wasn't this one of your cards?" she asked.

I took the card. Color began to fade in the background. The arms of the stick figure fleshed out. The skin turned a rosy peach and the hair thickened to black locks.

"Interesting," I said.

"Is this some sort of sick prank with you two?"

"No. Lucy's turned her deck into a talisman. It reacts to the person she is reading for."

"Like those necklaces that you made for us in Texas?"

"Yes, but those protected us against Ose's madness." I handed the card back to her and placed the braziers on the floor in a circle. "A talisman depends on your intent upon its creation."

"What are those for?"

"The circle for the ritual. It's to keep the power she'll manifest inside."

Marge snorted. "Why? She's just going to spout some mumbo jumbo."

"It's a little more than that. Lucy's going to call on the power of Apollo. It should give her the ability to answer your questions." If Lucy could pull this off, that is.

"You mean like the guy from Ancient Greece?"

"Yes. He's a spirit. A tulpa actually."

"What the hell is that? A demon?" Marge asked.

"No, it's a thought form. Human belief created him and other ancient gods. The more belief the more power they had."

"But all that's just myth. How can a myth help find my demon?"

"Apollo is known. He's one of the most well-known Greco-Roman gods and people still worship him today, so he still has some power."

"And those bowls are supposed to help keep him inside with her?"

I poured the herbs. "Braziers. And Lucy needs to empower it."

"Why won't it work like that binding circle you taught me to trap demons?"

I emptied the bag into the last of the braziers. "That was a symbol. The pattern and the writings powered the whole thing. At least enough to keep demons bound and powerless."

Lucy stepped out of her bedroom, carrying a large box with a bowl balanced on top of it. She wore a red shawl draped around her shoulders. "Are we ready, dearie?"

"Yeah. I'm not here for a tea party."

Lucy set the chest in the middle of the circle I had made and picked up the bowl. She pulled a knife from her belt and held both out to Marge. "I need some of your blood for this to work."

"What?" Marge said the word like she wanted to hurt Lucy with it.

"It's to attune the ritual to you. Otherwise it won't work."

"This better not be a curse."

Lucy smiled. "Why would I need that? You're already living on borrowed time."

Marge let out a half growl. "How much?"

"Just a few drops."

Marge raked her finger on the point of the blade and let the blood drip into the bowl. I handed her a handkerchief as she stepped back. Lucy took the bowl back to the chest and set it on the floor. I sighed, sat on the desk, and crossed my arms. There wasn't much for me to do now but sit and watch. I had to be here just in case something went wrong.

Lucy pulled out two candles with holders, a long wooden stick, and a lighter. She placed her bowl and the two candles back on the chest and lit the stick. She lowered the stick to the brazier sitting in the East and lit the herbs inside. She followed the circle clockwise, chanting softly as she lit the rest of the herbs. Smoke rose from the braziers and intermingled, creating a hazy veil between Lucy and us. A musky scent filled the air.

For a moment, I closed my eyes and allowed my second sight to take over. The room became a misty gray. Marge sat on the pillow, her impatience and anticipation flaring. She wanted this so much that it buried the disbelief she had. I turned my gaze to the circle and saw nothing but a thick gray curtain. I blinked and let my vision return to normal. Lucy sat before her chest and lit the contents of the bowl in front of her. She raised the veil above her head and leaned over the bowl.

"The Arabian vapor rises toward Olympus," she sang in a

light, breezy voice. "The shrill rustling lotus murmurs its swelling song, and the golden kithara, the sweet-sounding kithara, answers the voice of men."

She inhaled loudly, and her voice gained a slight burr to it. "And all the hosts of poets sing your glory, Apollo, famed for playing the kithara, son of Great Zeus. Beside this snow-crowned peak, oh you who reveal to all mortals the eternal and infallible oracles."

Lucy rocked back and forth as she continued to breathe in whatever fumes rose from the bowl in front of her. With a wheezing breath, she threw her head back and let out a rasping giggle. She sort of rolled to the side while still sitting and lolled her head to the right with her gaze landing on Marge.

"You have questions, Marguerite Devereux." Her voice started out a raspy whisper and rose to a high pitch. "Ask them."

Marge looked at Lucy as if she was crazy and glanced at me, opening her mouth. I gave her a slow, solemn shake of my head, hoping she would understand not to ruin her chances by making a smart ass comment.

She rolled her eyes and straightened her shoulders as she turned back to Lucy. "What demon has my contract?"

Lucy leaned back, cackling, and ran one hand up her chest to her collarbone. "Ah, yes, the deal of Deception. The Throne of Lust possesses your contract."

I blinked. Interesting. We'd believed Wrath was the one we were after. Apparently, we were wrong. Hell was divided into kingdoms, called Thrones, according to the Cardinal Sins. They were each ruled by a devil who was also called the Throne. Naamah was the Throne of Lust, and Allegra served her. Maybe this is what Lucy meant by our connection. My right hand twitched. This could be more beneficial than I thought. If we pushed hard enough, perhaps I could bring

Allegra to me. Marge glanced at me with her brow furrowed. I shrugged with my arms up. She sighed and turned back to Lucy.

"Who is the demon that killed Oulixes?" Marge asked.

Lucy ran her hands up her face and through her hair with a manic grin on her face. "Cambione absorbed the original holder of your contract and took everything that was his."

Marge looked back at me and mouthed "Cambione?"

I shook my head. I'd never heard of that particular demon. I would have to check my books to see if it was mentioned, but it was a long shot. Hell held so many and most weren't documented. There was a theory that demons were human souls damned to Hell, but I hadn't found any proof of that.

"Where can I find Cambione?" Marge leaned forward to where her nose was inches from the smoke.

Lucy raked her nails down her cheeks, leaving deep red marks in her skin. She slammed both hands on the chest and dropped her head. A low wheezing whine emanated from her. "Forty and eight three nine one by seventy-three and eight six oh four."

Blood ran in rivulets from her nose, her ears, and the corners of her eyes. Her cheeks drew inward so that the bones stuck out like pointed sticks. She jerked, and her body stiffened with her hands in a claw like position. She let out a throaty breath and the candles sputtered and the smoke from the braziers wavered before they began to dissipate. She went limp and collapsed to the side of the chest. Her whole aura looked wispy, as if something had drained it. The usually vibrant blues and yellows had faded to pale washed out imitations of their true color. She would need a few days to recover. Lucy's stamina was no match for something that drained on her soul.

"What the hell was that?" Marge followed behind me.

"The ritual makes her a little crazy, but her answers are accurate. We have a name and a location."

"Location? When did she say a location?"

I laid Lucy on the only side of the bed not covered with clothes and luggage, pulled the comforter over her, and brushed her hair from her face. She would be out for hours, but she'd succeeded.

"Well done," I whispered to her and turned back to Marge. "The numbers she gave. They were longitude and latitude."

"And where is that?"

"I can find out." I pulled out my phone and dialed Adrian.

"This had better be important," he answered.

"As if you were doing anything important."

"I'm hanging up."

"I need the location for some coordinates."

"What is it for?"

"Possible demon."

"Are you going after it now?" His voice held a tone of interest.

"Marge and I."

"I'm joining you."

"I thought you had important things to do."

"Give me the coordinates," he said with a slight edge.

I gave them to him. "Come and pick us up at Lucy's hotel."

"I'm on my way."

❧ 5 ❧

I stared up at the brown brick building across the street. Firelight tried to make its way through the dingy windows that lined the four stories. The world had given up hope on any safe habitation for this place years ago. Street lamps flickered on as the shadows swelled at the fading dusk.

"So, this is it?" Marge asked.

I nodded, scanning the street. It was a narrow two lanes with a few cars parked along the curb. A group of street rats stood on the corner in heavy jackets and sagging pants, laughing and talking to each other.

"How do you want to do this?" Marge asked.

"The blueprints show that there is a door in the back," Adrian said, looking at his phone.

"Let's go down the street and come up through the alley. If those kids are spies, they won't see which way we went," I said.

"We're here to kill the demon, right?" Marge asked.

"We've been over this. We're not going through the front."

"Fine."

We headed down the street, around the corner, and into the alley at the backdoor of the building. I climbed the rickety chain-link fence and hopped down the other side. I pressed my back to the wall of the building and rubbed my hand over the hilt of my sundang to calm the buzzing that raced through my veins. The loose chain clattered against the metal pole as Adrian scaled over. Marge landed next to him and brushed off her legs as she stood. Adrian pointed to the concrete steps and a small metal door that marked the back entrance. With a nod of my head, I crept to the door, slid my fingers in the crease, and pulled it open a crack, peeking in.

The hall was almost completely dark, with only the light from outside. I pulled out a small flashlight from its hook on my belt then shone it down the hall and over the dirty white paint that flaked from the walls. I slipped in and headed deeper inside, pausing at an intersection before a staircase for the others to catch up. I nodded to the right and pulled out my sword. Adrian pressed his back against the wall with his gun drawn. The pistol looked like something out of a science fiction novel. The grip looked like it belonged on a 17th century flintlock while the barrel and cylinder was that of a revolver. Two metal tubes traveled from the back of the gun to attach where the front sight should be.

Marge waved me along with a sour look on her face. I pushed open a door on the opposite side of the staircase. Bits of trash littered the worn carpet and dirt layered everything. The already muted colors faded as I scanned the room with my second sight and ghostly furniture replaced the barren shell. However, there were no demons lying in wait for us. I shook my head at the others and moved to the next apartment. We cleared the first floor in a few minutes, finding nothing. We stood in front of the door labeled basement.

"Second floor first," I murmured, and Adrian nodded.

I took a deep breath and crept up the stairs. Halfway up, I switched off the light. A pale yellow glow emanated from the hall above us and music thrummed from somewhere farther back, shaking bits of paint from the walls. The first room held a dirty mattress with the springs poking out of it in places. Needles, bits of paper, and cigarette butts were scattered across the floor. Marge scanned the room, her lips curled into a sneer.

"A drug den," she said.

"Come on," Adrian said. "Let's see if we can find the demon."

In the third room, we found the first living person. Living was relative. He lay on the floor, his eyes glazed and a vapid smile on his face. A syringe rolled from his hand and onto the floor.

I nudged him with the tip of my boot. "Hey."

His head lolled to the side.

I sighed and looked to the others. "This will take a while. How about we split floors? If we find anything we call. Otherwise we meet back here?"

They nodded and moved back to the stairs, arguing quietly about which floor they would take. I moved on. Two doors down, I found two girls that looked a little livelier. Very little. They leaned against one another in sitting positions in one corner of the room. A phone with a glassy front blared music, and their head bobbed out of time with it. I let my second sight take over and gasped. Muddy orange mixed with a dull gray and brown in their auras. Physically, the drugs had unbalanced them, but that wasn't the worst. The auras had withered and rotted, leaving small holes throughout.

What had caused such damage?

I crouched in front of them and reached for the baggie lying on the floor. Bile rose in my throat as I stared at the mustard yellow powder that clumped in the corner. Ose's grinning face came to my mind. The devil that had killed the Van Helsings' parents and older brother, had developed a drug to make humans easily possessed by demons. It had radical side effects, like warping the human to look more like the demon. It shouldn't be here. I'd destroyed Ose along with the drug.

One girl raised her gaze to me and smiled through her stringy bangs.

"Hey," she said.

"Hey," I replied. "You look pretty happy."

She rested her head against the wall. "This stuff is amazing."

"What's it called?"

"Blasphemy."

Well, some demon actually had a clever thought. "Where can I get some?"

She pointed her finger to the floor. "See the man downstairs."

I shook my head. "I didn't see anyone."

"He must be way down," the other girl said, and the two burst into laughter.

I stood and headed back into the hall. The rest of the floor was filled with much of the same. I stood at the stairwell with my arms crossed, waiting on Marge and Adrian.

"Well?" I asked when both had returned.

"More junkies up top," Marge said. "I couldn't find anyone handing the stuff out."

"Same for the fourth floor," Adrian said.

"A girl told me she got the drug from someone downstairs," I said. "Probably our demon."

"Basement then," Adrian said.

"Right." Marge grinned, nodding to an ancient contraption in the center of the hall. There were no doors, just a rusty metal gate. "Want to take the elevator?"

I wrinkled my nose. "I'm not going in that death trap."

"Come on. It can't be that bad."

We took the stairs. Marge liked to give me shit, but she knew the elevator would give away our position if there was a demon down there. Halfway to the basement, a purple haze lit the stairwell and a spicy musk clogged my nose. I paused, holding my hand up to the others. Two voices mixed together in a steady cadence. I couldn't make out the words. My grip on my sword tightened, and I hugged the wall as I sneaked down. Like the rest of the building, the basement was empty of any furniture or boxes, but someone had decided to paint the space with a glowing purple circle painted on the floor. Strange symbols lined just inside the ring, curvy and hooked in a primal fashion, like the ones on the back of Lucy's tarot cards. A triangle filled the center, and a man lay in the middle of it with his eyes closed and dirty hair clinging to his face.

Two demons stood outside the circle chanting. A set of horns peeked out from the hood of one, and a tail poked out from the bottom of the robe the other wore. The light of the circle pulsed with the rhythm of their chants. I felt the pressure building. Marge snorted and pushed past me, heading for the closest demon.

"No, Marge, wait," I hissed, and my hand brushed against her coat, but she slipped away.

Her kick caught him in the middle of his back, and his chant broke as he stumbled forward. He turned just in time to get caught in the chest with a sidekick. The force knocked him into the circle, and all hell broke loose. Literally.

When the demon's foot crossed the line of the circle, a reddish purple flame ignited. It licked his legs and traveled up his body in a flare. He barely had time to scream before he was ash. The fire filled the entire circle, incinerating the man in the middle within seconds and gouts flared out at the walls.

"Get out of here," I yelled to Adrian.

I ran to Marge, coughing as the reek of brimstone caused my eyes to water. The other demon had pulled out a dagger and swung it at Marge. She ducked and slammed her heel into his knee. He screamed. I grabbed his arm, spun, and tossed him into a burning part of the wall.

Marge glared at me. "He was mine."

I waved to the havoc around us. "No time. This place is going up and us with it."

I grabbed her arm and sprinted to the stairs. A piece of flaming ceiling chose that moment to come crashing down on us. Marge tackled me, and we went tumbling to the side. Bits of flaming plaster caught me in my shoulder and arm, burning holes through my jacket and searing my flesh.

"We're stuck," Marge yelled.

I swung my head to the staircase. The ceiling blocked our only exit in a purple inferno. I was going to die down here, burned by that freakish flame I hated. My breath caught in my throat, and I gripped Marge's arm. No, there had to be another way out, some small opening we could get through. I hopped to my feet and ran to the rubble. My hands dug at the debris, the flames searing my flesh. The more I pulled away, the more slid down to replace it. Marge yanked me back.

"What the fuck!" she said.

"There has to be a way out," I wheezed. The smoke was already clogging my throat.

I reared back and forth, but she held tight.

Her fingers dug into my arm. "Ok, stop. I'll try to find something to dig us out."

The fire covered the walls, lighting the room in a violet luminosity. The stone blackened and disintegrated in a matter of seconds where the flames kissed. The shadows flickered as the inferno surrounded us. It was too late. My legs gave out from under me, and I curled up in a ball. Marge hovered around our blocked exit, looking for some point to kick away.

She covered her mouth with her arm, her chest heaving in wracking coughs. It didn't matter. Soon, the rest of the world would topple down upon us.

The smoke drifted toward a corner near the ceiling where a hole formed. The concrete of the wall crumbled and mixed with the ash in the air. However, it didn't fall like it was supposed to. My mouth hung open as the tiny bits of debris shimmered, moved together, and began to form into a set of stairs as the hole grew. Adrian's nanites were hard at work creating an escape for us.

"You brilliant man." Not that I would ever admit it to him out loud.

I was on my feet in seconds. "Marge."

She turned, but I was already over to the steps. Adrian waved us up from outside a small hole. The steps remained solid under my swift run. I collapsed to my hands and knees on the gravel, gagging and gasping. My hands screamed at the rough grit that grated into the raw flesh.

Pain never felt so good.

We scurried down an alleyway like rats trying to escape a fire, except it was the police and their unwanted questions that we ran from. Moments after Adrian rescued us, we could hear the sirens growing closer. I was the first to bolt, followed by the other two.

Marge moved ahead of me with an unsteady gait. The debris had caught her as well, leaving her butt and the back of her legs a raw mess of burnt flesh. We stopped at the opening of an alley, six blocks away from the inferno while Adrian scanned the mostly empty street. A crowd had gathered on the corner to watch the blaze. I could only guess what they were whispering among each other. The place had been a drug den, so the police would most likely call this a chemical fire, but there would be the few who would wonder.

"Wait here," Adrian said. "I'll get the van."

I leaned against the wall with my good shoulder and glared at Marge. "You rushed in again."

"And?"

The van pulled up before I replied. I waved her to the

back with my mangled hands and turned to wrestle with the door. Adrian pushed it open from inside. I hopped in and managed to close it by myself. He eased the car into gear.

"What happened back there?" he asked in a voice as cold as the arctic.

"Rituals are volatile, especially summoning. They were pulling energy from another plane of existence. When Marge kicked him into the circle, it broke, and all that energy they had built up backlashed."

"But that circle that Adrian and Tres broke around the demon in Texas didn't do that," Marge said.

Adrian and Tres had gotten into a fight when we'd had a demon bound for questioning. It escaped when the circle had broken.

"It was a binding, a large symbol that traps the being inside it. The writings and sigils keep the entity bound. There's not a whole lot of power put into it, unlike back there." I jerked my head in the direction of the blaze.

"So what?" Marge asked. "We shouldn't stop a demon summoning?"

"You have to ground the power without breaking the circle. Though any sort of disruption has interesting effects. As with banishing rituals," I said.

"What were they summoning?" Adrian asked.

I shook my head. "Something from the Throne of Lust."

I knew that fire—dreamed about it often enough. Sometimes, instead of seeing the murder of my husband and child at the hands of the demon Allegra, I saw our home being consumed in purple flames. All that would be left would be me and Allegra. I was bound to her for eternity by this curse she laid upon me. I stared out the window and let the silence engulf the van as my chest tightened painfully. Once again, I was helping someone else, while Allegra roamed free somewhere. I took a deep breath. I had all the time in the world;

Marge didn't. Besides, this drug proved that events were deeper than just one demon.

Adrian pulled into the underground garage of the office and parked beside a black sports car. "Esais and Tres are here."

Marge made a limping rush to the door, and I was not far behind. I closed my eyes and counted to ten, letting out a slow breath. Each step sent a sharp bolt to the burns on my back. Marge shook her head at me and headed up the stairs. Esais and Tres waited in the infirmary, and their faces filled with concern when the two of us stumbled in.

"What happened?" Esais asked.

"Just a little fight with hellfire," I said.

"You should see the demons," Marge said. "Crispy."

Esais raised one eyebrow. "You found something?"

I pulled the bag of powder from my pocket and handed it to him. Tres pointed me to the two examination tables in the back of the room. I wrinkled my nose at the astringent smell of alcohol.

"I finally get to see the sexiness under all that leather." Tres peeled off my jacket and the long sleeved shirt beneath it.

I gasped at the sting of the fabric pulling away from my burned flesh. A rush of cool air soothed the raw agony. Marge hobbled to the other examination table, and with a strange hopping climb, she got on top to lie on her stomach. Esais leaned against the doorframe, studying the contents of the bag. Through winces and sharp intakes of breath, I told them what happened.

"So, this is the drug from Texas?" Esais asked with a frown.

"I think so, but I never saw one of the patients in Texas before they were possessed by a demon," I said.

"So you somehow screwed up," Esais said.

Tres stared at him with his jaw slack. I opened my mouth to give him a snappy comeback and froze when our gazes met. My flesh prickled as I broke out into a cold sweat. His eyes had paled to white, like quartz crystal, but that wasn't the worst. It was the look. He could end my existence with a thought, and no part of my curse would bring me back. Eternal peace was in those eyes, and damned if I didn't nearly fall to my knees and beg for it. I looked away, frowning. What was I thinking? This was Esais.

"You were there, too, Saint Esais," Marge said with a snort. "And this isn't Menrazine, unless people decided to free base an anti-psychotic."

"With this city, anything's possible," Adrian said as he pushed past Esais.

Esais stepped back into the corner of the room and stuck his hands in his pockets. His eyes had darkened to their normal steel blue color, and his face wore a troubled look as he listened. What the hell had that been about? He was upset the drug had been let out, but was that other just a part of his telepathy? I was going to have to watch him.

"And the demons in the basement mean the formula somehow got out," I said.

"We're going to need to analyze it," Adrian said.

He looked to his brother who shook his head as he swabbed a cotton pad over my wounds. I hissed as the alcohol seeped in, sending the burn through my veins.

"I can take a look," Tres said, "but I don't know what to look for."

He pressed his hand against my wound. The burning faded, and more comfortable warmth replaced it. After Tres was finished, there wouldn't even be a scar. Unfortunately, he would have to cause pain on another living being to balance what he healed. It was the way his gift worked.

"I can contact Jonah," I said. "He knows alchemy and can see if it's Brimstone."

"He's the one you sent Menrazine to so he could destroy it in the first place," Marge said. "Who says he's not the one who let it get in the hands of someone else."

Esais threw his head back and laughed. "Impossible. Jonah would be furious even hearing that."

"So? He could be lying."

Adrian snorted and shook his head while Tres cast a doubtful glance at Esais.

"Impossible," Esais said, still chuckling. "I've known Uncle Jonah my whole life. He wouldn't do such a thing."

Tres said, "The stick wedged up his ass wouldn't let him do anything dirty."

I opened my mouth and closed it. I'd known Jonah even before Esais was born, and there were things he'd done with alchemy that would make all three brothers blanch. Brimstone was a substance similar to sulfur, but like quicksilver, it held other properties. Hellish ones. We had determined before that the base of the drug was made with brimstone. Who's to say that he didn't want to experiment with this new drug? Knowing Jonah, he had probably already experimented with the stuff. Still, he wouldn't betray them, and he definitely wouldn't let something as dangerous as that drug out, unless by accident. I bit my lip and held my doubts to myself. I would talk to Jonah first.

Tres moved over to Marge and held up a pair of scissors. "Looks like we're going to have to get you naked."

Marge glared at him until the grin faded from his face. He leaned forward and started cutting her pants from her. Marge's jaw stiffened at the first touch of his hand. The red mass of raw flesh became smooth and white as his hands passed over it. With a silent chuckle, I stood up and stretched.

"There's another option," Adrian said. "Who analyzed Menrazine in the first place?"

I paused with my arms sill raised in the stretch. "John? I doubt it."

"Why do you say that?" Adrian asked. "What has he done to prove himself? Supply you with information every now and then?"

My lips pressed in a thin line. "He wouldn't betray me like that."

"What? Not after he slept with you?" Adrian smirked. "No, that doesn't ever happen."

Heat traveled from my neck to my face. "No, he's been there for me since I saved his life."

"People change," Adrian said.

"So, your precious Uncle Jonah could have, too." Marge held up her hands when all three brothers glared at her. "I'm just saying, we shouldn't rule him out because you consider him family."

"Look." Esais raised his hand. "I don't really trust John, either, but we need to prove this is the same . . . What was it called?"

"Brimstone would be the base. The new drug is called Blasphemy." I tried to keep the heat from reaching my voice. "I'll call Jonah and see if he can look at it."

"Does he have to come here?" Tres asked, looking like a child with his hand caught in the cookie jar.

"I think he'll be too busy to care what girls you're seeing." Esais chuckled.

"He'll still give me that disapproving look," Tres said.

"How about you concentrate more on fixing me and less on whining," Marge snapped.

Adrian chuckled and headed to the door. "Well, now that we're moving to unimportant talk, I have things I need to work on."

I glared at his back as he left. How could one man get me so riled up? True, he didn't know John like I did, but that didn't mean he had to suspect every person. John had always been ready to help me when I called, and he'd always come through.

So, why couldn't I push the tiny voice in my head saying Adrian and Esais might be right?

$\mathbb{H}$ 7 $\mathbb{H}$

I left Tres to tend to Marge's wounds. Esais remained in the doorway with his arms crossed and his forehead wrinkled in thought. With a deep breath, I traveled up the stairs to the second floor. The air in the hall was thick with the smell of new paint from the white walls. My feet made no sound on the new red carpeting as I found an empty room to call Jonah in private. He answered on the third ring.

"Ms. Di Luca." His London accent rang through the background noise of conversation. "What can I do for you?"

"You sound like you're in the middle of something," I said.

"I'm in Italy actually. I'm attending a conference at the Vatican."

I gritted my teeth and forced a laugh out. "Oh, your expertise has become invaluable."

"Possibly, a panel has been called on the fact Hell is using modern means to damn humanity. I'm here to present the Texas case."

"Why my case? Couldn't you find another for them to steal?"

"Gabby." His voice rang with an exasperated patience.

We'd been over this before. "The Church has changed over the centuries."

"They may not burn heretics at the stake anymore, but they're still judgmental asses."

"They are becoming more accepting."

"Only because their dirty laundry has been aired." They deserved it, too. The big group of hypocrites spent centuries persecuting others only to commit the worst of sins.

"What was it you wanted?" A change of subject. Smart man.

"I found a drug that has similar effects as Menrazine."

"That is unfortunate. I destroyed the batch you brought to me. Are you sure it was the only one?"

"Ose was working alone. He wouldn't have shared with anyone else." I bit the inside of my cheek. "You didn't keep any for your experiments?"

A small crackle of static filled the silence of his pause. "You believe I would have been foolish to risk such a thing?"

"I don't know, Jonah. You play with other questionable substances. Who's to say you weren't trying to find a better way to keep yourself alive?"

"I do what is necessary, but within limits. I wouldn't do something like that when we have seen only negative consequences." Jonah's voice held an icy stiffness to it.

"But that's how experimentation starts," I said. "If you say you didn't, I believe you."

"Who is in control of this new drug?"

I explained my night's adventures. "We're not sure if it is the same. We need your expertise to verify."

"So, you question me but still want me to verify?" Jonah sighed. "If this leaves the city, it has the potential to spread globally."

"I'm aware, Jonah, but we need to know what we are dealing with."

He cleared his throat. "I cannot leave. Send Lucy to me with your sample. I will look into it and contact you when I know more."

"She's probably still unconscious, but I'll leave her a message." My phone chirped in my ear, and I glanced at the screen. "Jonah, I have another call coming in."

"I will call when I know something."

I took a deep breath and switched to the other call. "Ciao, John. This is a surprise."

He chuckled, his voice sending a delicious shiver up my spine. "I hope it's a nice surprise."

"Well, that would depend on why you're calling," I said.

He sighed. "Unfortunately, it's not good news. What happened to the drug you took from Texas?"

The delicious shiver turned to ice. "It was destroyed. Why do you ask?"

"I'm working on an article for a corporation named Erebus. I'm in New York for a press conference. One of their subsidiaries, Acesco, is releasing some sort of super drug. I've heard rumors about the testing. The kind that makes me think maybe Menrazine isn't gone."

A sick feeling settled in my stomach. "I've run into a similar situation. As I said, what I had of the drug was destroyed." I paused. "What happened to the sample I gave to you?"

Horns honked and the indecipherable buzz of background conversation fed into the line. "I gave it back to you. Don't you remember?"

An image of Ose's long fingers reaching for me flashed through my mind followed by a rush of fear. Darkness surrounded me, and once again, I was in the coffin that the devil had trapped me in. I rubbed my eyelids and swallowed hard. Ose had driven me to the brink of madness, but I'd made it out. It was over.

"You might have." I tried to keep the shakiness out of my voice. "Texas is a little unclear for me."

"You think I would have sold the drug?" The quiet hurt in his voice reached me through the phone.

"No, but I had to check. I don't understand how it got out."

"It looks like I'll have to prove myself all over again." His voice lightened. "Care to join me for the press conference tomorrow? Say Nine AM?"

I smiled and swallowed the ache I felt. "That sounds like an excellent plan."

He gave me the address. "I look forward to seeing you tomorrow."

"Me too."

I hung up and tapped the phone to my cheek in thought. I would need something to find this company's secrets. Lucky we had an expert in technology just down the hall. Adrian sat at a desk in one of the offices, typing on a laptop with various tools and pieces of mechanical equipment scattered around him on adjoining tables. I blinked as one of the machines grew before my eyes. New chips formed on a board out of thin air and a round glass lens became surrounded by black plastic.

"Is this a camera?" I asked.

He glanced up from the laptop to the device I was pointing at and nodded before focusing on the screen again.

"It's really amazing seeing your tiny robots in action." I leaned in for a better look. "How are they building from nothing?"

He pointed to a pile of pipes, discarded cellphones, and CDs. "They're breaking down those on a molecular level. The molecules are being used to build the new device."

I tilted my head. "This still sounds a lot like magic."

He snorted. "When you get science this advanced, it

tends to seem like magic to those incapable of understanding it."

Did he just insult my intelligence? "But magic was the basis for modern science. What would chemistry be without alchemy? Astronomy without astrology? Even your robots could be attributed to ancient Jewish golem creation."

"We have moved beyond such antiquated practices."

"Have we? Vampires, demons, even spirits still exist, though science denies them."

"Most scientists do because they have no substantial proof. Magic doesn't always work for those who try."

"That's because they don't understand."

He smiled. "And that is the beauty of science. Once something is built, the common man doesn't have to understand how the device works to use it."

I opened my mouth to respond but stopped, realizing I didn't have an argument for that point. Summoning wasn't the only part of magic that had to be exact; it applied to almost any of the five magical practices of talismans, symbols, rituals, incantations, and alchemy. The symbols, timetables, and pronunciations were complex, and one mistake meant either the magic wouldn't work or that there would be dire consequences.

"You use magical symbols with your gun," I said.

"You were correct about the demons and spirits," Adrian said. "Until I can discover a scientific way to destroy them, I have to resort to less efficient methods."

"I'm sure your muse will give you an idea."

He sighed. "Once again, I mentioned the muse as a metaphor."

I shifted to my second sight. The colors dimmed to a dull gray, and the new equipment was replaced by that of a previous era. In place of the laptop was a typewriter. Certain time periods left an impression on the Eclipse, the spirit world. I turned my attention to Adrian and the colors blooming around him. Greens and yellows mixed with a small amount of red. He had a brilliant mind, but he still had a lingering anger. However, his emotions weren't what I was looking for. It was the woman standing over his shoulder.

She stood out amongst the gray haze of the spirit world. Her hair was in golden ringlets that flowed in a swirl design to the side of her head. A white toga hung on her athletic form and came to mid-thigh. Golden sandals adorned her feet, leaving her manicured toes open. She had an angular face, high cheekbones, and a pointed chin. Her lips moved, and Adrian's fingers flew over the keyboard.

"Right," I said. "And that part about hearing a woman speak to you in your dreams?"

"Lots of men dream that. Maybe I just need sex." He arched his eyebrow. "Interested?"

"Like I could ever compete with your robots. Maybe you should make yourself a woman."

"Perhaps. In any case, it is just a dream."

I sighed. One night, a couple of months ago, I'd gotten him to explain where he got his ideas. It took a bottle of alcohol. He rarely drank, but we were celebrating our victory over Ose and the destruction of the drug, so he'd made an exception. He described his muse as a vision from a dream. She'd been exactly like I'd just seen her, but the next day, he'd denied she was real.

"How can you rely on my ability to see demons but deny that I can see your muse?" I asked.

His eye twitched, and he stopped typing. "I'm not one of your emissaries. I don't have any special abilities."

"Except for the ability to create things way beyond any current scientific advancement."

He smirked. "Intelligence is hardly a supernatural thing."

"Are you sure? Solomon was granted wisdom by an angel."

He snorted and continued to type. "Solomon is long dead, and most of his story borders on mythical."

"He was real, but that's not the point. Spirits can grant intelligence."

"That's not something I want."

"Why do you hate them so much?"

He stopped and looked directly at me for the first time. "They come from the same place as demons."

"The Eclipse is vast. Not all spirits are like demons."

"Have you ever spoken to any of them? They could all be demons trying to fool you."

"I can tell the difference. I see them. I can see the taint demons leave on humans. Neither of your brothers nor you have that."

"That doesn't mean they should be trusted," Adrian said. "Eventually they will corrupt you."

I shook my head. I was getting nowhere again. I should've just been happy that Adrian finally accepted me as an asset and I was no longer a monster to him. I cleared my throat. "This isn't why I came in here."

He turned back to the screen. "Why then?"

"I need things to spy on this company called Acesco at their Expo tomorrow."

He stiffened and stopped typing. "Why Acesco?"

"John says they may have a version of brimstone."

"How convenient."

I narrowed my eyes. "Why would he tell me about it if it was him?"

He shrugged and opened a desk drawer. "Because he wants you to fall for whatever game he's running."

"Can you get me something or not?"

"You're probably not going to have time to set up room surveillance. You'll want something that will bug a person. I can come up with something that uses 5G signals, but someone will have to be near with a receiver. What time?"

"Around nine."

He nodded. "Meet me in the parking garage at seven."

"Wait, what?"

"I said someone needs to receive. Who else is competent?"

"So you're going to sit in a van and listen in. Kind of creepy," I said. "I will see you tomorrow then."

He rolled his eyes. "I count the time apart."

❧   8   ❧

Around nine, I left Adrian in his van in the garage of the Acesco building. John stood outside of the tall skyscraper with his hands in the pockets of his long coat. The wind ruffled his sandy blond hair, and he smiled at me when I approached.

"How are you so tan for winter?" I asked.

"It's sunny in Florida." His smile spread into a grin. He held up a set of laminated cards attached to a plastic clip. "Your credentials. You get to be my protégé."

"Sounds interesting," I said. "What do I need to do?"

"Look pretty."

I rolled my eyes. "What a job description."

He pulled me through the double doors into a large lobby with vaulted ceilings. My high heels clicked against the black and gold marble floor as I followed John into the small crowd standing by leather chairs. Men in buttoned up shirts with sports jackets and women in power suits huddled together in a buzz of conversation.

John turned to me. "So, how are you liking New York?"

I wrinkled my nose, scanning the crowd. "It stinks, it's

loud, and there are so many people. Worst of all, I can't see the stars."

He chuckled. "Too bad you can't live in the middle of nowhere."

I sighed. "Unfortunately, nothing happens there."

A thin man with hollow cheeks moved closer to us and pushed his glasses up his nose.

"Hey, Roda. Decided to lay off the small town crap?" He crossed his arms over his white buttoned shirt.

John pulled off his coat and draped it over his shoulder. "I go where the story is, Aaron."

I let my gaze linger over John's athletic body, admiring the way the tailored gray suit accentuated his broad shoulders. I cleared my throat and removed my jacket.

Aaron glanced in my direction, and his lips curved in a leer. "And who is this?"

"This is my new assistant, Gabby. She's still learning the ropes."

"So nice to meet you, Gabby. I hope we become good friends." He held his hand out to me.

His palm was damp, and he rubbed the space between my index finger and thumb. I pushed back a shudder and smiled at him. His gaze roamed from the black skirt I wore to where my red vest was pulled tight against my breasts.

"A pleasure," I said.

When Aaron held on longer than he needed, John cleared his throat. Aaron gave him a quick glance and released my hand.

A smiling blonde woman approached the group. "We're ready to get started, if everyone would follow me into the Atalanta conference room."

Aaron looked at the moving crowd and gave me a quick glance. "Well, if this putz can't help you, be sure to come to me."

"I'll keep that in mind," I said.

Aaron hurried to be one of the first to enter the conference room. I rubbed my hand on my skirt and brushed my tongue over the roof of my mouth trying to rid myself of the sourness. John raised one of his eyebrows in a quick motion and mouthed a silent wow before he sauntered towards the conference room. I chuckled and followed behind him. A small stage stood in the back of the room with a podium in the center.

I took a seat next to John in the middle of the room and scanned the conference area. The light green carpeting accented the honey wood panels lining the walls. Several reporters leaned over their chairs to chat with each other. A woman with red hair sat in one of the chairs behind the podium. Her skirt rode up her thigh as she sat with her legs crossed and talked with the man beside her. His face was narrow and ended in a pointed, reddish-blond goatee, which matched his combed back hair. His eyebrows were arched high in the middle, which gave him a wicked look.

The blonde woman stepped up the podium. "Welcome. You all have the privilege of learning about our new innovative product. Now, I'd like to introduce the mastermind behind it, Raina Benson."

The redhead stood and approached the podium to the sound of applause. A smile spread across her mauve lips. I narrowed my eyes and concentrated until a soft pop echoed in the back of my head. My peripheral vision blurred with a rainbow of colors. They pressed on me. I focused on the figures on the stage. Raina's hair and her blue suit faded away and was replaced by a shadow. Her features disappeared into a dark gray. A red glow emanated from the creature's eyes as she scanned the audience. No life pulsed in that aura. I swallowed as my throat became dry and a chill ran up my spine. Somehow, vampires had gotten a hold of brimstone. Adrian's sudden interest in this company made more sense.

". . . Percent of Americans live with obesity . . ." Raina's speech drifted through.

The man behind her shifted in his seat, but it wasn't actually a man anymore. His true face was one half comedy mask and one half tragedy mask. Two thin, long horns sprouted from behind the mask. A green light shone from the two eyeholes. His body was bright red and a thin whip-like tail moved behind his chair. Unlike the woman, life flowed through the body he wore. Well, the demon explained how the vampire had gotten her clammy hands on the brimstone.

"Our innovative new product boosts metabolism to amazing speeds . . ." Raina continued.

I closed my eyes and let my sight return to normal. As a dull ache settled behind them, I flexed my fingers, resisting the urge to rub my forehead. A television screen showed a smiling woman playing with a small child. They faded away and white and blue letter spun into existence forming the word "Synergy".

"Synergy stimulates the brain, suppresses hunger, and gives you that boost of energy . . ." Raina raised her hand to the screen. "We hope to have Synergy released to the public within a year. I'm ready to take any questions."

The audience stood in a rush and the room became almost deafening with the barrage of questions. Aaron stood in front, his face filled with eagerness. Even John held his pen up, trying to gain Raina's attention. I left him to it and pushed my way to the aisle where I waited in the back with my arms crossed.

After twenty more minutes of questions, Raina ended the press conference. She let the blonde take over while she and the demon walked down the aisle. I slipped out of the door, pulled a small spray can Adrian had given me from my purse, and got into an ambush position. The door swung open and hit me in the shoulder. Perfect. I gave a small cry, stumbled into Raina, and pressed down on the nozzle, squirting the contents onto her skirt. Adrian's nanites were now on her and ready to transmit to him. I stepped back with my eyes wide.

"I-I'm so sorry," I stuttered.

She glared at me and shouldered past me to the door. The demon paused, grabbing my arm to steady me. I gulped back the bile that rose in my throat at his touch and tried to put on a look of chagrin. He tilted his head at me and a slow smile spread across his face. He raised my hand, my fingers still curled around the small can.

"And what do we have here?" the demon asked.

9

The demon raised an eyebrow, waiting for a response from me. I blinked at him, putting on my best confused look on.

"My perfume?" I asked.

"You spray perfume on in front of a door?" he asked.

"No." I drug the syllable out. "I was putting it away when said door rammed into me by your boss. You should probably hurry after her. She seemed busy."

"Hmm, I'm sure I can catch up. Tell me, what is the scent?"

The door in debate swung open again. I stepped back to prevent getting hit and pulled my arm away, resisting the urge to rub where his hand had been. John stepped out with a searching look on his face. His face brightened when he saw me.

"There you are," he said. "I was wondering where you disappeared to."

He straightened up and cleared his throat when he saw the demon. "Forgive my assistant. Was she bothering you?"

The demon smiled. "We were just having a discussion about odd grooming habits."

John raised an eyebrow at me and glanced back at the demon. "Okay. Well, if you have a minute, can I ask you a few questions, Mr . . . ?"

"George Neumann," the demon said. "I can answer one question, so make it good."

John held out a small recorder. "Why has Acesco decided to begin a new weight loss line? Aren't there enough on the market?"

Neumann smiled. "Why, we want to change the world, of course."

He gave me a small wave and turned away, walking through the lobby.

"Thanks," I murmured.

"No problem," John said. "So, what now?"

"Now's our chance to learn anything interesting. Hopefully, before he starts telling Ms. Benson to strip," I said. "Come on."

We kept several people between us and the demon, watching as he stopped at the elevators and stepped in when the doors opened. With John behind me, I headed for the stairwell on the side of the wall. I took a deep breath, opened the door, and rushed down the steps. When I reached the parking level, I let out the breath I'd been holding. A moment later, John came up behind me.

"Why down here?" he asked.

I walked to the black van and pulled open the passenger door. Adrian glanced in my direction with one hand on the large set of headphones he wore as I slid in. He turned the dial on the van's radio to his left. John leaned over my lap with one hand on the head rest.

"Did it work?" I asked.

Adrian looked at me like I was a fool. "Of course."

"So, how are the rest of us going to listen?"

Adrian looked at John. "Get in."

I squeezed into the space between the seats and pulled my skirt as it rode up. John climbed into my vacated spot, shutting the door behind him. Adrian pulled the cord of the headphones from the rest of the radio, and the soft crackle of static filled the van.

"This had better work, Faust." Raina's voice drifted from the speakers. She spoke in short clipped syllables.

"Weren't you one of the testers?" a pleasant male tenor, the same as the Neumann we'd run into, asked. "Didn't your humans taste as delicious as promised?"

A muscle twitched in Adrian's jaw as he stared hard at the radio. John looked at me with eyebrows pulled together, but I just shook my head and mouthed the word *vampires*.

"The subjects did show an improvement in taste," Raina said.

"Then it works. All you have to do is sell it to the cattle," Faust said.

"I have yet to see this susceptibility to suggestion you spoke of."

Faust's quick laugh rang through the van. "Trust me. They'll be like putty in your hands."

"They had better. Mr. Durnovo doesn't stand for betrayal, even from your kind."

Adrian stiffened.

"I wouldn't dream of it," Faust said. "However, we need to tread carefully. There was a demon hunter at you little conference."

"Oh? Was she sniffing you out?" Raina's laugh was high and cold. "I'd say that's a problem you need to handle."

"Maybe, but she's been known to associate with a certain family of vampire hunters."

There was a long pause.

"I'm not too concerned. We have dealt with hunters in the past. We can squash these as well," Raina said.

"I have another meeting. Shall I see you later this afternoon?" Faust asked.

There was a shuffling of paper. "Don't keep me waiting. I want to go over the numbers of the latest group."

"Of course not." Faust's laugh was cut off by the thud of a closing door.

Adrian switched off the radio and leaned back in his seat, staring at the concrete wall through the windshield.

"So what was that about?" John asked.

"I'm betting Faust is the demon I saw at the press conference. It sounds like he's sold this Synergy to these vampires." I kept my gaze on Adrian, looking for any hint of acknowledgement.

"We have to get back to the office," he said. "I want to go over this recording again."

John looked between us. "I guess that's my cue to get lost then."

"Wait," I said as he pushed the door open.

I climbed out after him and moved from the van.

He smiled at me and brushed his thumb across my cheek. "I get the feeling he doesn't like me."

I shrugged. "Adrian prefers machines. He only tolerates people. Do you know anything about this Faust?"

He shook his head. "And by your question, I guess you don't, either."

"I know about the legend. I watched Goethe's play when it was released."

"So, a research session at my hotel? Or is this something you want to do with the Van Helsings?"

The van backed out of its parking space. Adrian stared at us, tapping his fingers on the wheel.

"One moment," I yelled before turning back to John. In a softer voice, I said, "I can meet you in a couple of hours."

He leaned in and kissed my cheek. "Room 302 of the Lexington Hotel."

I squeezed his hand before letting go. "I'll bring the books."

"Does that mean I'm supplying dinner?"

"Don't skimp." I grinned at him and climbed into the van.

Adrian sped out of the parking lot, and I grabbed onto the armrest not to slide out of my seat. He weaved in and out of the traffic.

"Is the office on fire or something?" I asked.

"I don't want you to miss your date," he said.

"It's not a date. It's research."

"Right," he said. "I'm sure you'll get a lot of work done."

"I'm talented. I can accomplish a lot in one night."

He snorted. "If you split your concentration between two jobs, you'll never excel at either."

"Two words. Time Management."

"Right."

"Don't worry. It's something you'll never see." I stared out the window for the rest of the ride.

Adrian pulled into the garage of the office without getting us killed. He slammed the door behind him and hurried into the elevator. I loosened the death grip I had on my seatbelt, climbed out of the van, and took the stairs. In the lobby, Esais leaned against an empty desk piled with boxes, his arms crossed and an easy smile on his face. Lucy stood in front of him with one hand on her hip and the other holding the stick of a lollipop that was in her mouth. Her duffle bag sat on the floor beside her.

"Wow, you look . . . all business," Esais said.

"I was doing some investigation with John and Adrian." I turned to Lucy. "How are you feeling?"

She grinned, though it didn't hide the shadows under her eyes. "You know me. I bounce back from anything."

I pressed my lips together in a thin line and gave her a level look. "Are you sure you're okay to leave?"

Lucy nodded. "I should be back in a couple of days."

"Oh." I grinned at her. "You don't plan on staying for a party with the priests?"

She rolled her eyes. "New York is much better than those stuffed robes."

"I don't know," I said. "In my day they were pretty lecherous."

Esais chuckled.

"That was five hundred years ago." Lucy glanced at her wristwatch and picked up her bag. "Well, I'll see you in a couple of days. Don't have all the fun without me."

"I'm sure there will be plenty of fun for you when you get back," Esais said.

Lucy left with a bounce in her step. Once she was gone, I turned back to Esais. "Where are Tres and Marge?"

"Marge said she was going to talk to her contacts in the city and see if they knew more about the Blasphemy. Tres is going on a date."

I snorted and headed to the stairs. "We should talk. Adrian's probably at his computer already. This one has him on edge."

Esais raised an eyebrow. "What did you find?"

"Vampires," I said.

His face became serious. Vampires were always a serious subject for the Van Helsings. Each member had taken an oath to hunt supernatural creatures that preyed upon humanity, but vampires were their specialty. They knew that one day they would face Dracula, thanks to the curse the fiend had laid on their family. As long as their legacy continued, he survived.

Esais followed me up to the second floor and into Adrian's office. Adrian looked up at us from his laptop and slid the headphones down with an annoyed look. I updated them on the press conference and described Raina's shadow body from what I could see of the Eclipse.

"So, what kind of vampire are we dealing with?" I asked.

"Strigoi," Adrian said.

Esais tilted his head and raised his brows at his brother.

"I haven't forgotten the training," Adrian said.

I looked between the two of them. "Well, would either of you explain what a Strigoi is? It's not one of Dracula's brood right?"

"No," Esais said with a tone of relief. "Though they are also a Slavic type."

"Strigoi are basically shadows of the dead. They have somehow managed to feed on enough blood that it's allowed them to take a physical form," Esais said. "They act and look like normal living people, eating, breathing, breeding."

I blinked. "They can have children?"

"The males can impregnate human women. Most don't carry to term, though."

"How do you tell them from humans?" I asked.

"Strigoi don't cast shadows," Adrian said.

"How do you know what kind she is?" I asked. "You didn't even see her."

Esais crossed his arms and looked to his brother with raised eyebrows. "You didn't?"

"He stayed in the van so we could get a good recording," I said.

"Well?" Esais asked Adrian. "How can you be sure?"

Adrian sighed. "I have had a run in with vampires from this company before."

"Seriously?" Esais asked. "When?"

Adrian typed on his laptop with his eyes narrowed on the screen. "Years ago."

Esais grinned and gave a whistle. "And I thought you'd run from the family business. Here you were hunting all on your own."

"If that's what you want to believe, sure," Adrian said.

"So what do you know about them?" I asked.

"Acesco is a subsidiary of a company named Erebus. Erebus is a multinational corporation that has its fingers in everything from weapons to pharmaceuticals. Looks like Acesco has moved up since I last dealt with them."

"So these Strigoi are working with a demon. You think it's brimstone?" Esais asked.

"I think it's too much of a coincidence for it not to be. That is, if Jonah can verify Blasphemy is made from brimstone," I said.

A chill ran up my spine as I felt something in the back of my head. A sort of black iciness gripped me. I rubbed my arms and glanced at Esais. He chewed his lip, his hand resting on his chin as he listened to Adrian. Memories began to rise. A vision of the bar in Texas where I first met the Van Helsing brothers filled my head, strong enough I could almost smell the stale cigarette smoke and beer. I closed my eyes and imagined a thick iron wall surrounding me. The chill disappeared as the presence faded.

"Was that you?" I asked Esais.

He blinked at me. "What?"

"In my head just now. Were you going through my memories?"

"No." He frowned and narrowed his eyes. "I don't sense any foreign minds. Whoever it was has retreated."

"If anyone was there," Adrian said.

I gave him a dirty look. "If the demons or vampires have a mentalist, we have to be careful."

"I'll handle it," Esais said.

I nodded. "I'm meeting with John to see if we can dig up some information on this Faust. It's time to crack open some old tomes."

"Do you need help?" Esais asked. "I was going on a date, but I can always cancel."

Adrian snorted and put his headphones back on. A smile spread across my face, and a mix of happiness and unease filled me.

"No, that's great. You deserve a bit of fun," I said. "Is this the boy from the club?"

Esais nodded, his smile making the room brighter. "His name is Viktor."

"You have to introduce us. For now, have a great night. I just need one favor."

"What's that?"

"Can I borrow some books?"

10

I closed my eyes and rubbed my eyelids. They ached after hours of squinting at the small, faded writing in these old books. I'd been lucky though. Out of thousands of demons, tales of Faust had been recorded. Understanding what it meant was a different matter. I sighed, pushed the book off my lap, and flopped back on the king size bed. John looked at me from his post at his laptop on the small desk beside the television across the room.

"That doesn't sound like the sound of triumph," he said.

"I found something, but it's vague," I said.

"Want to take a dinner break and talk about what we found? Maybe we can come up with something together."

My stomach rumbled, and I chuckled. "That sounds wonderful."

He picked up the hotel phone on the desk while I pulled the book to me once again. The words were hand written in a tiny, shaky cursive. My mouth moved as I translated the Latin into Italian. I shook my head; still this revealed nothing new.

John hung up and walked to the television and switched it on. The screen showed dancing lights as Beethoven's "Moonlight Sonata" filled the room. I smiled, closed my eyes, and my head swayed with the music. The mattress shifted, and his breath tickled my cheek. There was a small rustle of paper.

"Wow," he said. "How can you even read this?"

"Patience."

"So what have you found?"

I looked back at the book with a sigh. "Well, most of it is this tale of how Faust made a deal with the Devil."

John snorted. "Which one?"

"Lucifer, actually. I don't know what he got, but according to this account, he somehow tricked the Devil on his deal."

His hand slid up my leg to behind my knee. "How is that even possible? This is Lucifer we're talking about."

I shrugged. "According to this, he lived a happy life and died an old man."

"Well, that goes into some of the stories I've come across trying to read up on his legend. Are you sure he wasn't already old when he made the deal?"

"Maybe, but this passage says he got out of the deal but still became a demon. And this is where it gets weird."

"Wait, what was that about him becoming a demon?"

I looked up. "There's a pretty substantial theory that humans become demons."

"So, they're not all fallen angels?'

I grinned. "No, those would be devils. Demons are considered to be their children, but I don't think it's in the biblical, begetting sense."

There was a knock on the door. John stood up and opened the door for the room service attendant to wheel in a white clothed cart. He lifted the cover, allowing the steam to rise from the food. Two plates filled with thick cut steaks, roasted potatoes cut in small wedges, and bright green asparagus sat on the table. My mouth watered as the aroma of meat seared in garlic and butter reached my nose. The attendant placed the plates on the small table along with wine in the middle.

"Will there be anything else, sir?" the waiter asked.

"That will be all, thanks," John said.

John held out my chair for me before he sat down in his own. The first bite of the steak almost melted in my mouth, and I closed my eyes to savor it. John popped open the bottle and poured wine into my glass. I sipped, letting the dry, red liquid mix with the tang of the red meat.

"You didn't get this from here," I said.

John wagged his finger. "No, I had them special order it. So, how did Faust's story get weird?"

I waved my fork. "Well, since he tricked the Devil, when he did become a demon, he didn't belong to any Throne."

John leaned forward. "So, he's a free agent, like Ose?"

I shook my head. "Ose was originally from the Throne of Greed. He somehow managed to break free. Faust has always been a free agent and this account seems to warn about Faust's ability to make those he possesses into him."

"What does that even mean?"

"I don't know, but Faust can apparently possess other demons."

"Demons have no bodies. How is that even possible?"

I threw my hands up. "And now you see why I'm lost. Did you find anything interesting?"

"Nothing really." He set his fork on his plate, stood up, and held his hand out to me. "Come on. Let's take a mental break."

I took his hand, and he pulled me close, wrapping his arms around my waist. He rested his chin on my shoulder as we swayed to the music. I shuddered, breathing in his scent, and the clump of tense muscles in my back began to relax. I deserved a little bit of fun. After all, the others were out enjoying themselves instead of going over musty tomes.

Except Adrian. He'd probably work all night, the way he was acting. I smiled as I imagined him hunched over his computer, muttering to himself. Why was I thinking of him at a time like this? I was in the arms of the man I wanted.

I shivered as John pressed his lips against my shoulder. His fingers trailed up my back. I pressed against him, running my knee along his inner thigh. My lips parted in a half pant as warmth spread from my loins and into my stomach. His musk mixed with the spice of aftershave surrounded me, and I couldn't get enough of it. He swung to the side and dipped me to where I hung in his arms. We laughed as he lifted me up and carried me to the bed. I pushed the books aside and he climbed over me, staring into my eyes, his breaths ragged.

"That's one hell of a dance," he said.

"It's only just begun."

Our lips meshed, opening to allow our tongues to twine together and the heady aftertaste of wine and garlic danced on my taste buds. John pulled away with a shuddering breath. He unbuttoned my jeans and slid the zipper down one agonizing tooth at a time. John's eyes burned like a blue flame as they traveled up my body. He glanced at the wall and screamed.

I jumped, shattered from my haze of desire at the shrill sound in my ears. John scrambled from the bed, knocked over a chair, and pressed his back against the window while his eyes never left the wall. I rolled off the bed and faced the wall, ready to deal with whatever horror was coming out of it. A small black spider crawled across the wall.

I glanced over at him with a raised eyebrow. "Are you serious?"

He jerked his gaze to me. "Just kill it."

I slammed my shoe on the tiny creature on the wall and looked back at him. "Amazing. You're willing to go after demons but freak out at one spider."

"I can't stand them. They're just small and disgusting." He let out a long breath, closed his eyes, and gave a shaky laugh. "I guess I ruined the mood there."

The fire inside of me had cooled to a simmer. I opened my mouth to say we could rekindle something but stopped and studied him. The blood had drained from his face, giving a sickly grey to his tan skin. He gripped the window sill as his eyes darted from the walls to me. I knew that kind of fear. I fought it in every tight space and every crowd. It had taken me a long time to overcome it. I sat down, gathered the books to the nightstand, and leaned back against the headboard of the bed, patting the space beside me. He hesitated, scanning the room again, before joining me. He laid his head on my chest, and I ran my fingers through his hair in a gentle motion.

"Do you want to talk about it?" I asked.

"No." His voice held an edge of finality.

I sighed. As much as John was there for me as a sympathetic ear, it didn't extend the other way. He kept this wall up when it came to anything personal. He rarely spoke of his wife and her possession or the fact I'd been the one to save him from her. He said he'd forgiven me, but I never really knew if he held some sort of resentment.

"How much do you know about him?" A small voice whispered. *"Maybe Adrian and Esais are right."*

I tried to push the thought away, but it stayed with me in John's silence.

❧ 11 ❧

I stood in the parking lot of a group of warehouses by the riverfront and studied the metal buildings with their square, segmented windows. Several workers moved around the outside of the first building. I pulled my jacket tighter around me at the brisk wind that traveled over the waterfront. The overcast sky grew darker as the sun began to set.

"These look pretty crowded. Are you sure there's a demon here?" I asked Marge.

"Apparently we're looking for the abandoned one. Coker said he's heard some weird shit about the rave that happened here a couple nights ago."

"And who is Coker again?" Adrian's voice drifted from the small device in my ear. He'd given us a new toy to test out.

"He's a guy who keeps an ear out on occult shit for me," Marge said. "I get some good relics from him."

"So, he's like John," I said.

"Except he's useful. He actually found a demon," Marge said.

"Maybe," I said. "And John is tracking another demon that he found."

"Ladies, this isn't a competition." The tiny bud still carried the annoyance in Esais's voice. "Let's get to work."

I adjusted my sword, tucking it deeper into my long coat. Just touching it made me feel a little better. This was the first lead I'd had in a few days, and all the research for others was starting to drive me insane. Gazes followed us as we moved past the warehouse, and a few of the men, all with human auras, greeted us with whistles. The fourth warehouse stood closed and abandoned with boarded windows. I moved to the door and attempted to slide it to the side. It moved an inch before stopping with the clank of a metal chain. Some of the boards had been pried away from the windows above us, revealing only blackness from inside.

Marge pulled a collapsible grapple and rope from her belt and aimed it at the space below a window. The grapple flew through the air and hit the window ledge with a metal thunk. She pulled on the rope a few times before nodding to me. I used my feet to walk up the wall as I climbed, and once I reached the top, I signaled her to follow. The metal walkway shook with a steady squeak as I landed on it from the window. The only light shone from the few dingy windows, so I pulled out a small flashlight, moved to the t-section, and panned over the space around me. The walkway hung suspended with metal poles and was only about three feet wide with a small rail. Trash littered the concrete ground at the bottom.

"Ok, we're in," I said. "Can you hear me?"

"Clearly," Adrian said. "What have you got?"

"So far it's empty," I said. "Are you coming, Marge?"

There was a huffing of breath. "Hold your horses."

A shadow moved out of the corner of my eye, and I ducked down. A breeze ruffled the top of my head as a green, scaled hand swiped where my chest would have been seconds ago. I rolled back into the darkness and came up, drawing a knife from my boot as I shone the light on what attacked me. A being in rags glided forward. Its face was covered by a worn hood. I shifted to my second sight to see what sort of monster we were up against. The soul of the human who owned the body had been devoured by a demonic snake woman. A chill ran down my spine. I should have guessed from the scales and tail. A lamia. I had hunted one in Paris in the twenties with Dimitri Van Helsing, the boys' great grandfather.

I gulped back the bile that rose in my throat and let my vision return to normal. This was ridiculous. The rag covered creature turned in our direction, her clawed feet made a scraping sound against the grating. She stopped halfway at the intersection, her head turning at an angle impossible for a human. Green scales covered the creature's hairless head and traveled down her body.

"Gabriella Di Luca, I thought you would look more formidable. After all, you killed my sister."

I raised an eyebrow. "Was that a poor way of saying you thought I'd be taller?"

"I have waited over ninety years for this."

"I take it you mean Lola," I said.

"Was that what you called her? Must have been the human you killed with her," the lamia said.

"Is there a point to this?" I asked.

When she opened her mouth again, I flicked my wrist and flung my knife at her. She ducked to one side, and the knife bounced off the pole. It skittered across the walkway, over the edge, and hit the ground with a distant ping. She hissed at me, baring long fangs.

I smirked at her. "The conversation was growing dull."

The demon growled and came at me. I used one of the

poles to swing around so that I came up behind her, then drew my sundang. The light reflected off the wavy blade. The lamia brought her talons in an upward rake to my chest. I hopped back and brought my blade up in a defensive stance. The metal grating shook beneath me, and I pulled back to the intersection to allow Marge to come and stand beside me.

"Hey, scaly bitch," Marge said. "Are you Cambione?"

The demon paused and tilted her head to the side and her eyes narrowed to slits. "Who are you to know that name?"

"If you were Cambione, you'd know. We can do things the easy way or the hard way." Marge cracked her knuckles. "Please say the hard way."

The lamia gave a hissing laugh. "Come, human. I will rend your flesh from your bones."

Marge grinned. "The hard way it is then."

The lamia crouched and leapt at Marge with her arms outstretched and her claws flexed. She brought both hands down to attack Marge in two long crossing slashes, but the Cajun girl pulled back and raised her arms defensively with her hands in fists. I stepped on the rail, swung around a pole, and brought my sword across the demon's back. She screeched and spun to face me.

"Gabby, what's going on?" Esais asked from the ear bud.

"We've run into one of the demon hybrids," I said.

"Do you need help?"

I looked from the lamia stumbling around to Marge, drawing her leg up in a kick. "No, we can handle this."

Marge brought her foot down on the backwards joint of the lamia's leg. She let out a shriek and turned, throwing its arm back to hit her. She slammed against the rail and the entire walkway wobbled. The demon flailed its arms to try to keep her balance. I stood and brought my blade across the creature's stomach. She howled in pain as blood gushed from the wound, and light reflected off of her black claws as she raised a hand towards me. I ducked down, grabbed onto the railing, and half hung off of the side of the walkway. The demon took two steps back from me and clutched her stomach, but the blood ran through her fingers.

Marge jabbed her foot in the lamia's wounded leg again, and the crack echoed through the building as the saint's bones embedded in her boots did their job. The demon screamed and leaped into the air, rearing both her arms back. One caught me in the abdomen, and my foot slipped, leaving me dangling over the edge. My sword slipped from my hand as I struggled to hang on. Marge stumbled back as she was hit by the other hand and went over the railing. There was a thud and a loud crack. The lamia latched onto the wall and scuttled out the widow we'd opened. I hooked my foot on the metal grating, scrambled up, and lay on my stomach, panting. Marge lay below me with one arm twisted in an odd angle below her.

"Marge?" I called.

She didn't move.

"Damnit Marge, answer me."

She only did with silence.

I took the metal stairs to the first floor two at a time then knelt in front of Marge's motionless form. I breathed a sigh of relief when her chest rose and fell. Her forearm was bent backwards, and the flesh had torn at her elbow.

"Esais, we need Tres here, now."

"What happened?" Esais asked.

"Marge is hurt."

"Show me."

I blinked. I didn't remember Esais's telepathic range being so broad. In Texas, he was able to reach us from a few miles, but now I was almost twenty miles away from the office. His presence filled my mind, accompanied by his choir. Their voices flowed through me, and my heart pounded with their cadence. Images of climbing into the window and scouting the warehouse came to the surface. My heart sped up as images of the fight replayed like one of Lucy's movies. I came back to reality to find Esais and Adrian standing over me. Tres was already kneeling beside Marge.

I gaped at Esais. "What just happened?"

He smiled mysteriously. "Time is a tricky thing with memories."

I got to my feet and glared at him. "In other words, you kept my mind occupied until you arrived. You can't just go in my head and do that without me knowing."

He raised his brows. "I'm sorry. I didn't know it was such a problem."

Adrian's gaze met mine. "Slippery slope."

"What's that supposed to mean?" Esais asked.

"All gifts have prices. I wonder what yours will be, and how far will it drag you down?"

Esais's face went white. "For the love of God, I've read her mind before. I didn't think it was a big deal."

"I let you before," I said as a chill crawled up my spine. "Have you done it without me knowing?"

Tres cleared his throat. "Have you done it to us?"

Esais's eyes widened, and his jaw stiffened. "Of course not!"

"Not yet anyway," Adrian said. "But will the time come when you decide it's necessary?"

Esais narrowed his eyes as he glared at his brother. Adrian met his glare straight on with a mask of arrogance. If he pushed any harder, he might have been the first to find out what Esais's breaking point was, but maybe that was what he wanted. Tres gaped at both of them with his mouth open as his hands hovered over Marge's unconscious form.

I nodded to her. "How is she?"

"Multiple broken ribs, broken arm. She got lucky, though. There's no internal bleeding. I can heal it, but only if I get some action. This is building up." He held up his right hand.

Esais broke his stare and looked down at Marge and his brother. "Heal her so we can leave. I'm going to have a look around." He walked off without another glance at Adrian or me.

"I will take upstairs," Adrian said.

He walked off with an almost self-satisfied look on his face. Tres ran his left hand from Marge's shoulder down her arm as he straightened it out. The bone of the elbow shifted under her skin until it looked normal and the ripped skin smoothed together like putty. He stepped back, shaking his right hand as he massaged his forearm. In Texas, he had plenty of opportunities to use his power. I'd even seen him cause someone's flesh to tear open by itself. Ever since we arrived in New York, he'd been playing more than looking to his duty. I hadn't seen him heal anything life-threatening, nor had I seen how long he could wait until ill repercussions started. With the problems we had already, it was better to keep this one under control.

"How bad is it?" I asked.

"Not bad. Just a strong itch I need to scratch."

"We'll make sure that happens," I said.

"What happens?" Adrian returned with my sundang in his hand.

Esais came up behind him with his arms crossed and his eyes narrowed. His brooding expression looked a lot like one I'd seen from Tres on many an occasion. For Esais it looked odd. I guess he didn't like being called out for something he didn't believe was wrong. Adrian handed my sword back to me.

"*Grazie*," I said. "Your brother needs some relief."

"I thought that's what the redhead you left with earlier was for," Adrian said.

"Well, I was interrupted," Tres said. "She's probably found someone else now."

Adrian scoffed. "Oh, the sacrifices you have to make for the family cause."

"Like you know anything about it." Tres wrinkled his nose and gave him a sour smile.

"Enough!" Esais said. "We have other things to deal with. What was this thing you fought?"

"A lamia hybrid. Lamias like to eat children and search for a mate to breed their own children. It never really happens, though. It's like some sort of curse for that line of demons," I said.

"I'm guessing they're from the Throne of Lust?" Esais asked.

I nodded, frowning. More demons from that Throne. They were making a major play, and I seemed to have gotten caught up in the middle of it. Lust always plagued me, but was it any wonder. Allegra, the very demon who cursed me, belonged to it, and her master constantly tempted me into succumbing to them.

Esais rubbed his forehead. "And it got away with no way for us to find it."

I glanced down at the congealing blood on my sword. "Not true. Is Lucy back yet?"

"Tomorrow," Esais said.

I held my hand out to Adrian. "Give me a napkin or piece of cloth."

"And I would have that because?" he asked.

"You have tiny robots that make things," I said. "Come on."

He sighed, removed a piece of paper from his jacket pocket, and held it in the palm of his hand. The edges disappeared as if being eaten by an invisible fire. It grew smaller and smaller until it disappeared into nothing. A small white dot formed in the center of his palm. The white spiraled out into a cloth handkerchief. I shook my head. Modern Science couldn't explain that. I took the handkerchief and wiped my blade. I rubbed the cloth together, making sure all the blood soaked in.

"Lucy may be able to track the lamia with some of her blood," I said. "We just need to be patient."

"We are the picture of patience." Esais sighed and looked at Adrian. "What about you? Do you have anything yet?"

"No," Adrian said.

"What is taking so long?" Tres asked.

Adrian stared him down. "Infiltrating a corporate network takes time."

"In the meantime, we're stuck sitting on nothing while the demons run the city," Esais said.

My breath caught in my throat, and I sputtered. Once again, an arctic presence washed over my mind, numbing me from the inside out. My hand shook so hard my sword slipped, and I had to catch myself before dropping it. The pressure in my head grew, and I stumbled, grabbing onto Adrian for balance. I scanned the walkway above us, looking for any signs of my attacker.

"What is it?" Esais's gaze followed mine. "Is the creature back?"

The presence vanished.

I stared at him as I rubbed my arms. "Was that you in my head just now?"

His forehead scrunched up as he frowned. "No."

"Well, something was." I scanned the building with a shiver. "It was so cold."

He paled and swallowed hard. "Are you suffering any headaches?"

"No, it was just nosy," I said. "I thought you were looking into this thing."

"I am, but it seems to be interested in you. No one else has said anything." He looked to his brothers. "Maybe you're imagining it."

"I'm not imagining this."

"This past week has been pretty stressful. Maybe you should take some time off while we wait for Lucy," Esais said.

"I've been dealing with stress all my life and haven't had an issue," I crossed my arms and glared at him.

"Except in Texas," Adrian said.

I shook my head. "That was due to supernatural influence. This is probably the same."

"Either way, you can take a couple of days off. Visit John or something," Esais said. "We'll call you if the world ends or we find a lead."

I pressed my lips together in a thin line. "We got what we came here for. Let's get out of here."

"That may be the smartest thing you've said today," Adrian said.

I gave him a withering look and headed up the stairs. I was not going crazy, not like in Texas. Maybe it was some demon playing with me, like Faust. Just because I couldn't touch this threat, didn't mean it wasn't there.

John waited for me at the edge of the pier that overlooked the Hudson River. Snow crunched under my boots as I walked up to him, rubbing my arms as the cold seeped through my wool coat. He grinned at me with his nose slightly red.

"When I called, I expected to meet you back at your apartment," I said. "Not out in the middle of a frozen park."

"You sounded like you needed something more comforting." He pulled me close for a warm hug.

I inhaled his aftershave and felt warmed in a different kind of way. He took my arm and pulled me to the end of the pier to a telescope sitting in the middle. I looked at him with raised eyebrows.

"You said you couldn't find a place to see the stars," he said. "Well, I give you the stars."

A smile crept on my lips. "So this is why you brought me here?"

"Well, I do have a little information about the demons." He pushed me to the telescope. "First, enjoy."

I leaned forward and placed my eye in the eyepiece. A

group of stars shone brightly and so close against the deep black. I reached my hand out, even though I knew I was still thousands of lightyears away. A sense of longing filled me, an emptiness I couldn't explain. I wanted to join them in that vast emptiness.

"That's Canis Major. It holds Sirius, the brightest star in the sky," I murmured.

"I thought you might appreciate it," John said.

He moved closer to me, to where his chest brushed against my back and his breath warmed my cheek. It tingled along my chilled skin and spread through my body, causing a light fluttering feeling in my chest. My nipples hardened, rubbing against my bra. My lips parted as I drew in a ragged breath, spun, and pressed my hands against his warm chest. The stars were lifetimes away, but John was here with me now, so close his spicy aftershave filled my nose.

"It's . . . beautiful." I cleared my throat and turned back to gazing through the eyepiece. "So, what information do you have for me?"

"Well, I dug up a little more on Faust. Apparently, those he possesses do become him, and all have his ambition."

"I don't see much difference from other demons. Well, other than the ability to possess other demons."

"How about the fact he can possess multiple victims at once? Humans, demons, and God knows what else."

I tilted my head. "What?"

"From what I can understand, and you are much better at this demon stuff than I am, he can leave pieces of his essence in others. It gives him control over them."

"Wouldn't that weaken him? How the hell does he control more than one at the same time?"

John shrugged with his hands at the level of his shoulders, his mouth drooped open in a half-lost look. "You got me. I guess he doesn't have complete control. Like they have minds of their own? Apparently his puppets, not really sure what to call them, have been known to kill one another to gather more Faustian power."

I blinked. "Wouldn't that be counterproductive for him?"

"Hey, I'm only giving you what I know. I'll leave your brilliant mind to figure it out."

"That's . . . interesting." I stared into the sky, trying to digest this new information. "So, any idea what he wants with this drug? Is he looking for more demons to possess?"

John sighed and stuck his hands in his pocket. "No, but I think this Cambione is one of him. At least from what information I could get."

"That makes Faust the ringleader in this," I said. "I wonder if he has Marge's contract."

John shook his head. "Cambione probably still holds it. He's the one who claimed it."

"I still haven't found him. My leads have been taking me everywhere else," I said.

"Where have you been looking?"

I snorted. "Well, I'm sure you read about the weird purple fire in Brooklyn?"

He chuckled and shook his head. "Wrong place. Cambione is operating on a richer scale. He has someone as a go between for the lower end."

"The lamia," I said. "She's constantly on the move."

"He also has several runners in the club scene. You might try there if you can't find her."

I sat on the pier, wrapped my hands around my knees, and stared up at the night sky. There weren't any clouds. John had really chosen the perfect night to pull this off. He knew me so well and went to great lengths to try and bring me small bits of happiness. John sat and leaned in close to me. He rested his hand on my chin, turned my face toward him, and studied me for several moments. What could he possibly see? My face had to be as shadowed as his.

His voice was soft with concern. "You sounded really upset earlier."

I lifted one shoulder, trying to seem nonchalant. "Just a little argument."

"That tone in your voice means it's nothing little."

"It's just . . ." I pressed my lips together. "I'm either being stalked psychically, or I'm going insane. Again."

He frowned. "What do you mean?"

"I keep feeling this presence in my mind. I don't know where it's coming from. It's not—" I bit the inside of my cheek.

John didn't know about Esais's or the others' gifts. I doubted they wanted me spreading their secrets around, especially since they didn't trust John. Was I being a fool by placing so much trust in him? After all, hadn't the night in the hotel proven how little I knew of him?

John leaned forward. "Not what?"

I shook my head. "It's probably just in my mind. The others haven't felt anything. They think I need a break."

John gave my hand a gentle squeeze. "They don't know you like I do. Whatever it is, you'll beat its ass."

I chuckled. "You have a lot of faith in me."

"Of course." He brought my hand to his lips and kissed my fingertips. "You're my savior, after all."

"Even from spiders?"

His chuckle held a strained cord. "Yeah, about the other night . . . It's something I've never gotten over since I was a kid."

"That was a pretty big reaction."

He shuddered as he stared out over the frozen water. "They're always around, just watching and waiting, with their spindly legs and glittering eyes."

"I'm surprised this is the first time I've heard about this," I said.

"Well, we all have our secrets." He shrugged. "Besides, I thought this wasn't a real relationship, just friends with benefits."

"Even friends know a lot about each other, like their fears."

His lips pressed into a thin line. "This is more than just the spider thing, isn't it?"

"No." My voice had a slight edge to it. "It's just you know so much about me . . ."

"You still don't trust me." He stood up and paced. "For Christ's sake Gabby, what is it going to take?"

I swallowed the lump in my throat. "I . . ."

"Fine, you want to know about me? My favorite color is emerald green. I like Classic Rock, but you already know that since we've listened to it together. I live in a one bedroom apartment and bust my ass to bring you information to hunt demons."

"John, stop."

He spun and faced me, pointing his finger out. "It's really messed up, you know. You want me to get you this information, yet you don't trust me. How does that make sense?"

"I'm sorry," I whispered.

The air deflated out of him, and he sighed. He sat a few feet from me with his shoulders slumped. He met my eyes directly and spoke in a quiet voice. "Seriously, what do I have to do?"

"Talk about yourself," I said. "That's all I'm asking."

"And that will really make you trust me?"

I rested my hand on his. "It's a start."

❧ 14 ❧

I crossed my arms and watched Adrian type furiously at his laptop. Bits and pieces of old electronics lay strewn across the desk and the tables along the wall.

"Anything on Acesco yet?" I asked.

"That's what I'm currently working on."

I walked around to peer over his shoulder. "Well, what do you know about the main company?"

He sighed and half closed the laptop before I could read anything. "I will tell you when I have compiled everything. Shouldn't you be out chasing demons?"

"I'm still waiting on Lucy to get back to me."

"What about your boyfriend? Isn't he doing something?"

I shook my head. "No word."

"That must be a strain."

"My relationship is fine, thank you."

"I'm sure. You know trust is the key to any relationship."

"I do trust him."

"That pause in your voice says otherwise."

"Yes, we can all rely on your wisdom. Because you are such an expert on relationships."

"You would be surprised. I have a bit of experience in failed ones."

I opened my mouth, but nothing came out. That was interesting. He kept his face neutral as he typed away.

"This is not an opening for a heart to heart. I have work to do," he said. "It would get finished faster without people pestering me."

I wandered out, wrapping my arms around myself. My pace slowed to a crawl as I climbed up the stairs to the fourth floor. How much did I know about Adrian's past? His schooling in America, his incarceration for arms dealing left a whole lot of room for things that weren't covered. It was the same with John. I never knew he feared spiders. I was so focused on hunting demons, I never noticed how little he talked about himself. I let out a sigh. He couldn't have betrayed me, which meant I'd somehow lost the Menrazine in Texas during my bout with madness. Anyone could have picked it up. I swallowed at the sudden dryness in my throat. Marge jammed her shoulder into me as she stomped up the stairs past me.

"Hey," I exclaimed.

She glanced back at me with a death glare. Deep shadows lay in a valley under her swollen eyelids and her skin had taken on a sallow quality that was visible even in this dim light. She exited to the fourth floor and slammed the door shut behind her. I took the rest of the stairs two at a time and caught up with her in the small hall near our makeshift locker rooms.

"What's with you?" I asked.

"Nothing. I swear, you are so damn nosy." She threw her hands in the air.

I crossed my arms. "You look like hell. When was the last time you slept?"

She snorted and turned to the locker room. "I don't need a vacation like you did. I have a demon to find."

"And not sleeping has gotten you closer? Did you find Cambione, and I just wasn't informed?" I looked around and spread my hands wide.

She scowled. "Look. If you have any news, let me know. Otherwise, fuck off. I'm fine."

With that, she shut the locker room door in my face.

My phone in my pocket vibrated and started playing "Wandering Stars" by Portishead. I sighed and pulled it out. Lucy's name flashed on the little screen.

"Please tell me you were successful." I said.

"Not exactly." Her voice crackled over the phone.

"What do you mean, not exactly?"

"I think the drug is interfering with the dowsing."

"You couldn't find anything."

"No, it just keeps moving, and it takes forever to find a location."

"We're going to have to wait longer."

"No, the last location I managed to get was in Queens, but she seems to be on the move again."

"It's worth looking into. Give me the address."

I fumbled in my jacket for a pen and piece of paper as my heart raced in my throat. This wasn't what I was expecting, but at least it was a lead. There might be demons for me to kill even if the lamia wasn't there. I wrote down the address, hung up with Lucy, and stepped into the locker room. Marge glared at me with her shirt half over her head, looking more laughable than intimidating.

"Looks like you'll be earning that paycheck. We need to find Esais," I said.

"Cambione?"

"I doubt it."

She scowled and crossed her arms. "Then why should I care?"

"Because you'll enjoy it better than the punching bag." I sent my thought to Esais. *"Where are you?"*

"In Adrian's office. Come here, I want you to meet someone," he sent back.

"I have to talk to you anyway." I looked at Marge. "Come on. The faster we get this done, the faster we get out of here."

Adrian's office had become crowded. He still sat at his desk with a sour smile on his face while Esais stood on the opposite of the desk with his back to me. Beside him stood a young man with slender shoulders and dark blue hair that brushed the bottom of his neck. Tres leaned against the wall near the door with his cell phone in his hand.

Esais turned around and smiled at me. "Gabby, Marge. I'd like you to meet our newest member. This is Viktor."

The boy turned around and nodded at me with a smile.

"Hello," he said in a light Southern accent.

I took his hand in mine. "Gabriella Di Luca. It's a pleasure to meet you."

Marge looked him up and down. "New blood, huh. He doesn't look like much. How many monsters has he killed?"

Viktor's smile disappeared, and he scratched the back of his head. "I haven't killed anything, actually."

"So, why are you here?" Adrian looked to Esais. "Please tell me this isn't some sort of relationship whim."

Esais glared at Adrian. Viktor's face turned a deep red, and he cleared his throat, looking at the ground. There was a moment of silence where the whir of Adrian's laptop was the only thing heard.

Marge let out a choking laugh.

"Seriously? I should have guessed." She yanked her thumb behind her at Tres. "I would have thought the pretty boy, but he chases too many girls."

"Jealous?" Tres asked.

"Nope."

Esais turned his glare on Marge and Tres before returning to Adrian. "No, this is not because we're involved. Viktor has a gift that has drawn attention. He wants to know how to defend himself."

"Take a Karate class," Marge said.

"Not helpful," I said, turning to Viktor. "But she has a point. This is a life thing, not a job, or a hobby, and it will put you in more danger. If all you want is to protect yourself, we can give you basic tips."

He shook his head. "Oh, I want more than that, honey. Esais says I've been gifted, and I want to use it to help others."

"What kind of gift are you talking about?" Tres asked.

"It's easier to show," Viktor said.

He scanned the room until his gaze landed on a stack of plastic compact discs on the table and his brow furrowed. The discs rattled, shook, and lifted into the air. They circled around the room, making a rainbow pattern on the walls as they caught the light. Tres gasped. Adrian gripped the edge of his desk, and his smile disappeared. Esais crossed his arms and grinned.

"Damn, so he's another emissary freak, huh?" Marge said.

"Not exactly," I said. "He's a nephilim."

"A what?" Adrian asked in a cold voice.

"Like the biblical half angels?" Esais asked.

"Sort of. That's where they got their name, because I think some of the first were

born from angels." I tried to think of a way to explain. "You all know of Greco-Roman mythology, correct?"

We looked at Marge.

She glared at all of us. "What? I'm not stupid. I know. What do they have to do with this?"

"The emissaries would be the avatars of gods while the Nephilim would be the children of those avatars, like Hercules," I said. "I don't really know the extent of their powers, though."

"So, what else can you do?" Tres asked. "Besides parlor tricks?"

Viktor's brow furrowed again, and Tres rose in the air. His eyes widened and a muffled curse left his lips. His body was frozen with hands clutching his phone and elbows close to his sides. Viktor smirked and stood with his arms crossed as he surveyed his work. Tres lowered back to the ground gently.

"All right," I said. "But he still needs to be trained."

"I've already started on lore." Esais looked at Marge and me. "But I want the two of you to handle his combat training."

"We're busy," Marge said. "We have a demon to catch."

"Or four," I said. I updated them on my conversation with Lucy.

"So, the lamia's not there," Tres said. "Seems like a waste, but hey, have fun. Is this over? I have a date."

"Cancel it," Esais said. "You're going with Gabby and Marge."

Tres scowled. "Why can't Adrian go? Or you and the new guy?"

"I'm working," Adrian said. "Something you really need to learn how to do."

"And I need to train Viktor. That leaves you." Esais crossed his arms. "You'll have to play later."

Tres's shoulders slumped, and he muttered to himself. "Fine."

"Be ready in fifteen minutes," I said. "Marge, you're driving."

Tres snorted. "We're going to die before we get there."

❧ 15 ❧

"This is starting to become a pattern," I said as I stared up at the abandoned building in front of us.

"I guess they figured that if it works, why do anything different?" Marge said.

The address Lucy had given me belonged to a dilapidated brownstone, squished in between several others. A metal fence surrounded the porch of the first floor, though the gate lay on the ground. Graffiti covered any available space on the wall, including the boards that covered the windows. A set of rickety steps led up to the second story, green metal balcony, also covered in graffiti.

Tres pointed to the front door on the first floor and the boards that lay scattered around it. "Looks like someone has been here."

"Let's pay a visit," I said.

"I'll check around back," Marge said.

"We'll wait for your signal." I touched the tiny bud in my ear. "Can you hear us?"

"Every word, unfortunately," Adrian said. "If there's any trouble, we'll swoop in and save you again."

I snorted. "I didn't need saving. We needed Tres more than you, and since he's with us, we'll be fine."

There was a muffled crashing of wood from inside and Marge's voice echoed in the house and my ear. "All right, you bitches, it's time to pay up."

I sighed. "That wasn't exactly what I meant when I said signal."

Tres chuckled. "But it's definitely hers."

I flung the front door open, pulled out a flashlight, and moved in with my sword ready. The front room held only a threadbare, brown couch and a coffee table with the finish worn away in multiple places. I kicked aside a pile of trash and moved to the hallway. Marge rushed at me and stopped short a few feet.

"Oh, just you." Her voice held a note of disappointment.

"Nothing?" I asked.

"Not up here," she said.

"There's a door," Tres called from the living room.

I paused with my hand on the door. "They already know we're here. So be ready."

The door swung inward and revealed a set of concrete steps. A wall at the base of the stairs and the rail blocked any view of the basement, but a dim light beckoned from below.

My footsteps made no sound as I moved down the stairs. A long table was pressed against the wall opposite the stairs lit by a small lamp. Tubes and beakers of a variety of sizes sat in stands on the table filled with dark liquids, and fire heated a Bunsen burner in the middle, emanating a sickly sweet smell. A figure slumped in a chair in the corner of the room.

I moved to where I could see the darkened area under the stairs and shone my light. The beam caught the flash of a brown arm. Tres gave a shout from upstairs, and there was a loud thump.

I shone the light under the stairs again. Marge and Tres

could handle whatever they had upstairs, and I sure as hell wasn't turning my back on whatever was down here. The light caught the creature full on this time, reflecting her orange eyes.

She was short and stocky with most of her muscles in her legs. Tufts of fur sprouted all over her body, but the most prominent was a tan mane around her face and head. The cat demon snarled at me, flashing her pointed fangs, and pounced. I flung myself to the side, and she went flying into the table with a crash.

I dashed closer and slashed her across her back with my sundang. She yowled as her dirty white t-shirt became soaked with blood. She spun, grabbed a stool from under the table, and slammed it into me. I staggered and my hip slammed into the side of the table. Pain shot through it and raced through my upper leg. That would leave a bruise.

As the demon swiped her claws at me, I ducked and slashed my sword across her stomach. She grabbed the blade, yanked it from my hand, and flung it across the room. I ducked back to avoid the swiping claws of her other hand, grabbed a glass beaker from the table, and smashed it into her face. Her skin sizzled and popped, and she covered her face with a yowl.

I leapt for my sword and came up in a roll, holding it. The cat demon removed her hands from her face to reveal burnt fur and melted red flesh. She scanned the room with her ruined eyes. A loud series of thumps filled the room followed by a crash behind me as something heavy hit the bottom of the stairs. It sounded too hard to be human, or so I hoped. The cat demon growled and leapt that direction, coming to land beside the stairs with her nose twitching in a sniff.

Marge raced down the stairs, with the attention focused on the small stone creature at the base. I tackled my demon and wrapped one arm around her shoulders. She reared up, trying to throw me off, but I held on. I ran my blade across her throat. She gave a choking mewl and staggered backward as blood poured from the wound. I tossed her body to the side and turned my attention to Marge and her adversary.

The stone demon rolled off of the stairs and stood up. It looked as if a man had been squished to the size of a child, but it had kept its width. It leveled its gaze at Marge and she froze with her entire body stiffening and her joints locking.

I came up behind it and slashed my blade along its neck. Metal grated against stone to no avail. That was fruitless. The stone demon turned my direction, and I averted my eyes. It gave an annoyed rumble, like grinding stone, and slammed its fist into my solar plexus. The air gushed out of me, and I clutched my stomach, backing up. Tres raced down the stairs, past Marge's paralyzed form, and laid his right hand on the demon's back.

"Let's see if you still bleed," he said.

His eyes squinted for a moment. The sound of cracking stone filled the room, and blood seeped from around Tres's hand. The creature spread out its arms and spun. Tres flew back into the stairs, knocking Marge over in the process. I scanned the room. There had to be something to bash this abomination to death. My gaze fell on a fire extinguisher near the table. I dropped my sword and grabbed it. Tres got to his feet as the squat demon waddled closer to him. He held his right hand out with his fingers spread wide.

I slammed the fire extinguisher into the crevice of the stone demon's back. The crack widened, causing more blood to gush from the wound. It streamed down its back and stained the gray stone a dark red. The demon swung its arm at me, but I side-stepped it and bashed it again with the metal canister. It dropped to its knees, but I didn't stop. I kept slamming the extinguisher into it until the demon stilled. I stood over my fallen enemies, panting, and glanced over at Tres.

"Remind me never to make you mad," he said.

"This isn't angry," I said and glanced at Marge. "How about her?"

He knelt over her and started inspecting her. "Her joints appeared to have stiffened. Interesting effect."

"That particular kind likes to paralyze its victims and sexually assault them," I said. "Though I didn't know its physical form would turn out to be actual stone."

"So, you've seen these things before?" Tres asked.

I pointed to the stone remains. "This was a Trauco. The other"—I pointed to the cat demon—"was a Bajang. They're both less powerful kinds from the Throne of Lust."

"More from Lust," Adrian said in my ear. "I wonder what this purpose is for summoning this many."

"She always wanted power," I said. "I guess this gives her an advantage over the others."

"She?"

"The ruler. Naamah."

"So what were they doing there?" Adrian asked.

I limped to a crate by the table and opened it as Tres continued working on Marge. Bags filled with a yellowish powder lay stacked on one another. I picked up my flashlight from where I had dropped in during the fight and walked towards the slumped figure in the corner. A black slick liquid covered the figure from head to toe, shining a slight rainbow reflection from my flashlight.

An orang. Another demon from Lust. His head rested on his chest and his arms hung on the arm rests. A plastic tube came from one of the limp arms and was attached to an I.V. bag hanging from a metal stand. Blackish red liquid filled the bag. I reached forward and clamped my hand on the wrist. Nothing. I turned back to the table and scanned the contents of the still intact beakers. The same liquid filled several of them. I turned the flashlight back on the man, and a sick feeling rose in my stomach.

"They were making Blasphemy," I said. "And they were using demon blood to do it."

❧ 16 ❧

Marge jammed her foot into Viktor's knee and sent him to the ground for the third time. She hopped back with a satisfied smirk and brought her fists up. Esais covered his face with his hand and gave a loud sigh. I shook my head from my position beside Esais on the bench.

"Watch your left side," I said.

They'd been at this for almost an hour. Viktor was panting, and sweat poured from his face. He hadn't called for a break though. Every time Marge knocked him flat, he just got back up and took the position I'd taught him. He picked things up quickly for someone with not a lot of training.

"Your mind is jumbled," Esais said.

I glanced at him. "Are you looking in places you're not supposed to?"

"Not on purpose. You're being loud." He cleared his throat. "Do you want to talk?"

I chewed the inside of my cheek, debating on where to start. "John says he gave the remaining Menrazine he had back to me when we were in Texas."

"But you are having trouble believing him?"

I ran a hand through my hair and sighed. "I don't know. I was going mad there. It could have happened. And if it did, well . . ."

"You think this is your fault."

"Isn't it? Either way, I let that drug leave Texas. Now we have God knows how many demons in the city and who knows where else brimstone could be."

He sighed. "You shouldn't lay the blame at your feet alone."

"Who else? You, Marge? No one else put their trust in John."

"But you needed to find out what we were dealing with. Did you have any other options?'

"None that wouldn't have taken weeks."

"And we don't know that someone didn't walk away from the hospital that we didn't know about."

"Wouldn't you have sensed that?"

"Not if it happened while Ose had me unconscious."

I sighed. "Point taken."

He gave me a soft punch in the arm. "Stop wallowing. What do you plan to do about it?"

"Make damn sure that this doesn't get out."

He became very still, and his voice softened. "That may take great sacrifice. Are you willing?"

I stared at Viktor and Marge until they blurred to only two figures moving. What was I willing to sacrifice to fix my mistake? My life, definitely, though I'd learned long ago that was almost impossible. The lives of those I cared about? Not if I could help it, but Marge and the Van Helsings knew the danger of this life. My mind? I'd rather not spend eternity condemned to insanity. What was the risk involved if I let this get out? Human souls lost . . . a multitude of demons walking the Earth. I nodded to him. He sighed and patted my hand.

"Well, I believe we've tortured Viktor enough for now," Esais said. "I'm taking him out to dinner."

I looked over at Viktor and Marge. Marge had him on his knees this time with a sadistic look of pleasure on her face. He deserved some time off.

"Ok, that's enough for today. Be here at the same time tomorrow and we'll pick up again, barring any emergency."

Viktor nodded and turned to Marge with a grin. "Thanks for the fun, sweetheart."

"Oh, don't," I said. "You'll make her think she's doing something right."

Marge smirked. "He likes the way I teach."

"God help us." Esais stood and picked up the gym bag beside him. He moved to Viktor and kissed him. "You ready to get something to eat?"

Viktor grinned shyly. "Are you cooking?"

"Ugh," Marge said. "I'm out of here. Searching for demons has got to be better than this."

Scowling, she stalked to the elevator. Esais watched her go with a chuckle and wrapped an arm around Viktor's shoulders. They waved to me as they left, chatting to themselves. I moved to the center of the mat, closed my eyes, and rotated my neck, letting the tension fade away. I breathed in deeply as I counted to ten and exhaled. My body moved through the different stances automatically, and I let my mind wander. Doing this practice helped me focus on what was important.

The demons were using their own blood to create a drug. Who was the mastermind behind this? Faust or Cambione? Or they could have gotten it from another entity altogether. No, that felt too complex for this, too many fingers in the pie, so to speak. I had to kill the both of them and take care of this hydra. Unfortunately, I didn't even know what

Cambione looked like, and Faust was in the middle of a corporation full of vampires. Once again, I had to remind myself that patience was a virtue.

I took a deep breath and stood up straight with a more relaxed body and clearer mind. I grabbed a towel and wiped the sweat from my brow. I was at a loss on what to do for the evening. Marge couldn't patrol all of New York for demons by herself. With a soft hum, I changed clothes and headed to the first floor. Adrian pushed past me on the stairs, carrying a large bag.

"Where are you headed?" I asked.

"Out," he said.

"Obviously. But to where?"

He stopped and looked at me. "Out."

He continued down the stairs to the parking garage. I frowned, my forehead wrinkling. Adrian hadn't left his computer in days unless forced to. He had to have made a breakthrough with Acesco, but why was he hiding it?

I took the stairs two at a time until I reached the garage. He was closing the back doors of the van. I sucked in a quick breath and sprinted toward him. I slid into the passenger seat as he was starting the ignition. He turned his head and glared at me.

"What do you think you're doing?" he asked.

"Coming with you," I said. "You're being secretive, and I want to know what you are up to."

"I'm not your boyfriend," he said. "You don't need to follow me."

I gritted my teeth. "You don't need to be scouting dangerous places on your own. This has something to do with Acesco, doesn't it?"

"I'm perfectly capable of handling this myself. You would just get in the way."

I buckled my seatbelt. "Deal with it."

He stared at the steering wheel. "Fine."

He pulled out of the parking lot and into the night. Adrian parked three blocks away from the Acesco building, got out of the car, and opened the back of the van. I climbed out. When he handed me the bag he'd been carrying, I blinked at its lightness.

"Since you're here, you might as well be useful," he said. He pulled out a rifle case and slung it over his shoulder. "Come on."

He led me to an alley across the street from our target, pulled out a set of binoculars from the bag, and studied the building for several moments before handing them to me. I put the device to my eyes and scanned the building. Most of the windows of the five stories were dark as the employees had gone home hours ago. Adrian scooted forward and peered at the entrance.

"It looks like two security guards. One at the desk, one who patrols," he said.

"You can tell all that from a few minutes?" I asked.

He glanced in my direction. "No, I've been watching this place for days."

I blinked. So much for assuming he hadn't left our office. He reached into his bag and handed me a folded bundle. It rolled out to reveal a long black coat with a hood. I held it up to my shoulders and looked at him questioningly.

"The coat will render you virtually invisible. It bends light around you." He pulled one of his own out.

"You made this?"

He nodded. "I only had time to make two. One was supposed to be my backup. Let's hope both work."

Adrian set down the rifle case and opened it. He put the gun together in quick, sure movements. I paused with my arm halfway in the coat.

"Are you planning on sniping the guards?"

"I have to take out the security system. Then we will sneak into the building and deal with the guards." He knelt and positioned the rifle.

"So you're going to shoot out the cameras?"

"It's a dart containing some of my nanites. They've been programmed to infiltrate the security system."

I looked from his face to the rifle. He wasn't behind a computer this time. "How do you actually give commands to those things?"

He tapped his head. "I implanted a radio chip in my head that relays all my mental commands. Can we get on with this?"

"Right." I shut up.

He aimed to the left of the door and pulled the trigger. The gun clicked and made a whooshing sound, jerking his shoulder. He stood up.

"We should move. We have maybe half an hour," he said. "Head around back. There's a loading area we can sneak in through."

I nodded and took to the alley. One truck sat empty in the parking lot. The light above the door flickered. I leaned against the rail, keeping my gaze on the truck. Adrian shifted around behind me for several minutes before the door opened with the squeak of metal.

He held the door open for me. I pulled out my sword and stepped into the warehouse. A metal rail divided the walkway from the loading area below. It was mostly empty, with a few boxes scattered throughout. I waved to Adrian and climbed over the rail. I headed to the door across the room. With Adrian's guidance, we snuck through the halls to the front of the building. I crouched down, peeking around the corner.

One of the guards sat at the desk while the other leaned over, one hand resting on the marble counter surrounding the front of the desk. He chuckled at something on the screen of the television in front of them. The low babble of voices drifted to my ears. They didn't notice me crawl toward them until it was too late. I took out the standing man with a hand chop to the back of his neck. The other one gaped at me for a second before he stood, his chair toppling to the ground. He reached for his gun, but Adrian swooped in from behind me and slammed his fist into the man's face. The man dropped.

"Nice punch," I said.

"Practice with Tres." He moved down the hall. "Do something about them."

I pulled a handful of heavy duty zip ties from a pocket, making a mental note to get more. I left them zip tied and tucked away in a janitor's supply closet down the hall. Cliché, I know, but it worked. Adrian stood behind the security desk, typing away on the computers.

"The server room is on this floor. Lucky you. No elevator ride," he said.

I smirked at him. "I could have taken the stairs."

"Come on."

I followed him down one of the halls to a set of double doors. He swiped a card against a black square on the wall and the doors opened with a beep. The room held rows and rows of metal computer boxes that were almost as tall as I was. Adrian moved to the far corner of the room and sat down in front of a monitor and computer.

His fingers moved over the keyboard rapidly and a black window with green writing appeared. He pulled out a box with a cord and connected it to the computer. I moved to watch over his shoulder. A file came up with a head shot of Raina Benson. Her red hair was pulled back into a ponytail, and a pair of square glasses rested on her nose. A forced half-smile hovered on her lips.

"She looks a little different from the conference," I said. "Still cold, but less rigid."

"I guess she enjoys vampirism." His lips pressed together in a thin line.

"Were the two of you close?" I asked, and my heart sped up for some reason as I waited for his answer.

The small box to his side beeped, and he pulled it free. "We're done here."

He stood then walked out. We headed down the same hall we had entered. My gaze bored into his stiff shoulders as I walked behind him. He was so closed off. Honestly, learning anything about him was like pulling teeth. Why did I even care, though?

The dim lights flickered. A shadow pulled itself from the wall, stood upright as a person would, and blocked our way out. I took a step back, trying to wrap my mind around the fact a shadow had become three dimensional. I turned and found another shadow forming behind us as well.

Damn. Trapped.

❧ 17 ❧

"Vampires?" I asked.

He nodded but kept his gaze focused on the one in front of him. I put my back to him and pulled my sword from its sheath. If it harmed demons' actual forms, perhaps it would do something against these monsters. The vampire's form in front of me undulated, thickening until it became three dimensional. My own shadow reached up and slapped my sword out of my hand. Its black finger brushed across my skin, leaving a chill behind that burned my flesh and left a deep ache in my bones.

"Damn," I whispered.

"Throw this." Adrian put a small marble in my hand.

I didn't look too hard at what he handed me. I just lobbed it at the vampire. It shattered against the ground and a puff of yellowish smoke exploded around the creature. It contorted, and a harsh cough emanated from it. The smell of garlic filled the air. The figure rushed from the smoke. Pale skin had replaced the shadow along with straw-colored hair. Adrian jerked his arm and there was another sound of breaking glass and the stench of more garlic.

The vampire in front of me glared at us as he pulled a pistol from inside the jacket of his charcoal suit. I swore, spun around, and yanked Adrian to the ground with me. We hit the ground in a roll, and I came up on top with my face just inches from his. His breath warmed my skin. The boom of the gun firing echoed through the hall, and shots flew over our head. The other vampire jerked and stumbled backward. Adrian stared at the gun with his eye narrowed. The blond vampire gaped as the handle of his gun began to disappear. I rolled off of Adrian, leapt to my feet, and ran toward my sword. My fingers grazed the handle before I slammed into the ground with all of the air in my lungs leaving me.

As the second vampire sat on top of me, blood dripped from the wound of his chest and onto my face. I tried to squirm out from under him, but he tightened his knees around my thighs. He pressed one hand on my chest, forcing me against the floor while he jerked my head to the side and exposed my neck with the other hand. With a hiss, he buried his fangs in my neck. An icy burn replaced the initial jab of pain. The cry I would have made died in my throat as a numbness replaced any warmth I had.

My fingers fumbled along the edges of the stake on my belt. If I could just get it free. The vampire's grip on my head and chest relaxed as he began to lose himself in draining me. I pulled the stake out and jabbed it into the vampire's neck. He jerked away from me with a growl as his hand went to his throat. I writhed out from under him and scuttled to my sundang as he tugged the stake free. I didn't stop moving until I was on my feet and well away from him with my sword in my hand. Adrian wrestled with the blond vampire farther down the hall. The vampire in front of me hissed again and pulled out his own pistol. The shots resounded in the air. I dodged down, rolled forward, and came up in a crouch. My blade swung in an upward arc and severed the hand holding the gun.

The ringing of gunfire in my ears muted his screams. He clutched his stump to his chest with his face twisted in an almost comical visage. These creatures really could feel pain. Well, I would be sure to put him out of his misery. I leapt up and spun, letting my sword follow my momentum. It sliced through his neck and severed his head from the rest of his body. I expected more blood, but I was wrong. The creature's form dissipated into wisps of shadow and his clothes crumpled to the ground.

I stepped back, leaned against the wall, and panted. My hand moved to the burning wound on my neck, and my fingers came away wet with blood. Surprising. My blood felt frozen inside my veins. I didn't know how it could even flow. Adrian pushed the other vampire against the wall and staked him. He turned and his gaze sought mine. He moved to me, pulled my hand away, and inspected my wound.

"I have a first aid kit in the van," he said in a faraway voice before turning away.

I used the wall to prop myself up as we made our exit. Now that the adrenaline had worn off, the chill had returned, and I seemed to have a perpetual shiver. The night air drove me to my knees. I tried to stand but my legs wobbled and I collapsed to the ground again. Adrian glanced back at me and shook his head with a sigh. He wrapped his arms around my waist and lifted me up. His body radiated heat and I leaned as close as possible as we hobbled back to the van. I pressed my hands against the full blast of the heater as he drove for several streets before stopping to tend to my wound. At the touch of alcohol on the bite, I sucked air between my teeth.

"You're experiencing symptoms of hypothermia," Adrian said. "It's common from a Strigoi's bite."

"S-so, b-blood loss and hypothermia," I muttered. "I d-don't see how their victims survived."

"Many didn't. In the past, Strigoi used to be rare. They controlled their numbers in order to stay hidden. That's changed now." Adrian pressed his lips in a thin line.

"How?"

"Erebus, the parent company of Acesco, has taken to hiring groups of humans whose main purpose is to feed them."

I blinked. "So they're paying humans to allow vampires to feed off of them?"

His lips twisted in a wry smile. "Well, that and the possibility of immortality. Supposedly everyone has a price."

"How do you know so much about this company?" I asked.

"They're vampires," he said. "I'm a Van Helsing."

"So are Esais and Tres, and they sure as hell don't know about this."

"Are you sure about that? Why do you assume you know us that well?"

I swallowed hard and crossed my arms. I hadn't noticed when my hearing had started to return to normal, but it had left an ache in my head that only compounded the chill and my sluggishness. Adrian could have told his brothers about this, and this was their way of handling it.

"I know you well enough," I said. "Esais would have taken more active interest if he knew humans were being used as food."

"And he would have gone riding in to save people who chose that path?" Adrian taped the bandage to my neck and started the car again. "They made their choice. We need to focus on destroying the vampires and the drug."

I shivered at the possibilities Synergy could have on the

populace, or was that just the hypothermia. Wait. "No, it's more than that. You know Raina Benson. Who is she to you?"

"Another vampire to kill."

I sighed. "You're not going to tell me."

"It's none of your business."

"What about Esais and Tres? Is it their business that you're running off to fight vampires by yourself?"

"I don't have to answer to them. Or anyone. Despite what you think, I am a grown man."

"Really? Because you were all set on coming on your own tonight. What if you had had to deal with those two by yourself?"

"You were the one bitten." Adrian pulled into the garage of the office. "You should see Tres and see if he can do anything."

He slammed the door as he exited and headed up the stairs. I hopped out and sprinted to catch up. The parking garage blurred around me, and the world tilted. I leaned against the back of the van and swallowed hard.

"This isn't over," I called after him.

"Yes, it is." He disappeared behind the closing elevator doors.

❧ 18 ❧

With a deep breath, I knocked on John's door. My heart thudded in my ears as I leaned against the doorframe and rubbed my upper arms. The chill from the vampire's bite lingered despite Tres's touch. By the time he had allowed me to leave, Adrian had disappeared again. I'd been commanded to go home and rest, but how could I sleep with these questions burning in my mind?

John pulled open the door and blinked at me. "Gabby, hi."

I took in the wet tips of his hair and the way his shirt clung to his chest. "Did I interrupt anything?"

He glanced behind him and back to me. "Nothing that can't wait. What's up?"

"I thought I would drop by and see if you could help me get to sleep."

His eyes smoldered, but he frowned as he studied me. "You're shivering."

"Long story," I said.

He wrapped an arm around me as he guided me through the door and to the bed. "One that's obviously on your mind. Sit and I'll make you something warm. Then you can tell me."

I sat down cross-legged and pulled the blanket up around my shoulders. The thought of hot liquid coursing through me sounded delightful, but even more, I wanted John's body against mine. He moved to the small coffee maker and pulled out several packets from the little stand.

"Coffee or tea?" he asked.

"Tea," I said. "That coffee is awful."

He grinned. "You are such a food snob."

"Wouldn't this be a coffee snob?"

"But I know you."

I chuckled. He turned back to the coffee maker. I brought my knees up to rest my chin on them as I watched him. What had I been thinking in suspecting John? He'd always been one of my staunchest allies. He constantly put himself in danger just to find information I needed, and he always listened to me drone on about my problems.

He had secrets, but he wasn't the only one. Adrian's face flashed through my mind, followed by the picture of Raina. I shook my head and smiled up at John as he approached with a steaming mug in his hand. I wrapped my hands around the porcelain and breathed in the sweet scent of cinnamon and apples.

"I think the hotel stocked it special for the holidays," he said.

I laughed. "I forgot it was almost Christmas."

He shrugged. "I didn't think you paid attention."

"I don't really."

He walked to the window and pulled aside the curtain. The lamplight reflected off the glass and obscured the city he stared out into. I sipped the tea, and the hot liquid spread through me, warming my numb limbs.

"What are you looking at?" I asked.

"Nothing." He turned back to me with a smile. "So, do you want to tell me what happened?"

"Vampires," I said.

He raised an eyebrow. "You've pissed off that corporation?"

"Adrian and I snuck in to get more information. Humans aren't the only guards they have." I rubbed the tender spot on my neck where I'd been bitten.

"You're upset at being bitten?"

"I'm cold, not upset."

He sat down beside me. "You are. It's why you showed up at my door."

I sighed. "Adrian is hiding his previous relationship with Raina."

John gave a soft chuckle. "Of course."

I glanced at him. "What?"

"Nothing. So, he's got secrets. This isn't news."

"These are dangerous. She's trying to distribute the brimstone, and he's holding back. I think he wants to deal with her on his own." I stood up and set the empty mug on the table.

"He's a vampire hunter, Gabby. I'm sure he knows what he's doing."

"Not with Faust." I crossed my arms. "I feel like I'm dealing with this in the dark, and it might get one of us killed."

He came to stand a few inches away from me. "Some things you just need to let go of."

I met his gaze with narrowed eyes. "What do you mean?"

"You have issues with not being in control. You're upset because he's handling this on his own."

I threw my hands up. "Which is what I just said."

"You've said he was brilliant." He put his hands on my shoulders. "You need to trust in his skill. Or is there something more to this?"

I glanced away from him. "It just makes me uneasy."

"If it was one of the others, would you worry this much?"

"Of course I would."

He gave a sad smile. "All right. You need information. Leave it to me."

"I didn't come here to ask that of you."

"Are you sure about that?"

I opened my mouth and shut it. Maybe I had subconsciously. I'd relied on John for information so many times in the past. Lucy would have been too cryptic, and Adrian was family to her. For the most part, I could rely on John and not have to worry about the familial outburst that would happen if I told the others.

"Yes," I said. "I could use your help."

"Done." He brushed his thumb along the line of my jaw. "You know, there are other ways to warm you up if you're still cold."

My coat brushed against his shirt as I stepped closer. "And what do you suggest?"

His breath tickled my ear, causing a shiver to race up my back. "This room has a very large tub…"

"You look like you may have enjoyed it already." My voice came out with a slight burr.

"Not as much as I will with you."

In one swift motion, he scooped me up and carried me into the bathroom. John set me on the edge of the tub and kissed me on the cheek as he reached past me to twist the faucet on. A rush of water echoed against the crème-colored walls and white tiles, and steam rose, filling the room with a lavender scent.

When I reached to pull my coat off, John's hands covered mine.

"Let me do that," he said. "I'm here to take care of you tonight."

My lips parted with a trembling breath as he slid my coat

off my shoulders and tossed it to the floor, followed by my shirt. I lifted my hips, balancing on my hands, as John tugged off my jeans and silk panties. He crawled between my knees and trailed tiny kisses along my thighs, up my stomach, and to my breasts. His tongue darted out, tracing along the edge of my bra while he unhooked it from the back. I climbed in the tub and sighed as the heated water enveloped me, but it was nothing compared to the flame erupting within as I watched John drop his robe and walk toward me.

"Is there room for me?" he asked.

I scooted forward. "It wouldn't be any fun if there wasn't."

He climbed in behind me with his thighs cradling my hips and his arm snaked around my waist, pulling me closer so I could feel his growing hardness. The hair on his legs rubbed against my soft skin, sending delightful shivers through my body. I tried to turn around, but he held me still, and something wet and spongy caressed my shoulder blades. I gave a small moan as the tension in my muscles eased under his expert touch.

"Do you like that?" He nibbled on my earlobe, sending another shudder through me, and the sponge stroked across my ribcage and down my hip.

I turn so that I straddled him with my hand braced against his firm biceps. Beneath me, I felt his cock stir to full attention. I arched my back so my breasts thrust forward with my rosy nipples hardened to stiff buds.

"I thought I should make it easier for you to get the front," I said in a husky voice.

With a grin, he leaned forward and took one of my nipples into his mouth. I gasped and let my hands trail over his shoulders and down his chest. He caught them before they reached his waist.

"Oh no," he murmured. "I'm in charge tonight."

His hand slid down to toy with my clit as his mouth found

my nipple again. My fingers dug into his chest, and through sheer willpower, I managed not to lower them. How I wanted to explore every inch of him, though.

I bucked my hips slightly, sliding my slit over his shaft. His groan mixed with mine as my slippery lips rubbed over the head and my nub brushed against the silken skin of his cock. I lifted up so I positioned his cock at my entrance, but he grabbed my hips before I could thrust down.

"Not yet." His gaze locked with mine.

"I can feel that you want me." I wiggled my hips against him.

He sucked in his breath. "This is about you giving up control."

He shifted me so I once again glided down his shaft, and his thumb found my clit again while his other hand held my hips still. My blood raced in my veins at every flick of his fingers as the pressure in my loins began to build, sending an aching need through every molecule of my body.

"Please," I whimpered.

His chuckle vibrated against my ear. "I'm here to please."

He lifted me up and, with one powerful thrust, he impaled me. My rejoicing cry bounced off the mirror and walls as we became one. He cupped my neck and brought my mouth to his for a bruising kiss, and our tongues danced and swirled as he pounded into me, causing the water to slosh over the lip of the tub. Our fingers twined together as I rode wave after wave of pleasure, letting him guide me to the heights of ecstasy.

❦ 19 ❦

My dreams were interrupted by ringing. John's arm lay sprawled across my stomach, trapping me against the soft satin white sheets. He gave a soft groan and rolled away as I sat up in the bed, and, after wiping the tears from my eyes, grabbed my phone.

"Hello?" My voice sounded hoarse.

"Gabby, are you still in bed?" Lucy asked.

Pale sunlight streamed through the thick white curtains. I had slept for most of the day it seemed. I ran a hand through my hair and licked my dry lips.

"I had a long night," I said.

"Well, get up. I found her," Lucy said.

"Found?"

"The lamia. But we need to move now. I don't have enough blood to track her again."

I flung the blanket from my body and hopped out of bed. "We? Are you going?"

"I thought I would. I need to get out of this hotel room," Lucy said. "And I want to try out these new knives Adrian made for me."

"Fine. Where?"

"Meet me in the abandoned Subway tunnel on Worth Street."

"I'll try to call people to see if we can get more backup."

"Just hurry."

I dialed Marge's number as I pulled on my jeans and hiking boots. The phone went to voicemail. I slipped my shirt and jacket on and tried Tres and Esais. No answer. I grabbed my sword and my bag of supplies. John raised up on his elbows and stared at me blearily as he pushed his rumpled hair away from his face.

"Off to save the world so early?" He cleared his throat.

I smiled at him. "Something like that. Lucy has a lead."

He sighed and collapsed back on the pillows. "Damn, I was hoping to spend the day with you."

I sat on the edge of the bed and leaned over to give him a long soft kiss. "Duty calls and all that."

His hand cupped my cheek as his tongue ran across my lips. "I guess I'll have to dig up the dirt you want so you'll come back sooner."

"Or you could just call."

"As long as no demons threaten the world."

"Right. But you knew that came with the package." I headed to the door.

"I wouldn't have it any other way." His voice softened as he watched me turn the knob. "Gabby, be careful."

"Don't worry about me." I gave a two fingered wave and left.

"Esais, can you hear me?" I sent out mentally as I sprinted down the stairs.

Silence greeted me. Strange, usually he answered me. I pulled out the tiny communication device and stuck it in my ear, pausing at the door that led to the lobby.

"Are you listening?' I asked.

"I wouldn't say I'm waiting to hear your voice," Adrian said.

I breathed a long sigh. "At least I got someone. Look, Lucy found the lamia."

"Excellent. You can now redeem your poor record."

"My record's not poor."

"One lamia. Zero Gabby. I'd say that's a poor record."

Bastard. "Are you coming?"

"No, I am in the middle of something."

I hailed a taxi on the street, hopped in, and gave directions. "Would that *something* be staring at your computer screen and a certain red head you refuse to give information about?"

"Either way, I will not be joining you. But I'll be here to speak if you need advice."

"I think I can handle it, thanks."

The cabbie pulled up on the corner of Worth Street. I handed him cash and climbed out. The street was slightly busy for this time of afternoon. I stuffed my hands in my pockets and headed to the abandoned subway. I slid past the barriers and flicked on my flashlight. Lucy waited for me at the bottom of the stairs. She bounced a little on the balls of her feet and waved me over.

"Which way?" I asked.

She pointed left down the subway tunnel. "Down there."

"Lead the way."

She climbed off the platform and waited for me to follow. "Careful of the third rail, dearie, we don't want to electrocute ourselves before we find the demon."

I trailed the light over the graffiti on the walls and down the dark tunnel. I took a long, deep breath and climbed down after Lucy. We walked close to the wall, and I concentrated on Lucy's back. After twenty minutes of walking, she stopped and held up a small silver pendant. It was an inverted teardrop, the point stained with a dark substance. It quivered pointing to a maintenance door covered in rust. She pushed at the door several times before it opened with a creak that echoed through the tunnel. I followed her in and down a set of metal stairs that quavered and squeaked under our weight.

"What are you expecting to do to her?" I asked, trying to focus on something beside the walls that were so close together.

Lucy stopped and grinned at me. She pulled out two small, round punching knives sheathed in her belt. She fit them between her middle and ring fingers and curled her hands into fist so the blades stuck out. I shone the light on them. A small round symbol was engraved at the base where the blade met the handle. I'd seen it before.

"Those are the blades Adrian made?" I asked.

She nodded.

I tapped the earpiece. "You're giving out weapons now?"

"Well, everyone needs to be able to fight in a city full of demons."

"I didn't know you could produce that."

"Why couldn't I? It's just a symbol."

"It's more than just a symbol. I've told you this before. They take precision." I fiddled with the handle of my sword. It didn't feel so unique anymore. "Have you given any to Marge?"

"No, these are the first."

"So, you're putting Lucy in danger and hoping they work?"

"They work on the bullets, the symbol hasn't changed. I'm just looking for any differences."

The pendant in Lucy's hand vibrated again, and she sheathed her knives. "Come on. I don't want to lose her trail."

We turned down a hall, and the walls became a crumbling brick. The floor came to an angle with a dip in the middle. My feet became immersed in stagnant water, and a stench arose. I gagged and focused my light ahead of us. My heart pounded in my head so hard I swore it thudded through the corridor. We twisted and turned through several halls until we arrived at a small room. There were three other tunnels connected to it. Lucy's pendant began to spin like a fan at full speed. She stared at it, biting her lip, her brow furrowed.

"Problem?" My voice had risen several octaves.

"Hmm, it should give us a path . . . but . . ."

I wiped the sweat from my brow and drew a shaky breath. Why was it so stuffy down here? I almost missed the bite of the winter wind. I rested my hands on my knees and bent my head down, counting to ten. I looked up again and the world turned gray. Lucy's aura sparkled with a mix of excitement and confusion. Something flickered in the corner and darted our direction.

"*Merda.*" I leapt up and shoved Lucy from the center.

She stumbled to the side with a grunt, leaving me to face our attacker. I gasped. The lamia slithered towards me on a long tail with her scales scraping against the stone. Her eyes glowed with the malevolence as she grinned in anticipation.

I tried to dodge, but she was too quick. Her tail closed in around me, trapping my arms to my side. I struggled, my breath caught in my chest, my eyes wide. I whimpered as the coils tightened around me. Lucy moved in and threw two quick punches at the creature's tail, leaving blistering wounds where they struck. The lamia hissed and backhanded Lucy. The girl's small form flew across the room and slammed into the wall with an echoing thud. She stood and staggered, rubbing the back of her head. The lamia looked down at me with her long fangs extending over her pale lips. Lucy came from behind with her fist raised. She jabbed one of the punching knives into the middle of the lamia's back. The demon half turned her torso, reached behind, and grabbed Lucy's arm. A snap echoed through the room, and Lucy cried out.

"Gabby?" Adrian said from the earpiece. "What's happening?"

I gave a choking grunt as the tail constricted again. My breath came out in short pants, and the world started spinning. The lamia looked down at me and bared her fangs in a sadistic grin.

"Gabby, breathe," Lucy said. "I'll get you out of there but you need to focus."

What the hell was she saying? I was focusing on the fact that this snake monster was trapping and squeezing the life out of me. I was going to die in this tiny hall, just like a grave, a coffin. I screamed, and the lamia laughed.

"Count to ten with me Gabby," Adrian said. "Breath in and one . . ."

Two, the air filled my lungs. The scales scratched at my skin, and my prison grew tighter. My chest ached, and I felt a pop from inside me. Lucy pulled out a large bottle and tossed it at the tail. It burst and sizzled with a puff of steam rising. The lamia let out a shriek, and the coils loosened, allowing me to scramble out and to the far corner of the room. I patted my side and found it empty. My sword was somewhere under all that snake.

I pulled a canister from my belt and lobbed it. White smoke surrounded the lamia, and she screamed again. She rushed from the holy water mist and right into Lucy. I hurried to my sword.

Lucy brought her right blade up to bury it in the lamia's chin. The creature snatched her head to the side and brought the back of her hand up to smack the blade aside. She reached for Lucy with her other arm, but Lucy rolled off to the side and came up in a crouch. I welcomed the adrenaline that pumped through me and abated the pain in my side. I moved forward to block the demon from pursuing Lucy.

I brought my blade up to slash diagonally across her stomach. Her nails clacked against the metal as she caught the blade. She hissed at me.

"You were so talkative before? Did you lose your tongue?" I asked.

The forked tongue in question flicked out from between her pale lips, and she snapped her teeth at me. "No need to converse with the dead."

"I doubt you could kill me. Lola was inadequate. You're not much better." I jerked the blade away from her and spun low to deliver a quick slash to the lower part of her tail.

Lucy snuck around to her other side and jabbed both of her blades under the creature's ribs. She screeched and flicked her tail so that the tip slapped against the back of Lucy's knees. The girl toppled over with a grunt, and the demon slid her scales over her until she covered Lucy. I brought my blade across her abdomen, hoping to cut deep and disembowel her. She slithered to the side, and the sword only gave her a shallow cut. Green ichor from the wound and a sickly sweet smell mixed with sulfur filled the air. Lucy pulled herself free and stood, panting. We glanced at each other, and with a slight nod, we rushed her.

I spun around and leapt up, trying to latch onto her shoulders. Lucy went in low, aiming for her stomach. The demon grabbed me and swung me into Lucy. We both went flying and crashed in the wall.

The lamia's jaw distended, and she gave a hissing roar, her eyes narrowing into slits. She rose up and bashed her fists into the ceiling. The walls shook, and a rumble filled the room. Small stones fell from the brick. Her second strike hit her mark, causing the room to quake. Bricks, dirt, and rock tumbled down around her.

We were bathed in darkness.

$$\text{❧ 20 ☙}$$

I choked and sputtered as the dust clung to the inside of my lungs. I pulled myself up, trying to untangle my limbs with Lucy's. She groaned and shifted away from me as she sat up. Blackness surrounded us, and my flashlight lay buried.

"Do you have a light?" I asked.

Her clothes rustled, and a small, pale blue light erupted, giving her face an eerie glow. Blood ran from a jagged cut across her forehead and over her eyebrow. The bleeding quickly stopped, and the cut sealed itself starting from the outer edges.

I stood and held my hand out to her. "How's the arm?"

"Fine," she said.

"Adrian, can you still hear us?"

"The earbuds are sturdier than that," he replied. "What happened?"

I scanned the pile of broken bricks, concrete, and rock that stood before us. If the lamia had survived, there was no getting to her.

"The lamia brought the room down on us," I said.

"Do you need to be evacuated?'

I turned to the open tunnel behind us. It wasn't the one we came through, but at least it was a way out. I touched my side and winced. Hopefully we wouldn't become lost down here.

"Not yet," I took a deep breath and counted to ten. "Lucy, can you get us out of here?"

"I think so. Not sure."

"Great," I said. "Let's go. I'm starting to itch."

We walked for what seemed like hours all the while the ache in my side grew to a sharp pain. Lucy stopped at one tunnel crossing and looked at the compass in her hand. I leaned against a wall and panted, sweat dripping down my face.

She put a hand on my arm. "Just a little farther."

"I'm going to need Tres," I told Adrian.

"I'll call him," Adrian said. "Esais and Viktor are here. I'm coming to get the two of you."

The brickwork became newer as we walked, and soon we turned and found ourselves in a hall with metal steps and a maintenance door. We stepped into the subway tunnel, and I breathed an almost sigh of relief. Just a little farther, as long as we didn't get run over. The tunnel was dark, but we stayed close to the wall just in case.

Lucy gave me a boost onto the platform, and I groaned, lying on the dirty tiles in agony for several moments before I held my hand to help her up. I leaned on her heavily as we climbed the stairs. I breathed in the first breath of night air and savored it with its smell of exhaust and oil.

"We made it out." I tapped the ear bud. "We're on the corner of White and Centre Street."

"I'll be there in a few minutes," Adrian said. "Try not to draw attention to yourselves."

I glanced at Lucy's dirt-streaked face and our grimy clothing. He had a good point: people were already giving us side-long glances as they passed. I pulled Lucy back into the entrance off the subway tunnel and leaned against the stair railing as we waited. Thank god it wasn't long before Adrian pulled his van to the curb. Lucy helped me into the back, where I stretched out in the long seat while she climbed into the front. Adrian sped out into traffic and soon had us in front of the office. Once inside, I stared at my hated foe, the elevator. My gaze traveled to the stairwell, and my side flared with pain at just the thought of it.

"Come on," Lucy said. "I'll be inside with you."

I remained where I was. I could still feel the lamia's scales scraping against my skin. I didn't want to be trapped again. Lucy took my arm and gently pulled me inside the elevator. I squeezed my eyes shut and counted toward ten. I reached seven when the doors slid open with a ding.

Tres stood in the hall with his brothers, Viktor, and a curvy redhead who pouted her hot pink lips and clung to Tres's arms. They all looked in our direction as we stepped out. Tres pressed his lips together into a frown.

"Bring her inside," he said. "Delilah, wait here."

She crossed her arms over her ample breasts and gave him a glare. "This had better not take long. You said dinner." She tapped her red heeled shoe on the carpet.

I leaned close to Lucy. "Is he dating courtesans now?"

Adrian, who caught the last words, snorted but managed to hold his laughter. Everyone, sans Delilah, filed into the room. Esais and Lucy helped me onto the examination table. Tres ran his hands over my abdomen, and I gave a small hiss as he pressed down on the sore spot of my side.

"Cracked rib," he said. "Should be easy to fix."

"She got away," I said. "Again."

"Well, we have more of her blood. So I can always dowse and find her again."

"That hasn't worked out very well," Adrian said. "I have another plan. I have looked over the information from Acesco, and there are three warehouses ready to ship Synergy."

My skin under Tres's hands began to tingle and warmth spread through me. It tickled in my veins like tiny bubbles. The stabbing ache faded under that warmth. I breathed a sigh of relief and sat up.

"How soon?" Esais asked.

"Soon enough. We should move immediately," Adrian said.

I coughed. "Does that mean tonight?"

He looked me up and down with a long sigh. "Tomorrow night, then. We will need everyone because we're going to have to hit all three warehouses at once."

Viktor raised his hand. "Does that include me?"

Adrian's jaw tightened and he looked to Esais. "Well?"

"He needs to get some field experience," Esais said. "I'll be with him."

"And me," I said. "He hasn't had nearly enough combat training to leave the two of you alone."

"Then Adrian and Lucy will take one and Marge and Tres will take the last," Esais said.

Marge groaned. "Not the pretty boy."

Tres made a face. "I'm not looking forward to it, either."

"This isn't a social gathering," Esais snapped. "Work it out."

My phone buzzed in my pocket, it was a miracle it still worked. I pulled it out and checked the screen before I held it up for Lucy to see.

"Your father." I hit the answer button. "Hello, Jonah."

"Gabby, do you have a cold?" Jonah's voice crackled with a slight static.

"Just dusty," I said.

"I dread to ask. I've finished analyzing this Blasphemy. The base is indeed brimstone," he said.

Esais nodded to me once and moved closer to Adrian. The two of them began speaking in low voices while Viktor looked on with his brow furrowed. Tres moved over to Lucy while continuing to bicker with Marge. Lucy shook her head at him and moved closer to me with a questioning look. I held one finger up and turned my back on the group.

"I've pretty much surmised that," I said. "Did Lucy tell you about the other possibility we found."

"She did. I'm quite interested in this company."

I glanced at Adrian and chuckled. "They seem to be popular."

"Yes, well, the conference is wrapping up here at the Vatican in two days. I shall come to New York after."

"You're getting out from behind your desk?"

Lucy raised her eyebrows.

"I have a feeling you will need my legal expertise as well as my occult advice," he said with a long sigh. "Also, has anyone had a chance to study a human under the effects of this Blasphemy or the other one, what was it called?"

"Synergy," I said. "I saw what their souls looked like. Almost like it was being eaten away. I guess that's what makes it easy for the demons to possess them."

"And it just spirals out once possession has taken place. Hmm," Jonah's voice trailed off for a moment. "If possible, could you find one of the users who haven't been possessed?"

The abandoned building the demons had used for a drug den flashed through my mind. If there was one, there was sure to be others. "It shouldn't be too difficult to find one."

"Very good. I think it may prove useful, in learning more about this. Try to keep the children out of too much trouble before I arrive."

"Of course," I said.

"Please let my daughter know I will call with the details of my arrival."

"She's right here, if you wish to speak with her."

Lucy lifted up her hands and shook her head, backing away slowly.

"Unfortunately, I have a meeting to attend. I will speak with her later."

"Very well, Jonah. Thanks for the information."

"Well?" Esais asked as I hung up.

"The good news is we aren't dealing with a new way to turn humans to demons. Same as Texas," I said.

"Is there bad news?" Tres asked.

"Depends on how you feel about Jonah coming here in person," I said.

His shoulders slumped. "Horrible news then."

"Yeah, yeah, whatever," Marge said. "Are we done with this sewing circle?"

Esais crossed his arms. "Not yet. Adrian had a plan for tomorrow."

"You will each have eight charges you need to plant in the warehouse. Once they are planted, we will send a signal that will cause the charges to explode simultaneously in all three locations."

"That's it?" Marge asked.

"Patience is a virtue," I said.

She snorted. "Not one of mine."

"Obviously," Esais said.

Adrian glared at us all with his one eye. "There will be some sort of security, most likely guards, cameras, and an alarm system. I will also provide you with nanites to infect the system for a short period. Make sure you finish within that time."

"How long do we have?" Tres asked.

"About twenty minutes."

Tres shrugged. "That's not too bad."

"You say that now," I said.

"OK, so cut security, run in, plant bombs. Got it," Marge said. "Anything else?"

"For now, no," Adrian said.

"Please make sure you're not endangering human lives," Esais said. "We don't want them caught in the explosions."

Marge shrugged. "They shouldn't be there and working for vampires."

"They probably don't know," Esais said.

"Their fault for being blind." Marge pulled the door open. "Later."

Delilah stood from her spot on the wall and walked to the doorway. Marge shoved her to the side with one hand and continued down the hall, ignoring the protest and scowl she received. Delilah turned her brown eyes on Tres and gave him a petulant look.

"Are you done with your little meeting?" Her voice took a high pitch. "I'm starving."

"We just need to do the secret handshake," Adrian said.

It was my turn to hold back the laugh that rose in me as Tres glared at his brother. Esais just shook his head and took Viktor's hand.

"I suggest everyone get some rest," Esais said.

I grabbed the remains of my jacket and headed out. I was in need of a hot bath and a warm bed. How had I ever missed all this action? As much as that thought came, I knew deep down I lived for times like these. Even if I broke my curse, I doubted I would live a normal life. This was all I knew.

✾ 21 ✾

The security guard slammed his car door shut and switched on his flashlight. He passed it over the parking lot and rubbed his large stomach. I ducked down behind the car the three of us were hiding behind as the light made its way in our direction. Esais narrowed his eyes, staring off into the darkness.

"Two guards," he whispered. "Both human."

"I guess they don't want to spring for the undead kind of protection," I said.

"Eternity as a security guard? Not the kind of thing I would sign up for," Viktor said.

I chuckled softly.

"I'll handle them, you get to the camera," Esais said.

I pressed my body against the wall of the warehouse and crept to the door. A small black camera was bolted in the wall above the door, impeding any further movement. I touched the small bud on the inside of my ear.

"Camera at the door," I said.

"Can you reach it at your height?" Adrian's cool voice echoed in my ear.

"Funny. I'm not that short."

"Put the device I gave you on it. The nanites should do the trick."

I climbed to the stoop while keeping as close to the wall as I could. It took me rising on my toes, but I managed to plant the device on the camera. The small red light blinked off. I waved to Viktor and Esais. They did a half-bent, fast walk to the guard.

Esais shook his head. "No keys."

"I doubt they would really trust these humans with access to their merchandise," I said.

"I got this," Viktor said.

His hand hovered a few feet from the door and a click echoed from the handle. He pushed it open and motioned for me to go first. I pulled out my sword and new flashlight and stepped inside. The dim lights hung over rows of metal shelves filled with cardboard boxes. They towered over me as I walked between them. I shivered, scanning the tops of the shelves. Something could be crouched up there, ready to ambush whoever walked in uninvited. I shone the lights over them and found nothing.

"Clear so far," I said.

I moved past the shelves to a more open area of the warehouse as Esais stepped inside, followed by Viktor. The center was mostly clear of shelves and the floor descended in a ramp down to the loading dock where three large, metal doors stood shut. The air conditioner rumbled to life, its rattle echoing through the open building. I nodded to the stairs along the left of the wall leading up to a landing. A metal bar guarded the walkway that led to several offices. Esais slit one of the boxes open with a knife and pulled out a white bottle. On the label stood a woman in a sports bra with her hands on her hips. Synergy was written across the bottom in yellow dynamic letters. I raised my flashlight up the shelf, spanning the rows of boxes stacked, and gave a low whistle.

"This is a lot," I said through the earpiece. "Adrian, Marge? What have you found?"

"A shit ton," Marge said. "The warehouse is full of it."

"Boxes and boxes," Tres said.

"Ours, too," Lucy said.

"How did they make so much so fast?" I bit the inside of my cheek and stared at the wall.

Esais looked to me with a troubled expression. "If it comes from demon blood, they have a lot of demons somewhere."

Adrian said, "They are using the Blasphemy users."

A chill ran through me. "All they have to do is take them from the drug dens, like the one we found."

Viktor cleared his throat. "Or from the nightclubs. There has been a rumor going around in the club I work at about an awesome new drug."

I swallowed hard as a sick feeling rose in the pit of my stomach. "Let's get to burning this. If this spreads around the globe, I don't know if we can stop it."

A truck rumbled outside. I froze, waiting for it to pass, but it only grew closer. Esais stiffened and grabbed Viktor, pulling him behind one of the shelves. I crouched behind another one and cut off my flashlight.

"We have company here," I whispered.

"We have some of our own, dearie," Lucy panted in her microphone with the background of grunts and gunshots. "But it looks like they were already here."

The engine of the truck cackled and puttered in its mechanical laugh and was accompanied by a steady beep right outside the left metal, roll-up door in the loading dock. The roar of the truck was cut, and two doors slammed. The click of a lock echoed through the warehouse, and the door slid up with the screech and rattle of metal. Boots thumped across the concrete, and the room was bathed in a yellow light. A tall, thin man with a long, pointed nose stood at the power box. He nodded to the second man, this one with a thick barrel chest, who pulled a ramp from the truck.

"Grab those boxes over there," the thick one said. "The bitch queen will have our asses if we don't hurry."

I switched to my aura sight. In the corner of my eye, I could see Esais's bright radiance which eclipsed Viktor's sparkle. I turned my head and focused on the two newcomers. Both were devoid of any color. Their shapes had disappeared, leaving behind only shadow.

"Vampires," I sent to Esais.

"They're taking the drug out," Esais sent back.

"Looks like it." I clutched my sword tighter and pulled out one of Adrian's garlic smoke marbles. *"I'm ready when you are."*

The thin man drew closer to us. A few more steps, and he would see me with just the turn of his head. I shifted on the balls of my feet, ready to spring at Esais's word. The vampire pulled a box from the shelf one row down from our hiding spot and turned to walk back to the ramp. He took two steps, froze, and clutched his head with a pain-filled cry. There was another cry from the large vampire at the truck. Excellent. He'd gotten both of them. The box tumbled, stopped only a few inches from the ground, and slammed into the thin vampire. He stumbled back and blinked, looking around in panicked surprise.

I tossed the smoke bomb at his feet. It flared to life in a quick flash, and the scent of garlic and sulfur filled the air. The vampire stumbled out of the smoke and pulled his gun, his gaze landing on me. He fired off several shots. I dove behind the shelf, hitting the ground. The bullets hit the boxes with a dull thud.

"What the fuck is going on up there?" the other vampire called.

"*I thought you had him?*" I asked Esais.

"*Their minds are slippery,*" he said. "*I will deal with him.*"

The thin vampire moved until he was only a foot from my cover. He turned his head back. "Just a pest, I have her trapped."

I lunged at the vampire and swung my sword at his neck. He stumbled back with wide eyes, his aim going sideways as he fired his gun again. The shot echoed against the concrete as bullets careened into the boxes above us. Esais hopped over the rails and disappeared from my view. There was another shout from the vampire below, and I grinned at my opponent. It was time to send the dead to their eternal slumber. If it had to be with blades and stakes, so be it. He raised the gun at me point blank.

"Let's see *this* miss you," he said.

I spun my wrist and brought the blade up again, severing his hand. It and the gun clattered to the floor. The vampire looked at the bleeding stump and his face twisted, the cheeks becoming hollow. His roar bounced off the metal walls, becoming louder and louder. Viktor leapt out of his hiding spot with a stake clutched between his hands. He raised it and jammed it into the vampire's back. The creature spun around with black veins creeping into the whites of his bulging eyes. The shadows that belonged to the shelves bent and flickered, twisting into thin whips.

"What the hell?" he snarled.

"Damn," Viktor said. "That's harder to aim than I thought."

"Try the front," I said.

In a flash, the black tendrils ensnared Viktor's arms and legs, forming viselike grips. He fought against them, but they tightened around him until he could barely move. The bonds lifted him off of the ground, stretched him out spread-eagled, and started pulling. The damn vampire was about to draw and quarter Esais's lover. Not if I had anything to do with it. I brought my sword up in an angle slash along his back. He ducked out of my swing and grinned, flashing his fangs.

Viktor continued to struggle against his bonds, but they had stopped pulling. I feinted to the left, twirled, and came up behind the creature. His momentum brought about his doom quicker as my sword was already swinging at his neck when he tried to turn and face me. Small tufts of shadow drifted where he once stood. Viktor dropped to the ground with a mix of a groan and exhalation of breath. He stood slowly, rubbing his shoulders, eyes scrunched up and my lips pressed together. The other vampire shouted in pain from the dock. At least someone seemed to be doing well.

"Esais?" Viktor called, and he ran towards the loading dock.

I pulled myself off the ground and joined him. Esais had another stake in his hand, and he seemed to be facing the vampire. Half of its face was in ruin from what looked like acid. I hopped down and joined Esais. The vampire snarled at the two of us and leapt at Esais. He slowed in midair. Esais slipped underneath him and rammed the stake into his heart as I ran my blade through his neck. His body didn't even hit the ground.

I sheathed my sword and pulled out the charges. "Let's set these and get out of here."

We each took two and split up. I took the upstairs with the offices while Esais and Viktor divided up the ground floor. We crept from the warehouse and across the parking lot like the shadows we'd just fought.

"Mission successful, here," I said. "Everyone else alive?"

"Yes," Adrian said in a grim voice. "Are you away from the warehouse?"

"Yeah, we're three blocks away," Esais said.

"We're done," Marge said. "Why did I get the warehouse with no action?"

"Look on the bright side," Tres said. "You get to push the button and get a light show."

"Send the signals then," Adrian said.

Esais pulled out a small remote and pushed a button. It gave a small beep. Yellow and orange lit the sky from the direction of the warehouse and a large boom reverberated through the night. Smoke billowed up like a giant cloud. I crossed my arms and watched with a smile. I was starting to like fire; it had a certain beauty in its finality.

"We shouldn't stay here," Esais said. "We'll meet back at the office."

"Great, you're buying drinks," Tres said.

I chuckled and followed Esais and Viktor back to the car. I couldn't blame Tres for wanting to celebrate. We'd finally had a victory in this whole mess. I wanted to hold onto this feeling of triumph for as long as I could.

Tres met us in the lobby when we arrived. "Any injuries?" His gaze landed on me in particular.

I rubbed my shoulder. "Just sore this time."

He gave me his charming smile. "Well you know, I could give you a massage. Rub the aches away and a few others."

"Mmm, still haven't given up, I see," I said.

"I'm still alive, aren't I?"

"Stick to your courtesans," I said. "They probably appreciate the flattery."

Esais gave a soft chuckle and shook his head. "I'm going to grab a sandwich. I'll meet you upstairs."

"Me, too," Viktor said. "I'm starving. Does hunting always build an appetite like this?"

"Only the good ones." I glanced at Tres. "Where's Marge?"

"She said she had better things to do than sit around and talk. If we need her, call."

I shook my head. "And Adrian and Lucy?"

"They just went upstairs to talk." His phone buzzed and he put it to his ear. "Hey, beautiful. Give me a little longer."

I left Tres to his current flavor and headed up the stairs.

Now that we had a victory, we needed to keep the momentum going. Adrian had to have had more information, maybe on where they were making Synergy.

Adrian's voice left his room. "Is this from your mother?"

I stopped at the hint of cold accusation. Damn it, Lucy. She'd said she would be careful. I warned her of this, and Adrian, out of all of them, had discovered her secret. At least with Esais or Tres, there could have been a little more understanding.

Lucy sighed. "Look, it's not a big deal. I'm still the same Lucy you've always known."

"If we ever really knew you. You've been hiding this our whole lives, haven't you?"

"So, I heal really fast. That's actually a boon to being a hunter. You don't have to worry about me being injured. Tres doesn't have to expend energy. It's really useful."

"So, this would make you immortal, like Gabby."

The elevator dinged, and Esais, Viktor, and Tres stepped out, chatting and laughing. I stepped into Adrian's office. Lucy turned with her mouth slightly open and her eyes wide. Adrian sat at his desk with his chin resting on his hands.

"Maybe this is a conversation that should be shared with everyone," I said, keeping a pointed gaze on Lucy.

"You knew about this?" Adrian asked.

"Know about what?" Esais asked from the door.

"Wow, things look a little tense," Tres said. "This must be good."

Lucy looked directly at me with an annoyed glare. She closed her eyes and let out a deep breath. "Fine. I guess you were right."

"Who was right about what?" Esais asked, looking around. "What's going on?"

"Apparently, Lucy has been hiding a gift of her own all

these years," Adrian said. "I watched her get almost eviscerated by a vampire only to have the wound disappear."

Esais and Tres turned confused looks at Lucy. She raised her arms in a half shrug and chuckled.

"What can I say? I'm difficult to kill. Not like Gabby, of course, but I get by," she said.

"So, you're an emissary?" Esais asked.

"No, I'm like your boyfriend who's hiding in the hall. You can come in, dearie. Let's all join in on this little drama."

Viktor stepped in the doorway, rubbing the back of his neck. "Sorry, hun, this didn't seem like my business."

"Why have you never told us?" Esais asked.

"Because there are some things in my life I don't like discussing," Lucy said.

"But you can heal yourself." Tres's eyes were alight. "This is part of what you are."

"Reckless," I said under my breath.

Lucy gave me another silent glare, which she then turned on the brothers. "Well, I wasn't the only one to hide things from this family, was I?"

Esais cleared his throat and stuck his hands in his pockets while Tres looked down at the floor. Adrian met her gaze unflinching. He would, of course. He was still in denial that he had any power at all.

"I mean, I had to hear about your abilities from Gabby when she called me last month. So, don't play that betrayed act with me." Lucy let out a huff and crossed her arms.

"We haven't seen you in years, Lucy," Esais said. "I mean the most we had was phone conversations with you and Uncle Jonah."

"Yeah." Tres snorted. "Not really the best way to have that conversation."

Viktor stepped forward and gave her a wide grin. "Great to meet another one. Do you know any others?"

She looked him up and down before a smile of her own crept to the corners of her mouth. "No, I haven't looked. I've never really been interested."

Viktor's smile faltered a little. "Well, just know you're not alone."

"She never was," Tres said.

"You honestly have no problem with this, do you?" Adrian sighed. "Of course not."

"Why do you have such a problem?" Tres asked. "It's Lucy."

Adrian stood, resting both hands on his desk. "Because all these gifts are poison. We know nothing about the entities that supposedly granted them. There's no such thing as a free lunch."

Esais swallowed and crossed his arms with a long sigh. "We have no idea if they even ask a price."

Adrian shook his head. "This is going to turn on us, eventually."

"If you say so," Tres said. "As much as you hate them, these powers have saved our asses, or your asses, more than often."

"For now," Adrian said.

Tres shook his head. "So, what now? The warehouses are gone."

"We need to find the factory they made the Synergy in." I looked to Adrian. "Where is it?"

He sat back down and began typing on his laptop. "I'm still looking into that. This information is heavily encrypted."

"So we're back to waiting," Tres said. "Excellent. I know how I plan to wait."

"Actually, no," I said. "We still need to find Cambione. John mentioned that he runs in a more expensive crowd than the dens, and his runners usually hit clubs."

Viktor nodded. "Like I said, there are rumors. And I noticed some new regulars."

"So, we start there," I said. "We find one who can lead us to Cambione. Also, we need to find someone on the drug for Jonah. He wants to study the effects before they are possessed."

"So we're adding kidnapping to breaking and entering, and arson." Viktor chuckled. "Life has gotten a lot more interesting."

"Don't forget supposed murder," Tres said.

I shrugged. "Call it that, but maybe we can find a way to help these people. They're as good as dead after they get possessed." I looked to Adrian. "Can you come up with somewhere we can hold the ones we bring back?"

"I suppose I could multitask," he said.

"Try to be gentle. These people don't really know what they've gotten into," Esais said. "We'll split up. Tres and I will join Viktor while he works."

Lucy crossed her arms and grinned at me, her annoyance forgotten. "Looks like I get to show you around my favorite spots."

❈ 23 ❈

I scanned the few patrons of the bar. "This place seems pretty empty."

Lucy chalked the tip of her pool cue. "Yeah, most are at Paradise Lost for the Sons of Salem concert tonight."

"Paradise Lost, really?"

She looked up and smirked. "We're heading there next."

"Why not first? That sounds like the best place."

She shrugged. "It hasn't started yet, so I figured we could check this place first."

The worn, green felt dragged against the calluses on my fingers as I arranged the multi-colored balls into a triangle on the pool table. The light reflected off the balls from the hanging lamp above the table. I scooted out from between the tables, grabbed my own pool cue, and motioned for Lucy to start the game. She leaned over, positioning her cue stick aiming for the white ball. The colored balls clinked as the white one slammed into them then spread across the table.

Layers of posters, flyers, and Polaroid's covered every inch of the walls. I wrinkled my nose at the charcoal, concrete floor. It had probably been closer to white at one point, but years of neglect would do that. A boy with spiked green hair fed coins to the jukebox and pressed a few buttons. Megadeth blared as he made his way back to the bar and slapped his palm down several times. The bartender's stretched t-shirt slipped up off his large stomach as he walked to the boy. At the other end of the bar, a couple leaned in close to one another, laughing and slamming shots.

"All in all, things turned out alright," Lucy said. "You didn't really have to nose your way in."

"I still think you're lucky that Esais and Tres found out as well." I took her place at the table, aiming for the number two ball. "You still haven't told them everything. You and Jonah."

She cleared her throat. "That's a bit more complicated. I don't know how much Dad wants to talk about that, and it would raise a lot of questions if I just talked about my part."

"Well, you both should consider it."

She chuckled. "You are just tired of being called an old woman."

I grinned at her. "I'm still older than both of you combined."

The white ball sent the number two spinning towards the center left pocket. It slid in with a thump. I stood and scanned the bar again, this time with my second sight. The pinks and oranges of lust swirled around the couple. Ahh, young love. The bartender had a dull brown of boredom. The boy's aura was a mess, however. All throughout the dull gray of illness and the bright red of anxiety was rot I bumped Lucy's hip with my own and cleared my throat. When I gave a slight nod to the bar, she glanced at me and then behind her. The boy tapped his foot against his stool and downed the last of his beer.

"Dealer?" she murmured.

I shook my head. "I think he's waiting for one."

"Then we wait, too. Your shot."

I approached the table, took my shot, and missed. Lucy took over again. I tapped my fingernail on my pool cue as I watched the boy for a few more minutes. He looked like he would bolt at any sudden movement. I needed to approach this a little more gently.

"I'm going to get us some beers." I headed to the bar and slid in the seat next to the boy. "Two Guinness."

The boy looked me up and down and gave a thin-lipped smile.

I smiled back. "It's quiet in here."

"Won't be after the concert." The bartender set two mugs in front of me.

I looked back. "You're not interested in the band?"

"I'm waiting on someone," he said.

I nodded and tried to look disappointed. "Ahh, a girlfriend."

He stared at me for a moment and laughed. "No, no. Just someone I've got to meet first. Though if you're going and you want to meet up, I'm all for that. What's your name?"

I grabbed the mugs and stood up. "Gabby, and I'll think about it."

Lucy was leaning against the table. "Well?"

I handed her the beer. "We wait."

I sipped my beer and set it down. I wanted to keep a clear head, but it would have looked odd to be at a bar and not drink. After fifteen minutes of switching back and forth on the pool table, Lucy nudged me.

"Isn't that?"

I looked up and blinked at the familiar redhead that came down the steps from outside. "Tres's courtesan."

Lucy snorted. "That's too pretty of a word. Whore works fine."

She did look the part as she unzipped her leather jacket to

reveal a black bra underneath. She nodded to the bartender and sat two stools away from the spike-haired boy. He flicked his gaze to her and said something. I moved around the table and bent over, so I could look like I was focusing on the game and still keep an eye on the two of them. The rot had eaten away at her aura, worse than the boy next to her.

"She looks a lot different than she did the other day," Lucy said.

The short dress she'd worn at the office was an entirely different style than her hard rock leather now. Her attitude here was more laid back, less impatient. The bartender set a small glass in front of her. She downed the liquid and gave a high pitched laugh.

"If she's the dealer, maybe it's not a coincidence she was with Tres," I said.

"You don't think Tres . . ." Lucy said.

I shook my head. "But he has a weakness for women and demons play on weakness."

She stood and pulled out a cigarette and nodded up the stairs. She and the boy headed out.

"Well, dearie, I feel like a smoke," Lucy said. "Care to join me?"

"Sure," I said.

I paid the tab and headed up the stairs with Lucy. When I stepped outside, a brisk wind blew through me and carried the sound of the cars on the street to my ears. Delilah and the boy stood near an alley several buildings away. She glanced at us as she slipped something into his hand. Her eyes widened, and she turned to rush away in the opposite direction.

"I got her," Lucy said. "You get the boy."

I moved so I was blocking the stairs of the club. "Did she have anything good?"

He shifted his gaze around and tried to look confused. It

came out more of a shady expression. "What are you talking about?"

I tilted my head and raised my eyebrows. "I'm just looking for something good. Did she have any?"

"Oh," he smiled. "Yeah."

"Damn," I said. "Do you know where she was headed?"

"She said something about the concert."

I smiled and stepped to the side. "Thanks."

He nodded. I brushed against him as he walked past me and slipped my hand in the pocket of his coat, grabbing the small packet inside. I walked down the street in the direction Lucy had headed. She ran up to me.

"I lost her," she said with a pant. "She got in a taxi."

"It's fine," I held a small plastic bag filled with yellow powder. "I know where she's headed. Let's get Marge in on this. If we're lucky, we might have a chance at Cambione tonight."

The bass of the music vibrated the sidewalk as we approached the club. A neon sign reading *Paradise Lost* flickered in the night. Marge stood apart from the line with her arms crossed and one foot tapping. She wore a black leather jacket and jeans. Her brows were scrunched together as she scanned the street.

"This had better be worth it," she said as we joined her.

I narrowed my eyes at her. "Why? Have you found Cambione yet?"

She scowled.

"So, any lead is worth following. But if you want to continue sitting on your ass as your time ticks away." I gave a broad wave down the sidewalk.

"Ladies," Lucy said. "Let's not waste time arguing."

"Why not? What's a little more time to waste?" I asked.

"Someone's on edge," Marge said. "So why here?"

Lucy explained Delilah in short clipped words as we stepped in line. I closed my eyes for a moment. When I opened them, an array of colors greeted me. Most were muted and muddied, people looking to ease the pain of their daily lives with alcohol and drugs. Still, the ones in line were all human. I sighed and let my sight return to normal. Staring through the looking glass too long at so many people made my head hurt.

"And Tres has become even more useless," Marge said.

"Don't be so certain. This girl may be our only lead." I rubbed my left temple.

The bouncer eyed the three of us; Marge in her jeans, Lucy in her short skirt and boots, and me in my leather pants. He grinned at Lucy and waved us in. She patted him on the shoulder as she passed. A haze filled the air, making the already dim room harder to see in. The smell of smoke invaded my nose and clogged my lungs. I coughed. A large dance floor took up most of the club with the stage in the back of the room. On the stage, a band tried their hardest to blast my eardrums to oblivion. The singer half-growled, half-screamed indecipherable lyrics into the microphone while bodies pressed together in below him, jumping to the beat.

"Do you see her?" I yelled to Lucy.

"Hold on." Lucy climbed on one of the barstools and started scanning the crowd.

"Found her," she called.

She hopped down and darted between two bikers, making her way to the dance floor. I pushed my way through, keeping an eye on Lucy's pigtails. She grabbed the arm of the redhead and dragged her to the edge.

"What the hell?" The girl glared at Lucy.

"You know what," Lucy said. "Does Tres know you're dealing drugs?"

"And?"

Lucy glanced around the club with an annoyed expression. "Let's talk outside."

"No, Sons of Salem are on. You got a problem, talk with Tres."

Marge grabbed the girl's arm and twisted it behind her back. She used it to steer Delilah toward the restroom. Several people shot looks at us as we passed, but most moved after seeing Marge's expression.

"Ow, ow. Hey, let me go." Delilah twisted and turned, trying to break free of Marge's grasp.

Marge spun her around and pressed against the wall of the bathroom. "OK, bitch. Where the hell are you getting the Blasphemy from? Are you spying on us for Cambione?"

Delilah's eyes widened, and she began to stutter. "I don't know what you're talking about."

The door to the bathroom slammed open and a group of girls with multicolored hair came in. They paused, glancing at us, before moving to the stalls and sinks. Delilah shoved Marge back with both of her hands and bolted through the open door. I grabbed for her, and my fingers caught the bottom of her jacket. She yanked hard, causing me to lose my grip, and slipped through a group of leather-clad drunks.

Marge turned her glare on Lucy. "You couldn't have predicted that?"

"I'm a fortune-teller, not a seer." Lucy followed me out the door.

I switched to my second sight. The rot-eaten aura darted and weaved through the rainbow, making a path to the exit. "She's leaving."

I maneuvered through the crowd after her. The cold air blasted my face as I stepped outside. Delilah was running across the street, almost at the corner. I took off after her with Marge and Lucy close behind me. It didn't take us long to overcome her. She was in five inch heels after all. I slammed into her and rode her to the ground. She slapped at my face but I grabbed her wrist. She opened her mouth to scream and I punched her. She reeled back, slamming her head on the concrete.

"We really should move somewhere more private," Lucy said. "We're attracting attention."

I nodded to the subway entrance. "Help me, Marge."

Delilah didn't resist as we led her down the stairs. She held her head and moaned. I sat her on the bench, and she put her head between her legs.

"You bitches are psycho." Her voice was muffled at that angle, but I could hear her New York accent now that we were out of the club.

"This could go easier for you," I said. "Answer Marge's question. Did Cambione send you to spy on us?"

She glanced up at me, her hands gripping the sides of the bench. "He said he'd make it worth my while. Pay me extra, you know."

Marge leaned in and gripped Delilah's shirt in her fist. "What have you told him?"

"Just that you people are fucking insane. Talking about monsters and shit."

"You sell Blasphemy. You had to have seen weird things," I said.

She opened her mouth and then closed it, shaking her head. She pushed Marge's hand away from her and stared at the ground.

"Where is Cambione tonight?"

"He'll kill me," she said.

"That's very cliché, dearie. You do have options to prevent that," Lucy said. "Such as getting on a bus and leaving."

"Besides, I can make you wish you were dead." Marge turned her head from side to side and a loud pop echoed through the subway station.

I kept my expression impassive and pushed down the queasiness that came with the thought of Marge's methods. Delilah looked scared enough that we shouldn't have to resort to torture. The girl looked at us, her mouth opening and closing several times. Tears left black stains down her face, and her blue lipstick was smeared across her cheek.

"Fine," she said. "He throws a party in the penthouse of a hotel. It changes every night."

"And tonight?" I asked.

"It's at the Surrey. I was going after the show but . . ." She looked at the three of us and shook her head.

"Is there a code to get in or anything?" Marge asked.

Delilah sat up and crossed her arms. "6669."

I rolled my eyes. "As clever as most demons."

She blinked. "What?"

I darted forward and swung my fist at her. She started at my movement, her eyes widening and her mouth opening, but she had no time to duck out of the way. My blow caught her in the temple, and she slumped against the bench.

Lucy blinked at me. "That was a bit harsh."

Marge let out a choking laugh. "Wicked."

"Get the Blasphemy off her." I stepped away and put the small comm in my ear. "Adrian, I need to pull you away from your computer."

A sigh reverberated through the little device. "In trouble already?"

"Oh, ye of little faith. We have a location, and I need you to pick up our captive."

"Oh? And where am I making this pickup?"

I gave him directions and tapped the earpiece again. Marge stepped up and searched her pockets. She pulled out three bags of yellowish powder and shook them at me.

I nodded and grinned. "Well, ladies. Once Adrian takes Delilah off of our hands, we can hunt."

"About damn time." Marge's eyes glittered as she cracked her knuckles. "I've been waiting for this."

❧ 25 ❧

We took a taxi to Manhattan. There was no way I would get in the cramped underground subway. It was just an opening for trouble. I stepped out of the car and let my gaze travel up the hotel. The lights of the city reflected off the glass windows and shone on the white and red brick of the building.

"Well?" Marge asked.

"We need to assess what we're getting into," I said.

"Are you planning on scaling the outside?" she asked.

I continued to stare at the building, biting my lip in thought.

"Oh, hell no. That's fifteen floors up."

"Then we go undercover," Lucy said. "This will be fun."

"Fine," I said. "Party girls, I take it?"

Lucy brushed a stray lock of her hair out of her face. "Just follow my lead. Gabby, take off your shirt."

"What?" I glanced around the street as a couple passed. "Here?"

She waved her hand. "In the elevator or something."

She swaggered to the door, blowing a kiss at the doorman

as he held the door open for her. He didn't notice. His gaze was focused on some place in the distant sky. I frowned at his large pupils and waved my hand in front of his face. He didn't look in my direction.

"Gabby," Lucy hissed.

I walked inside and blinked at the white opulence. The floor was a white and gray marble with a rectangle in the center that looked like a looping dragon. The Surrey was one of New York's upscale hotels. Only the best for the best or at least those who had money to pretend they were the best. The lobby was empty except for the concierge and the bellhop.

"Excuse me," I said. "We're guests for the Presidential suite."

The concierge turned in my direction, but his eyes looked past me.

"Passcode?" he asked in a monotone voice.

"6669," Lucy said.

He set a plastic card on the counter. It had a darkened strip like a credit card, but the hotel's logo was on the front. He pointed behind us. "Take the elevator to the top."

"Thanks," I said.

I glanced back at the hotel employees as we left the desk. Both stared at the floor with blank expressions. Their bodies swayed from side to side ever so slightly.

"I think they're hypnotized," I said. "The doorman, too."

"That explains how people can come and go without the staff questioning it," Lucy said.

"They probably got the whole hotel," Marge said.

"Let's continue under the assumption that everyone might be a potential threat," I said.

I stopped and stared at the metal double doors. *Merda.* Climbing the stairs in a building this tall would take too long. I took a deep breath and pushed the button. Lucy patted me on the shoulder. We stepped inside. I stood in the middle, closest to the doors. My stomach dropped as we rose. The lights at the top counted off each floor we passed. I breathed in slowly and exhaled, swaying a back and forth. My face was on fire. I closed my eyes and swallowed hard.

"Gabby, take your shirt off." Lucy reached over and yanked Marge's shirt up.

"Hey!" Marge pulled it back down.

"You have to look the part at least," Lucy said.

"Fine," Marge let her pull the shirt back up.

I slipped my long jacket off and checked that my sword was tucked in its sheath on my back. I pulled my shirt over my head and put my jacket back on. "So, we have at least one demon that can hypnotize. I'm betting on a succubus."

"Two with Cambione," Lucy said.

"I'm hoping for more," Marge said. "A real party. Just remember that Cambione is mine."

"There probably will be . . ." I put my hand on the doors to steady myself. Floor ten. "Bystanders there."

"They're druggies," Marge said. "They chose to be here. Fuck 'em."

"Just because they wanted a good time doesn't mean they deserve to be hurt," Lucy said with an edge in her voice. "They didn't know what they were getting into."

I spoke with an equal edge. "Maybe they should learn there are consequences to their actions."

"So now you're anti-drug?" Lucy asked.

"It's a crutch, and not everyone has your stamina."

The elevator dinged. I stepped out without waiting for Lucy's reply and breathed in the sweet air outside that death-trap. One of the two doors in the narrow hall held the sign for the stairs while the other vibrated with the thrum of loud music from within. I knocked and stepped back, checking to make sure my sword wasn't obvious under my jacket. It opened, and a demon dressed in black lingerie to offset her violet skin greeted me. Two tiny horns peeked out from the ebony curls that cascaded down her back. Warmth filled my loins and spread through the rest of my body. Marge gave a sharp intake of breath and Lucy stepped closer with her mouth slightly agape and her cheeks red. I gritted my teeth. Fucking succubus.

Her gaze traveled from our faces and down our bodies, lingering on our breasts and hips. "New meat."

I widened my eyes and let a giggle escape my lips. "Love the costume."

She smirked and held the door open. "Thanks. It's like a second skin."

We stepped inside, and she sauntered to a couch in the middle of the room. She straddled one of the men sitting on the couch and ran her hand under his blue t-shirt. He flashed his white teeth in a grin and ran his hand up her thigh to her rump. Her tongue darted out from her full lips, and she trailed it over his jawline. Another succubus, this one with a pale lilac shade of skin, was lip-locked with a man. Her fingers gripped his short hair as she rocked her hips against him. I cleared my throat and adjusted the collar of my jacket. The air hung moist and heavy with the musk of lust.

"Make yourselves at home," the first demon said as her playmate kissed her neck. "There are party favors in the kitchen."

"The good stuff?" Lucy asked.

The succubus laughed. "Oh, you'll have to wait for Cambione for that."

"And when will that be?" Marge asked with her lip curling, though she had a slightly glazed look in her eyes.

I elbowed her. "You know. I could use a drink."

I pulled Marge into the kitchen and Lucy followed. The

counters were filled with a multitude of liquors and crystal glasses. I spun on Marge, glaring at her.

"You need to stay calm." I kept my voice low. "Patience."

"But." She let out a deep breath and ran a hand through her hair. "What the hell is wrong with me?"

"Succubae exude an air of lust," I said. "Especially for those that are attracted to women. Then they seduce and drain the life out of their victims."

Marge's face turned crimson, and she scowled at me. "We should just fucking kill them."

"I know, but this is our chance at Cambione. Don't screw it up like last time."

She snapped her mouth shut and crossed her arms.

"Let's worry about getting those men out before the fighting starts," Lucy said.

"That's not going to happen," Marge said. "Those demon bitches aren't giving up their meals."

"She's got a point," I said.

"You don't care?" Lucy leveled her gaze at me. "They know nothing of what they've gotten into."

"The same could be said for anyone who gets involved with demons," I said. "There are always casualties."

"Let's try to make less, then," Lucy said. She held my gaze for several moments.

"Fine," I said.

Marge rolled her eyes. "What are we going to do then?"

"We should assess the situation more," I said.

"What's there to assess? We wait any longer and they'll be fucking them into husks," Marge said.

"Are you all right?" the demon called.

"Fine." I grabbed a glass and poured liquor from a random bottle. I paused at the door and nodded at Lucy and Marge. "Come on."

The lilac succubus had stood up and was leading her prey

to one of the doors to the left. His eyes had a glazed look about him, and he blinked several times. He gave her a dopey grin, sat in one of the chairs at the glass dining table, and pulled her down for a kiss. I walked around the couch, my mouth opening to say something, when the door behind them opened.

The man who stepped out paused upon seeing us and ran a hand through his white blond hair. His abdominal muscles glistened in the low light, like he'd been oiled. If I had felt warmth earlier, now it was like fire. My nipples hardened, brushing against the soft fabric of my bra. I drew a shuddering breath and reached under my jacket. Lucy gave a low moan behind me. I pressed my lips together and narrowed my eyes at the incubus in front of us. It would be a cold day in hell before I fell to these petty tricks. His gaze raked over the three of us, and he grinned.

"Well, well," he said. "If it isn't my Marguerite. And you've brought the famous Gabriella Di Luca."

A chill ran down my spine. "Cambione, then."

He gave a little mock bow.

"Give me my contract." Marge stepped in front of me. She tried to level her a hard scowl, but couldn't quite pull it off with the semi-glazed look in her eyes.

"Oh, but that merchandise has already been sold," Cambione said.

"Who has it?"

He wagged his finger at her. "That would be telling."

"The hard way then," I said.

I darted to the side, pulling my sword from the sheath on my back. My boot landed in the side of the succubus in the chair, and she fell from the lap of her prey. My sword slashed across her throat in a quick move, and there was a flash of purple from the wound as she fell limp, her eyes staring at nothing. The stench of brimstone filled the room. The man in the chair started screaming while Cambione and the other succubus blinked in surprise. They expected more banter. I was over it. It was best left in Lucy's movies.

"Capture," I told Marge as she leapt over the couch at Cambione.

The violet demon stepped in front of her and unsheathed her claws. Cambione smirked and crossed his arms. Lucy circled the couch, blocking the demons' escape and produced two punch daggers from her sleeves.

"I have some claws of my own," she said.

I pulled out a knife from beneath the jacket I wore. I'd taken a page from Adrian's book and inscribed a binding symbol on its blade. He'd expect the sword and pay less attention to the knife. Once we had Cambione trapped, I would leave him to Marge. He smirked at me as I approached and stepped to the side to push the door behind him open. The lamia sprung from the darkness with her yellow-eyed gaze locked on me.

26

The lamia flew through the air at me. I jumped to the side to avoid her attack, and she crashed into the table. The boy screamed as her tail slapped him from his chair. He slammed into the wall with a loud crack and slumped to the floor. The lamia rose from the destroyed wood with her claws spread and a glare for me.

"Cambione has told me you can't die," she hissed. "I think I will rip your arms off and watch you suffer."

Lucy stared down the succubus with her eyes glazed and her breath coming out in short pants. The demon grinned at her as she traced her tongue along her lips. Dammit, Lucy needed to get it together. Somewhere in the background, a man was screaming. The lamia blocked my view of Marge. She jeered at me, and I could smell the blood on her breath from the five feet that separated us. I went low, aiming for the upper part of her tail and twirled so that I came up behind her. She flicked her tail at me. It hit me in my hip and sent me stumbling into one of the walls. Cambione rushed past me, sliding the patio door shut behind him. He gripped the side of the wall and began to climb it.

"Son of a bitch," Marge yelled.

She had the succubus in a grip by her head. Marge slammed the demon's face into her knee and twisted the creature's neck. She let the body fall and sprinted to the patio. I glanced back in time to dodge the lamia's claws aimed at my face.

Marge ran back through the room. "He's headed for the roof."

"Marge, wait," I called.

The lamia wrapped her tail around my foot and flung me into the couch. It broke under my impact with a loud crack, and the man who had been huddling there and screaming bounced and tumbled to the floor. I scrambled to my feet before the demon could pounce on me. She crashed into the couch, turning it into nothing more than splinters and torn fabric. The man crawled backward until he was pressed into a corner. His nostrils flared as he gawked at the snakelike monstrosity in front of him. I'd have to deal with him later.

The lamia's hand flew out to strike my face. I ducked down, and it hit the wall, smashing through the plaster with a loud clatter. She jerked her arm free and turned to face me with another hiss.

"Stand still. I thought you were supposed to be brave," she said.

"Oh, I am. I'm just not stupid enough to let you catch me again."

I leapt into the air and landed on her back. She twisted and clawed at me, but I held on tight. I dragged my blade across her throat. Black blood poured down her chest, and she made a gagging sound. She flung her shoulder back and dislodged me from my perch. Purple smoke puffed from the gash on her neck, and she dropped on the floor with her tail flopping for several moments. Lucy stood over the body of the succubus Marge had killed. She blinked at me with a confused look on her face.

Marge met us halfway up the stairs. She scowled down at us, her fists clenched. "Did he come this way?"

She slammed her fist in the wall, cracking the plaster. She stood there for a moment, just staring at the wall. Poor girl. I'd been in her place multiple times. I would have Allegra in my grasp only to have her slip away, laughing. I took a step towards her.

"Don't," she said. "Just go upstairs and look at the circle on the roof."

I nodded and slid by her, pulling Lucy with me. Cambione or one of his demon lackeys had painted a circle in the center of the roof. It was actually two concentric circles with a large triangle in the center. In between the circles were symbols painted with quick almost messy strokes. They had a very tribal look to them. At the Cardinal directions was one of the symbols I'd seen on the back of Lucy's tarot cards. It represented the Throne of Lust. I walked the entirety of the circle.

"Summoning circle, like the other one," I said.

"Looks like they are calling more up each night," Lucy said. "That's a lot of demons, even for this city."

I sighed. "Once again, our main culprit has escaped."

"We have some leads however."

I snorted. "Not good ones."

Lucy looked around. "Maybe the men downstairs know something."

Marge stood in the same place we'd left her. She'd made a fist-sized hole in the wall. She rubbed her bloodied hand and watched us descend the stairs. She didn't say anything but followed. Both of the men had remained where I'd left them, one huddled in the corner while the other sat slumped against the wall with his chin resting on his chest. I checked for a pulse. It was faint. Lucy hauled the huddled one up and set him on one of the chairs.

Lucy looked at the man in the chair. "Tell us how you knew the party would be at this hotel."

He blinked at her. "What? What the hell was that? Who are you people?"

I moved next to Lucy. "Focus. How did you know about the party?"

"I g-got a text," he stuttered, running a hand through his hair.

"Yeah, that ain't happening again," Marge said.

"What else have we got?" Lucy asked.

"Computers," I said. "Adrian should be able to take a look if he's not too caught up in his little project."

"It shouldn't be too hard to get the files from the concierge," Lucy said.

"Yeah, I doubt these zombies will miss them." Marge looked over the remains of the room and the two men. "What about this?"

"We'll take them with us," I said. "I'm sure Jonah would love to have more than one person to test." My gaze traveled to the remains of the lamia and two succubae. "We're going to have to clean this up."

"How the hell do you propose that?" Marge asked. "The cab driver ain't going to look the other way when we drag a snake body out."

"Looks like I need to call Adrian again." I let out a sigh and crossed my arms. That was not a call I was looking forward to. Hopefully, by now, he'd gotten our first guest situated. I pulled out my phone. "You two deal with the computer. I'll handle our cleanup and exit"

After a short conversation with Adrian, I began dragging the bodies together. His arrival sped things up and, thanks to his tiny robots, the room looked as if hell had not come to earth. We loaded the bodies, both living and dead, into his van where it was parked in the delivery area of the hotel. I stared out the window as we drove back to the office.

Somewhere, Cambione and a whole nest of demons were hiding. I just had to find them and end this infestation.

❧ 27 ❧

A heavy haze hangs in the room, casting odd shadows in the purple light. The air is filled with soft sighs and little moans. Arms wrap around me from behind and fingers trail up my stomach to my breasts. My nipples harden as the thumbs circle around them through the sheer gown, sending a delicious chill down my spine. I swallow and wet my dry lips with my tongue, allowing a moan to escape my lips. A deep heat is building in my loins. I lean back against a solid chest. Teeth graze my earlobe, and a man's chuckle echoes.

No, something isn't right. That chuckle is too light and too triumphant for anyone I would trust. I pull away and turn to face him.

Cambione crosses his arms and smirks at me. "Well done. I see the stories of that strong will of yours are true. But then, you wouldn't have resisted Mother for so long if it wasn't."

A low moan catches my attention. On a bed of silk in the corner of the room lays Marge. A succubus, her skin the color of roses, lies next to her and trails her hand down Marge's abdomen. Marge arches her back as the demon's hand slips between her thighs.

"She was almost as strong. It's taken several dreams to get to her."

His smooth face becomes marred with a scowl. "Of course, it took me having to lose valuable tools. No matter. You and Marguerite will make better substitutes."

The world shifts, and I am lying on a bed. The silk beneath me slides along my bare skin, sending a shiver up my back. Cambione hovers above me. His knee spreads my thighs apart. I catch my breath sharply, and my hips rise in anticipation. Coldness erupts in the pit of my stomach as I stare into his pale violet eyes. It moves through my body, dousing the fire he'd lit in me. I sit up, push him to the side, and climb from the bed. I march over to Marge and the demon and yank them apart, causing the succubus to tumble off of the bed with a surprised yelp. I wasn't going to fall for this game, and I'll be damned if I let Marge fall prey either. I wrap my hand around her wrist and drag her through the haze to a wooden door that seems an eternity away.

"You're right," I call behind me. "I've resisted your mother. You're nothing compared to her."

"Maybe I haven't used the right incentive." His voice floats from in front of me. John materializes from the mist and gives me his light grin. "Would this be better?"

My heart pounds in my chest, but I narrow my eyes. "I'm not fooled by cheap imitations."

I step around him, lugging Marge with me. She stumbles along with dull, lust-filled eyes. I fling the door open and step through to our freedom.

The last thing I hear is Cambione's laughing words. "Oh, how little you know."

I paused in the foyer of our office and rubbed my hands together, blowing on them. The temperature had dropped when the sun set, and already the melting snow was turning to ice. Last night's dream had left a chill colder than any winter. This wasn't the first time the Throne of Lust had invaded my sleeping world. Naamah, or Mother, as Cambione had called her, tended to do it more often than I cared to admit. However, this was the first time I'd had someone else with me. I had to find Cambione and kill him before he broke Marge's mind. Our new guests would be the perfect place to start.

The door opened behind me, and my hair whipped around my face at the wind that came in uninvited. I smiled at the two people who entered. Lucy struggled to push the door back in place while holding a large plastic bag. Her father held another and brushed small flakes of snow from his long black coat. He removed his bowler hat and looked down at me, laugh lines crinkling as he returned my smile.

"Jonah." I took his hand in mine. "How was your flight?"

"Don't get him started again," Lucy said. "He complained during the entire taxi ride."

"It was the poorest excuse for first class that I've seen," Jonah said in a crisp London accent.

He turned his gaze to me, and I was caught in his clear gray eyes. His salt and pepper hair was trimmed from when I'd last seen him months ago. His beard was short and neat. He hadn't aged much since I'd met him, but he had one of those youthful faces. I chuckled to myself. Youthful with a little help, that was.

"How have you been? How did the conference go?"

Jonah let out a long sigh. "Long-winded. There was a lot of skepticism, of course. Some priests actually believe that the demons are just as hidebound as they are."

"So they're as useless as always," I muttered.

"Don't discredit them. The Pope is a forward-thinking man. I expect to see changes in the near future."

I wrinkled my nose. "I'll believe it when I see it."

"Where are the boys?"

I glanced around. "I just arrived myself. Adrian is probably upstairs, though."

"And were you able to procure what I requested?"

I smiled. "Upstairs. We have three that Adrian has made accommodations for."

He nodded with a smile of his own and squeezed my hand. "Shall we, then?"

They didn't try to push me to take the elevator. Lucy and Jonah knew me well enough not to fight me on the little things. We climbed the stairs to the second floor which Esais had claimed most of as the library. It had taken him months to fill the shelves with old books of different creatures and lore of magic. Before Viktor, I think he'd chosen it as his sanctuary. Now he rarely seemed to be around long enough to enjoy it. The library once again went neglected as I unlocked a door across the hall from the stairs. When I opened the door, shouting met my ears.

Tres turned his glare from his brother onto me as I stepped inside. "Did you think I'd just let you lock my girlfriend up like a lab rat?"

Tres threw his hand out in the direction of the three occupied cells against the wall. Delilah sat on the cot of hers with her knees pulled up to her chest and tears running down her cheeks. They were probably fake. Her gaze fell on me, and she made a small squeak, pressing herself against the wall and making herself as small as possible. Adrian had spent hours turning several old offices into a secured guest facility. Each cell was blocked off from the center of the room by a large pane of shatterproof glass.

I raised an eyebrow at Tres. "You know she used you to spy on us for a demon right?"

Tres's jaw worked, like he was grinding his teeth together. "That means she deserves to get locked up?"

"It would be stupidity to let her go. Who knows what she's told Cambione already," Adrian said. "Did the two of you have a lot of pillow talk?"

Tres stiffened as redness crept up his face. "Fuck you, Adrian."

"I'm more interested in what she knows of Cambione," I said. "Besides, she's dealing and using Blasphemy. Jonah needs to study someone."

"Why not the other two?"

Jonah cleared his throat. "More individuals would produce better results. I need to know how long brimstone stays in their system and how much damage has been done to them."

"I'm a doctor. I can do that," Tres said. "*Without* locking them up."

"You were more interested in sleeping with her," Adrian said.

"Besides, we're looking for a more alchemical effect," I said.

Tres clenched his fists. "If Esais was here, he wouldn't stand for this."

I glanced at the door. "Where is Esais?"

"Not here," Adrian said. "He's once again slipped off the radar. All of them."

Jonah walked to stand in front of Adrian and inspected him with pursed lips. "I don't remember you being this tall."

"Well, I'm not Esais," Adrian said. "But I may have gained a few inches since you last saw me."

"Yes, your time in America at school." Jonah sniffed. "Among other things."

"You can say prison," Adrian said.

Jonah stiffened, and I cleared my throat. He glanced in my direction, but Adrian kept his gaze on the older man. This was the consequence Jonah had to pay for keeping his distance with the brothers. His decision wasn't unwarranted with the secrets he wanted kept. However, nothing was staying hidden with this family. Adrian may not be as forgiving of Jonah.

Lucy pushed past me and put her hand on Tres's shoulder. "I know you're upset, dearie, but I think you're pushing your anger in the wrong direction."

She turned her gaze to Delilah in her cell.

Delilah glared back and yelled, her voice muffled by her glass prison. "These bitches are lying and crazy. I don't deserve to be here."

"Who do you believe?" Lucy said. "Your family or—"

"Forget it," Marge called from the doorway. "He's gonna believe the piece of ass."

She leaned against the doorframe with her arms crossed. She was dressed in a one piece black vinyl bodysuit with a black corset over top. She tapped the heel of her high heeled boot and smirked at me. Oh, hell. Tres's eyes widened and his mouth dropped open. Adrian blinked and shook his head.

Lucy gave a low whistle. "Trying a new look, dearie?"

Marge tilted her head to the side and smiled at Lucy. "I think it suits me. Wanna give it a try?"

"Excuse us." I grabbed Marge's arm, not unlike the previous night, and yanked her out into the hall, shutting the door behind us. "What the hell happened to the girl with the 'fuck all' attitude?"

Marge shrugged. "Wasn't working out."

"You need to fight him and the dreams. I thought you wanted to stay out of hell."

"What's the point? I'm damned anyway. We don't even know who has my contract."

"Cambione is still alive. We still have a chance."

She crossed her arms and snorted. "Yeah, how well has that worked out for you? I don't have centuries."

"So, you're just going to give in and become . . ." I waved my hand up and down. "This."

"I might as well stop denying what I want," she said.

I eyed her outfit again. "I'm not even sure what that is."

She seemed to have accessorized with her usual hunters gear along with—was that a whip?

The door swung open, and Adrian looked out at us. "I hate to bust this little chat up, but I need to speak with the two of you." He turned his gaze to Marge. "That is, if you haven't traded in demon hunting for a one eight hundred number."

She smiled at him. "I'm still down for hurting things."

He stepped out, followed by Lucy and Tres. Tres had his shoulders hunched, and he wouldn't meet any of our eyes.

"Jonah needs time to examine our guest." Adrian's gaze scanned all of us. "I have the location and blueprints of the

Acesco factory. I figured we can get out of his way and put an end to one of the drugs."

"How are we going to do that?" Lucy asked.

"I'm in," I said.

Marge snorted and crossed her arms. "You sure your old bones can handle it?"

"Better than you in those boots," I said.

She scowled.

"I'm staying here," Tres said. "You have them, you don't need me."

"No," Adrian said. "I'm not leaving you here to bother Jonah with your whining."

"Besides, how long has it been since you hurt something?" I asked.

Tres muttered and leaned against the wall, looking at the floor.

Lucy turned to Adrian. "So what is the plan?"

❦ 29 ❦

The Acesco factory occupied an entire city block. It was a three story L-shaped monstrosity surrounded by a fifteen foot, white brick wall. A small guard shack with a window stood outside the only gate and it was occupied. As I lay flat on the roof of another building across the street, I scanned the walk through the binoculars.

"One guard on the outside," I said. "The fence is lined with metal poles and it looks like cameras. We can probably get the gate open if we take the guard out."

Adrian sat hunched over a black rifle case. His head was down, and he fiddled with something close to where his eye should have been. He turned to the rest of us with his eye patch in his hand. What looked like a small camera lens protruded from his eye socket. It was attached to a metal casing that was flush with his skin around his eye. Tres snorted.

"Are you bionic now?" he asked.

"Something like that," Adrian said.

"What the hell is that?" Marge asked.

"Something I came up with to allow me to quantify patterns."

"That's a bit vague, dearie," Lucy said. "What sort of patterns?"

"Energy, life. If it works correctly, I should be able to differentiate between a vampire, a demon, and a normal human," Adrian said.

A remnant of our conversation about magic drifted through my mind. "Does this allow you to see spirits?"

"Perhaps." Adrian turned back to the rifle case, pulled out several pieces of a rifle, and began to put them together. "I will handle the guard. Gabby, handle the gate and security system."

I blinked at him. "Aren't you the technological genius here?"

He took a small black cylinder out of the case and held it out to me. "Even you should be able to do this. Just place it on the computer. The nanites and I will handle the rest."

I glanced around at the others. "I guess they just get to sit around."

"For now," Adrian said. "They would wreck something."

"Hey," Lucy said. "I rarely wreck anything."

I slipped on a black ski mask, climbed onto the fire escape, and took a series of ladders down to an alley. I pressed my back against the wall and stared across the street. The figure inside didn't move as a car sputtered down the street with its motor echoing in the air. After the taillights vanished down the hill, I traversed to the shack in a crouching walk. The guard sat slumped in his chair with his chin resting on his chest. I squeezed in the security station behind him and leaned over to reach the computer built into the desk. A loud amalgam of a snort and snore emerged from him. I paused with the small black cylinder in my hand, but he continued to sleep.

I pressed the cylinder to the front of the computer and backed up to the wall. The three monitors that hung from the ceiling blinked through the two floors of the underground parking lot and on several angles of the three story building.

I touched the communication bud in my ear and spoke. "It's on the computer. How long will this take?"

"It should only be a minute for the nanites to do their trick." Adrian's cool voice echoed in my ear.

I backed to the doorway as I continued to watch the monitors. The screens flickered with tiny white lines and froze. I pulled off the black ski mask covering my face and sucked in a long breath.

"It's frozen," I said.

"We're on our way," Adrian said.

I pressed the green button on the wall near the door and the front gate slid open with a metal squeak. Lucy crossed the street first, followed by Adrian and Tres. Marge stalked up last with her hands jammed in the pockets of her windbreaker and her hips swaying as she walked in those heeled boots. A scowl marred the delicate features of her face. I slipped through the gate as it began to close. Adrian headed down the road to the underground parking garage.

"Why can't we just bust down the front doors again?" Marge nodded to the right where the visitor parking spots sat before the double glass doors.

"Stealth, guile, the police," I said. "We've talked about this before."

"I stop paying attention in your little meetings once you say whose ass we are kicking."

I snorted and kept walking down the ramp. Yellow lights flickered over the empty concrete as we paused at the single metal door that led into the building. Adrian pulled out a card with a dark strip on the back and ran it through an electronic reader connected to the handle. A beep and a click echoed through the garage, and he pulled the door open. I inhaled and counted to ten, letting the others travel up the spiraling concrete stairs first. My hand hovered over the sheath of my sword. Marge hissed behind me.

She waved her hand at me in an impatient manner. She always acted like she had somewhere better to be, though the only place she had to go home to was a shabby apartment with bad television. She should be enjoying this place. The possibility of a fight was high. Then again, that was probably why she was waving me on. Adrian waited for us at the top and closed the door behind us.

"Second floor," Tres said. "Shoes, formal, lingerie."

Lucy sniggered.

"The servers should be down that hall." Adrian pointed to the left. "We need to wipe them of the information."

"Lead the way," I said.

We followed him around the corner. Two figures dressed in blue guard uniforms appeared at the end of the hall. They stopped at the sight of us, one of them reaching for the gun on his belt. I pushed Adrian behind me, drew my sword, and crouched in a sprinters run.

"Vampires." Adrian drew two stakes and tossed one to Tres.

Marge ripped off a metal canister from her belt, pulled a ring pin, and rolled it down the hall. A pale mist, blue in the light, rose from the opening and around their feet. A mix between a roar and a scream burst from the guard on the right. I charged in, keeping low to the ground, and swung my blade at his leg. Black smoke erupted from the deep gash on his calf, and he toppled over. He clutched his leg and let out a monstrous cry again. Adrian didn't give him a chance to continue. He pushed the creature to the floor and jammed the stake into his chest. The vampire convulsed. His skin blackened, and he shrank until nothing remained but wisps of shadow in a security uniform.

Tres rushed forward, his hand extended to touch the second guard's shoulder. The guard grabbed him, spun, and pressed Tres against the wall. Black claws extended from the fingers that wrapped around Tres's neck. Lucy uttered an expletive and grabbed the guard's arm. The guard caught Lucy in the chin with his elbow and sent her flying into the opposite wall.

I brought my sword high and swung it at his neck. The blade passed through as he shifted into a shadow, and Tres slid through his immaterial fingers and to the ground, choking and coughing. The shadow floated in an amorphous mass between us. I gripped my sword tighter. It would do nothing to the monster now, but I needed to get to Tres.

A holy water grenade passed through the shadow, spraying mist as it went, hit the wall, and landed in Tres's lap. Smoke rose from the shadows, and it undulated in a frantic rapid pattern before it disintegrated. I straightened up and held my hand out to Tres.

"Are you all right?" I asked.

He stood with a hoarse groan. "Wonderful. Can we get this over with?"

"Don't worry," Adrian said. "Your girlfriend will still be in her cage when we return."

Tres glared at him. "Fuck off, Adrian. I don't need this right now."

"Is it possible you could save your bitching until we are not in a factory full of monsters?" I asked.

Tres turned his glare at me, and I stared him down. His shoulders slumped, and he looked away, pressing his lips in a thin line. I'd stared down much worse than a child in the middle of a temper tantrum. Marge gave a soft snort of amusement and sashayed down the hall with her heels clicking against the tiles. She stopped at the door at the end.

"Is this what you're looking for?" she asked.

Adrian joined her. "This is it. I should only be a few minutes."

Adrian swiped his card again and entered the room. I remained at the end of the hall, watchful for any more guards. Tres leaned against the wall and kept his arms crossed. He wouldn't meet anyone's gaze and stared off down the hall. Lucy chewed on her lip and looked between him and me. I shook my head. He could pout for all I cared, as long as it didn't get one of us killed. It wasn't my fault he'd chosen the wrong woman to sleep with. He was learning that the hard way now.

"This is boring." Marge picked up one of the grenade canisters she'd thrown.

"Sorry to disappoint you," I said. "Not everything in life can be high action."

Adrian came back out. "Done. Third floor has the labs."

We headed up the stairs. I busted out of the tiny death trap with my hand gripped around my sword. A white, empty hallway greeted us.

"Were there only two guards for this entire place?" I asked.

"Most likely not," Adrian said. "Keep an eye out."

The hallway split to a turn to the left and continued straight. I paused at the hall and peered around the corner. Two doors stood across from each other, both with electronic key cards. Windows lined the walls, revealing the inside of the rooms. The room on the left was filled with rows of white pod-like machines that were attached to a metal tube hanging from the ceiling. The room on the right held a table with computers built into it. Another glass window covered most of the far wall and overlooked a dark room.

"What are those pods?" I asked Adrian.

"They produce the actual pills." Adrian pulled out several small cylinders and turned to the rest of the group. "Take these and place them inside the machines. Once they are set, I will command the nanites to travel through the tubes to destroy the formula."

"If you could do that, why did you have us burn the warehouses?" Marge asked.

Adrian stared at her as if she was stupid. "I could not be at all three at once, and I don't have the range to control them from such distances."

"You need to figure a way around that." I grabbed three of the cylinders.

"I could set up a relay system, but that would be difficult, time consuming, and irrelevant."

"Do we need some sort of suits when going in here?" Lucy asked.

"That's more to keep the drug sanitary," Tres said. "Since we're trying to mess them up, no point."

Lucy shrugged and took a handful. Adrian split the others between Marge, Tres, and himself. He ran his card through the slot and held the door open. We slipped inside. I took the second row, opened the porthole like door, and attached the device to the inner side.

"I thought we'd be killing more things," Marge said. "This is janitors' work."

"I'm sure they are saving something special for you," Tres said.

We finished and exited the room. Adrian stared at the pods for several moments and nodded. He turned to the other door and we gathered in the small room. He typed a few strokes on a keyboard and the monitors lit up as well as a row of buttons. The room past the window held ten tall, cylindrical pods along the walls of the room. Humanoid figures floated in clear liquid with tubes attached to their arms and masks over their heads.

"What the hell?" Marge said.

She leaned forward to peer through the glass, her hand landed on one of the backlit buttons. A screen at the top of the pod closest to us lit up with a list of numbers. Blood flowed through one of the tubes and was deposited in a glass jar attached to the side of the pod.

"I think we found our source," Adrian said in a grim voice.

"Open the door," I said.

I moved to the first pod and studied the gray furred female with my aura sight. The bajang possessing the body glared at me with its liquid silver face twisted in rage. The human's aura was in shreds, and the demon had started to consume the human soul. Every pod was filled with an angry hellspawn.

I put my hand on the glass. "Can you see it, Adrian?"

"The patterns read as a human and a possessing demonic entity." His voice came over the speaker.

Tres pushed past me and moved to the next pod. He pushed a button on the top, and the screen lit up. "Vitals appear to be normal . . . and they're awake."

I leaned forward and inspected the glass. Etched on was a Star of David surrounded by two concentric circles. Astrological planetary symbols lined the space between the circles with their precise lines and curves.

"They're bound," I said.

Lucy gave a low whistle. "They went through a lot of trouble for this."

Marge walked to a pod on the opposite side of the room. "How do we get this open so we can kill it?"

"There may be a way to destroy them all," Adrian said. "A kill command."

He stared at the computer with a look of concentration.

A shadow rose up behind him and another moved in front of Lucy. I opened my mouth to warn them, but I was too slow. The shadows materialized into two guards. The one in front of Lucy tackled her, pushing her against the wall. Adrian half-turned, but the vampire behind him slammed his head into the computer. Adrian slumped over the screen, and his hand hit the keyboard. The lights in our room turned red and a loud beep echoed through the speakers.

"Release activated." A monotone female voice filled the room.

The first vampire's eyes widened. He shoved Adrian to the ground and typed something rapidly. The door slid shut. I ran to it and pulled on the handle, but it stuck fast. The vampire that held Lucy turned and yelled something to the other. Lucy slammed the back of her arm into the inside of his elbow. She slipped out from under him, flicked her wrists, and her punch daggers slid into her hands. The vampire turned back to her with a look of surprise.

"Gabby." Tres backed to the center of the room with his gaze on the pods.

The lights on the panel blinked on all of them, and tiny words flew across the screen, too small for me to make out. Marge and I joined Tres in the center of the room, our backs to each other. As the doors opened, a metallic smell filled the room and liquid splashed against the tiled floors and covered our feet. There was a mechanical whirring, and the demons slid from their positions in the pod to the ground.

"Finally," Marge said with a short laugh. "And I thought this was going to be a bust."

"You wanted violence," I said. "Here you go."

The first demon to notice us was a bajang. She was smaller than the one I'd fought in the abandoned apartment, and dark brown fur covered her body. She snarled at us, her muscles tensing and her claws extending. She leapt at us with a growl. I moved forward and brought my sword in an arc over my head. The blade sliced through her stomach as she passed over me. Blood sprayed on me, and she tumbled to the ground a few feet past Tres. Three small stone figures surrounded us, with their eyes beginning to glow. I looked to their feet and backed up.

"Avert your gaze, Marge," I said. "We need you for this."

"Not happening again." Marge flung a canister to the ground.

Mist, red in the flashing lights, rose around us. Guttural hisses filled the room, and the demons rescinded, their figures becoming slightly hazy in the mist. The pounding of stone on metal rang through the air, and I spun around to the secondary door in the back of the room. A short, stocky truaco demon bashed into the door with its stony shoulder.

"They're trying to escape," I said.

"On it." Tres took off through the mist.

"Wait," I called.

I reached out a hand to catch him. My fingertips slid along his shirt, but I couldn't get a grip. Damn it, Adrian was already unconscious. I wasn't about to lose Tres. The mist cleared after several feet, leaving only the emergency sequence of the lights. Tres had his hand on the back of a short stone demon at the door. Cracks formed from his fingers, spreading up along the truaco's shoulders and lower back in a spider web pattern. It shuddered and let out a cry like that of a rumbling avalanche.

A sharp crack came from Marge's direction. A black tip of her whip flew past me and into another bajang, wrapping around her ankle. The creature yowled as she was jerked off of her feet and back to Marge. The bajang hissed and raked her claws into the girl's shoulder. She scowled and slammed her foot down on the demon's knee. She could handle that. I needed to get to Tres.

A humanoid figure blocked my path. Its body was covered with dark oil that gleamed with a reddish shimmer in the flashing lights. Another orang, except this one was alive. I swung my sword in an upward arc. A slash appeared, extending from its left hip to right shoulder. The oils spread across the wound and covered it, leaving no trace of the wound behind. It snatched my arm, and its hand melted into liquid that covered my hand. I gasped and tugged, but the stuff was like being trapped in quicksand or tar. Pulling would do no good. I darted around to the side of it, turned, and, using the small momentum I'd gained, flung it into the mist. I was pulled off my feet and after it. We both hit the ground. The oil began to bubble, and the demon's body was subsumed into convulsions. The liquid trapping my hand slid away as the creature dissolved into a slick puddle.

Marge stomped the crumpled figure on the ground with a crazed look of pleasure on her face. I got to my feet with a shake of my head and went after Tres once again. He'd been pulled away from the door and was stretched between two of the fluid orang demons. A truaco slammed its stone fist into Tres's midsection. Another truaco pounded the door. The handle gave way with a loud pop, and the door banged open. The demon clomped out of the room. No time for him.

"Marge, use another can," I yelled.

She gave a grunt of exertion. "I only have one left."

"Adrian can make more," I said. "As long as we get out of this alive."

I jabbed the pommel of my sword into the truaco's head. His fist stopped in midair and it turned his head in my direction. I ducked my gaze away from his face and aimed for his shoulder. It raised its arm to knock my hand away. The goo surrounding Tres's left hand contracted, and a crunch sound was covered up by Tres's scream. Both orangs pulled in opposite directions.

"Marge!" I said.

"Fine."

The can landed at my feet in a clang, and the mist spread with a hiss. The truaco rumbled and stumbled away from us toward the door. He barreled into a bajang who was trying to escape. The bajang landed on the ground and yowled as the truaco stepped on her in its haste. Marge didn't waste any time and pounced on the fallen demon. She rammed her foot down on the creature's neck. Tres pulled free of the melting orangs and clutched his hand to his chest.

I ran down the hall to the observation room and flung open the door. Lucy stood over a fallen vampire with a stake in her hand. She rammed it into his chest, and he burst into tendrils of shadow. I knelt beside Adrian and, with my heart racing, I touched the side of his neck. His pulse thrummed against my fingertips. I let out a sigh of relief. Footsteps sounded from the door. I spun with my sword ready. Tres stood at the threshold, panting, his hand cradled against his chest. Marge was a few feet behind him. I stood up and moved to Lucy, crossing my arms over my stomach. She looked at me with a worried frown. Tres ran his good hand over Adrian, lifting his head up and moving his eyelids.

"Well?" I asked with my voice slightly hoarse.

"Concussion. He needs a hospital. And so do I." He lifted his battered hand. "I can't do anything with this."

"Worthless," Marge muttered.

"We can't take him to a hospital with that." I pointed to the device that now took the place of his long missing eye.

"Tres looked down at him and his shoulders slumped. "Well, someone will need to take him home while I go to the hospital."

"Can you wake him?" I asked. "Otherwise, leaving here is going to be difficult."

He slapped his hand against Adrian's cheek in three sharp taps. Adrian groaned, his eye blinking rapidly. He tried to sit up but ended up laying back again with his hand covering his face. Marge leaned back and glanced down the hallway with narrowed eyes.

"We need to move," she said. "Several of those demons escaped."

"Hopefully they'll occupy the guards." I moved to stand over Adrian. "Can you walk?"

He sat up slowly. "I will manage."

"I'll help him," Lucy said. "Give him a shoulder to lean on."

"Fine." I looked to Tres. "How about you?"

He gave me a faint smile. "I can walk."

"Marge, lead the way. I'll take the rear," I said.

We crept through the hall, wary of demons and vampires.

Shadows flickered and growls echoed from one end of the hall. The door to the stairwell hung open with the handle and lock a busted mess. Marge pulled it open and leaned over, peering inside. She waved her hand forward and headed down the stairs. She stopped at the bottom and turned the handle. It rattled, but didn't open.

"Move," Adrian said.

Marge stepped aside. Adrian's hand dropped halfway through his wave, and the metal on the door began to disintegrate. What was left of the handle popped off under the force of Marge's foot. The overhead lights flashed red as we sprinted through the garage. Marge shot her grapple and climbed over the wall. A few moments later, the gate opened. The guard still lay unconscious at his post. We didn't stop running until we reached the van three blocks away. Lucy snatched the keys from Adrian, prodded us into the seats, and then took off. The tires screeched as she turned the corner. I grabbed the armrest to keep from sliding into Marge.

A cacophony of voices filled my head, followed by Esais. *"What has happened to my brothers?"*

I squeezed my eyes shut and rubbed my temple. *"They're all right. We're headed to the hospital."*

I mentally replayed what had happened at the facility.

"Which hospital?"

"Lucy, where are we going?" I asked.

"New York Methodist Hospital," she said.

"I'll meet you there." Esais said, and the song stopped assaulting my brain, leaving only a dull throb behind.

Lucy took another sharp turn and ran through two red lights. "Almost there."

"Try not to get pulled over." I rubbed my head again.

Lucy pulled into the parking lot of the hospital, and the tires screeched as she stopped in front of the Emergency entrance. "You help Tres. I'll take Adrian home."

I slid the door open, hopped out, and walked around to the passenger door to help Tres. Marge squeezed past the gear shift and claimed Tres's vacated seat. She stared up at the four story square building with a bored look on her face.

"I'm with Lucy," Marge said. "No point in me waiting here."

"Thanks for the help," I muttered.

She looked at the three of us with a smirk.

"You got this. Besides, I'm sure Esais will rush to his brother's side as soon as he finds out." She looked into the parking lot at the two approaching figures. "Oh look, here he comes now."

Lucy sped away with a squeal of tires, and I turned to face the music with a deep sigh.

Esais raced toward us with Viktor in tow. His mouth tightened into a thin line, and he swallowed hard as he looked over Tres. "I'm sorry."

Tres laughed a hoarse laugh. "The world's not ending. We just need to get patched up."

Esais gave him a strained smile. "Let's get you checked in."

Esais took Tres's arm and guided him through the doors. Tres rubbed his wrist the entire way to the doors. Viktor watched them go and let out a long sigh. I paused and turned his direction.

"Are you coming?" I asked.

He gave me a fleeting smile before he crossed his arms and looked down at the sidewalk. "Not really sure if I belong here."

"I know it feels strange, but I think Esais would want you there."

He shrugged. "Maybe, but does Tres? He hasn't really been chatty. And you have to admit that Adrian hasn't exactly welcomed me with open arms."

"That is his issue. He's like that with everyone," I said. "And he's not even here now."

He sighed and ran a hand through his hair. "I just don't want to come between them. They're really lucky to have each other."

"You don't have any family?" I asked.

He gave a bitter laugh. "None I want to call family."

"That bad?"

"I was a freak to them. A blasphemy." He shook his head. "Ironic, really."

I blinked. "Why ironic?"

He cleared his throat. "Nothing. Never mind. Thanks for listening, Sweetheart, but I'm freezing. I'm going to try and find some coffee."

I chuckled and stepped up so the door opened. "Well, if you want to talk any more, just let me know."

Esais sat in one of the black plastic chairs along the wall. I wrinkled my nose at the stench of old blood under the astringent sanitizer. I sat down next to him and crossed my ankles. He stared at the floor with his fingers laced together on his knees.

"Did Viktor leave?" Esais didn't look up.

"He's getting coffee."

Esais ran both hands down his face. "This is my fault."

"They're hunters. They're going to get hurt."

"I should have been there." He gave a harsh laugh. "I thought I could have a private life. Obviously, I'm not meant to."

I reached over and touched his arm. "They're not children. You don't need to hold their hands through everything."

"When I don't, this happens."

I leveled my gaze to his. "Don't you dare guilt trip yourself into giving up what little happiness you have. Both Adrian and Tres are fine. You can't be with them all the time."

He opened his mouth to speak when Tres opened the door near the nurse's window. His hand was covered in a white cast, leaving only the fingers free. I blinked. That had been fast. I glanced at Esais.

"Did you push him ahead of others?" I asked.

"I had to do something," he said. "He didn't take the place of anyone in danger."

"Good to know," I said.

He met Tres halfway across the room. "So?"

"Broken, what else?" Tres shrugged. "It will take some time to heal. Looks like I'm out of commission for a while."

"Will you be able to do anything for Adrian?" I asked.

"Not at the moment." Tres snorted. "He's got a concussion. He needs to be watched over for the next couple of days. I'm sure he'll be back to his irritable self by tomorrow."

Esais nodded and gave a faint smile. "I guess I'll be spending some quality time with him then."

"Just don't change his music," I said.

Esais stared down the hall. "All right. Let's get out of here."

"What about Viktor?" I asked.

He cleared his throat and looked to the ground. "He's going home. It's just going to be us for now."

I stared at him, but he wouldn't meet my gaze. I threw my hands up and followed them out to the van. It was no surprise Viktor felt alienated. This wasn't helping. However, all I could do was offer the advice. I had too many crises to play matchmaker.

❧ 31 ☙

The next day, I sat with my feet propped up on a desk in the office Jonah had commandeered. He leaned forward and peered at his tiny handwriting in his leather bound journal while he held a small vial in one hand. White foam fizzed at the top of it, like a shaken carbonated beverage.

"Have you found anything?"

"A few things," he said.

I sat up a little straighter. "Well?"

"I will explain everything to everyone once." He pressed his lips together in a thin line. "That way I will be less suspected of anything."

I sighed and sat back. "You're still upset."

"You thought me capable of causing this."

"What do you expect? You aren't exactly on the straight and narrow like the brothers believe." I wave a hand at the various vials and jars of ingredients on the edge of his desk. "You use vampire blood. Who knows if you would decide that brimstone could have some useful application?"

His hand gripped the desk tightly. "The vampire blood is so I can continue with my oath. I have no legacy. Lucy is . . ."

"I know," I said. "But it was questionable."

"Even if I did, I'd never let it spread to such a degree that it has."

"I apologize." I crossed my arms and leaned back. "However, you haven't been exactly truthful to everyone. Do you ever plan on telling them?"

He picked up a pen and wrote in neat strokes. "Now does not seem like the time."

"I know you were able to keep things secret by avoiding seeing them often, but you can't hide forever. They've probably already noticed, especially Esais."

"I will consider it once this crisis has been taken care of." His phone buzzed and he put it to his ear. "You've returned? Good."

He hung up and looked at me. "Lucy has brought dinner. Could you gather the others so we can speak downstairs?"

"Marge isn't here," I said.

"Someone else can update her later."

I climbed to the third floor. Adrian sat at his desk with his head wrapped in a white bandage. He glanced up from typing at his laptop and nodded to me. I froze as my heart fluttered. What was this? I shoved my hands in my pockets and leaned against the doorframe.

"How's your head?" My voice sounded hoarse.

"It would be better if people stopped asking me," he said.

"Sorry," I said. "Esais been bothering you all night?"

"He hovered some. He finally fell asleep a few hours ago."

"Jonah wants to speak with all of us. Lucy brought dinner."

Adrian stiffened. He shut the laptop and stood, straightening his shirt. I chuckled. The Van Helsing brothers could be fearless in the face of vampires, but Jonah gave them the air of children with their hands in the cookie jar.

I stepped into the hall and searched the empty offices. Esais lay on a small portable mattress with his arm curled under his head. The air became cold and thick with an oppressive presence. I stiffened and pressed my back against the wall. Something heavy pressed on my mind and sent an ache through my entire body, causing my body to stiffen. Tears flowed down my cheeks as memories surfaced. Esais coughed and gave a moan. The pressure abated as he sat up, rubbing his face. I turned my head from him and sucked in a long breath of air. Could that have been him, or was I imagining things like he claimed?

He blinked at me. "Are you watching me sleep?"

I chuckled softly and glanced at him from the corner of my eye. "I came to wake you up."

"Good, because that would have been creepy."

"Jonah is here. It looks like he bought dinner for us."

He stood and stretched with a sleep-filled smile on his face.

"Food sounds good." He smacked his lips together and wrinkled his nose. "I think I'll freshen up first."

"Can you find Tres then?"

"Sure."

I turned to the door with a nod.

"Gabby, what's wrong?"

"Nothing." My voice was just above a murmur.

I rushed from the door and down the hall, almost running into Adrian. He placed a steadying hand on my shoulder and looked past me from where I came.

"Running from your ghosts again?"

I shot him a glare and moved to the stairwell, but he grabbed my arm and pulled me to the elevator. I bucked, but he held tight.

"One floor. You'll be fine," he said.

I pressed against the back corner of the elevator with my hands flat against the wall. My stomach felt like it rose when we started to descend and the walls drew closer in. I closed my eyes.

"Inhale," I thought. *"One. Two. Three. Exhale. One. Two. Three."*

"So what had you running down the hall like a vampire was on your tail?" he asked.

I swallowed hard. Should I tell him? Would he believe me? "I think there's something wrong with Esais."

"He's just upset that he's not Superman."

"What?"

He shook his head. "Why do you think something's wrong with him?"

"I keep sensing this mental presence when he's around, but he acts like nothing is wrong."

"And you're sure it's not in your mind? You have been under stress lately."

"That doesn't mean I'm imagining things," I muttered.

Of course he didn't believe me. I had no proof. Hell, I wasn't sure if I believed me. I continued to breathe as I forced the images of being trapped between floors from my mind. Adrian had his little machines. He could always make a way out for us. I would be all right. The elevator dinged and the doors slid open. I rushed out of them and leaned against the desk in the lobby.

"Congratulations," Adrian said. "You've lived through one floor of the elevator."

I glared at him. "I'm not in the mood to be taunted."

"Who said I was taunting you?" He put a hand on my arm. "He has been acting differently. It is possible this is something from his 'gift.' Or he's just caught up in the newness of the boyfriend. Why don't we keep a closer watch on him?"

I nodded, crossed my arms, walked down the hall, and opened the door. Three round metal tables spread across the black and white tiled floor. A black counter divided the front from the kitchen. Adrian moved to help Lucy take cardboard boxes out of the sacks and set them on the counter. The smell of spiced chicken and tomato drifted through the air. Jonah was already seated at one of the tables and spoke on his phone. I opened one of the boxes and steam rose from the rice inside, warming my face and leaving behind little beads of water.

"Greek?" I asked.

Lucy nodded. "Dad got a feast for us."

The door opened with a squeak, and Tres stepped in with his arms resting on the back of his head, followed by Esais. Tres's eyes had a drooping quality and he wore a wide smile on his face. Esais's hair had a slight ruffled look to it, though it looked as though it had been set that way on purpose.

"I'm here, so we can get this party started," he said.

"Surprising," Adrian said. "You're actually on time for something."

Tres made a sarcastic sad face at his brother and walked to Jonah. He spread his arms wide. "Uncle Jonah, thanks for the meal."

Before Jonah could reply, Tres pulled him into a tight hug, patting him on the back. Tres stepped back and wrapped an arm around Lucy's shoulders, giving them a tight squeeze with his good hand. Esais held his hand out to Jonah and leaned close to speak with him quietly.

"You're in a good mood," I said to Tres. "How is your hand?"

"I'd probably be in agony, but the pills they gave me are awesome." He grinned and wiggled the fingers of his casted hand. "And I can still be a little useful. Watch."

His hand brushed my cheek, and a small scrape I'd gotten

from the fight the night before. A warm tingle spread through my face. My fingers ran across my smooth cheek. He grinned.

"Only little stuff, so try not to be yourself," he said.

He stepped past me to inspect the counter. A loud smack echoed through the room followed by a sting that erupted from my right butt cheek. I turned to glare at him, my hand clenching in a fist. He sidestepped out of my reach and winked at me. His gaze drifted over the food.

He sighed. "I could really go for some mici or even good sliade from home. What about you, Adrian? Are you too accustomed to American fare?"

"Pot and kettle," Adrian said.

"What is that supposed to mean?" Tres asked.

"Your choice in women. Your hunter instincts are horrible."

Tres glared at him, his face turning a bright red.

"We all make mistakes," Esais spoke up. "He'll know better next time."

"Right," Tres smirked. "Now I'll have to do a background check on every girl I date."

"That's not a bad idea," Jonah said. "I could arrange that."

I coughed to cover the laugh at the look of dread on Tres's face and held up my plate. "Shall we eat?"

"Yes, I'm starving." Lucy set her plate, piled to a peak with meat and rice, on the table.

"Speaking of our guests." Esais sat across from me. "How long do we plan to keep them against their will?"

"Until we find a way to cure them." I took a large bite, savoring the warm roasted chicken and spices.

"If that's possible," Jonah said.

Esais frowned, his eyebrows furrowing. "There isn't another way?"

"We could let them go, become possessed and be forced

to kill them. This way, at least they have the protections of the office." I turned to Jonah. "So, what have you found out?"

He cleared his throat and patted his mouth with a handkerchief. "As I said, both samples of the drugs contained brimstone. They looked to be from the same formula."

"It has to be Faust," I said. "What have you found from our guests?"

"The brimstone has been changing their physiology, metaphysically that is."

Adrian frowned. "How do you mean?"

"I doubt it could be something any physician would be able to see. For instance, they all display severe allergic reactions to holy water, but all normal ingredients that are in holy water give no reaction."

"I think I said it before, but it's weakening their souls," I said. "Probably how they can be possessed so easily."

Jonah nodded.

"I believe the change is allowing them to become malleable for the demons to change their form." He stared at the wall, his gaze growing distant. "Now we have the possibility of this becoming an international incident. What can you tell me about this company?"

Adrian straightened and began going over what we'd learned. My phone vibrated from the pocket of my jeans and "Wandering Star" echoed through the room. I gave an apologetic smile in response to the glare Adrian shot me and stepped out into the foyer. John's name flashed across the screen.

"Hey," I said, the warmth I felt coming out in my voice. "I was just starting to miss you."

"I need to see you." He spoke the words in a shaky rush. "I think I may be in trouble."

A chill ran up my spine. "What's wrong?"

"Not over the phone. In person."

"All right? Do you want me to meet you at your hotel?"

"No, some place public. Rubello's in twenty minutes."

He hung up, and I stared down at my phone, trying to shake the sick feeling rising in my stomach. He'd sounded desperate, like a man out of options. Something had gone wrong. I just hoped it wasn't something that would snowball into a disaster.

32

I took the small set of stairs down to the darkened bar and wrinkled my nose at the stench of old cigarettes mixed with fresh ones. Rubello's was one of the few public places in New York where smoking was still allowed inside. It had something to do with it being called a Cigar bar. Lucy had explained it to me a few nights ago, during our patrol of different clubs, but I'd only half paid attention. John waited for me at the bar with a lit cigarette in his hand. I sat beside him, clasping my hands together on the counter. He didn't look up from his whiskey glass.

"Since when do you smoke?" I asked.

"I needed something for my nerves." He glanced behind him with narrowed eyes. "Is there anyone here who is a blasphemer?"

I raised an eyebrow. "A what?"

He waved his hand in a circular motion with his palm up. "Someone using the drug."

"Oh. Interesting term."

I glanced around. The booths along the wall were filled. Men and women in business suits chatting and laughing over salads and glasses of wine. The world faded around me and a pop went off behind my eyes. I blinked at the myriad of hues that shifted around the patrons. Some of the auras touched and blended with each other, all were slightly muddied from inebriation, however none held the corrosion effect of Blasphemy. I turned my attention to John. A dark anxious red mixed with a muddied gray of fear swirled around him. Whatever this was, it had him pretty bad.

"They're clean," I said.

He let a huge sigh, and his shoulders slumped.

"What's this about?"

"Cambione's after me. I think he's sent several of his flunkies to follow me."

My heart pounded in my ears, and my chest tightened. "Are you sure? How can you tell?"

"I've seen the same people hovering for the last couple of days."

"Are any here now?"

He shook his head.

"That's really strange. Why you? I mean, I was the one who had a direct confrontation. He should be after me."

"Yeah, well maybe he knows about us."

I swallowed, my mouth dry. "I've put you in danger."

He gave me a faint smile. "It's all right. I knew what I was getting into."

"Could it have been whoever gave you the information?"

John's foot tapped against the barstool in a nervous tattoo. "The thaumaturgist I talked to tries to stay away from demons. It had to be Faust. He knew me from the conference and after I've been looking into your whole Raina, Adrian thing, he's probably not too pleased."

I straightened. "Did you find anything out?"

"Of course that's what you'd want to know in all this." He drained his whiskey glass in one swallow. "Not a whole lot you couldn't find out if you knew how to use the internet. Adrian used to work for Erebus."

"That's the main company for Acesco, right?"

"Yeah, big on weapons and tech. Their president started to branch out and bought a few other companies about a decade back. Anyway, an interesting bit of information I did find, Adrian got put on some sort of special project with Raina. That is until he ran off with some company secrets and got involved with arms dealing."

I bit the inside of my cheek. "What was the name of the project?"

"Apotheosis."

"Like deification? What were they working on?"

He shrugged. "Who knows? The rest you're going to have to find out for yourself. I've got other problems."

The bartender stopped in front of us and pointed to John's empty glass. "You want another?"

John's laugh sounded forced with a bitter edge to it. "Sure. It might be my last."

I frowned at him as my chest tightened again. "Don't say things like that."

His shoulders slumped and he stared at me with dull eyes. "Why not? My best bet is to make sure the bastard is dead."

"Then we'll kill him."

"Do you know where he is? I sure as hell don't and it's probably not the best idea for me to go looking for someone who's out to get me."

"I'll find him and get his attention," I said. "You lay low."

He snorted. "I don't think that will work. He's already set his sights on me. I doubt he'll just let me go."

"I don't think he's that relentless."

John gulped down his new drink and muttered. "It's too late."

He really wasn't giving this one up. "Then come back to the office with me. We have protections."

He rubbed the back of his neck as his brow furrowed. "As much as I'm sure the Van Helsings would love putting me up, I'd rather not be a sitting duck. I'll just lay low, keep moving."

I swallowed the lump in my throat. "I won't be able to protect you if I don't know where you are."

He laid his hand on top of mine. "I'll call you to let you know I'm all right."

I nodded, looking at his hand. It shook ever so slightly and felt light, like it was disappearing, and I wouldn't be able to hold onto it. I'd gotten John involved in this, and now I couldn't keep him safe. No, I could. I just had to do what I did best. Kill the demon who threatened what I cared about.

"I can at least get you somewhere safe," I said.

He shook his head. "Sorry, but you have this habit of attracting the wrong kind of attention. Just kill him. Soon, Gabby."

I stood and pulled my hand away. Any words I wanted to say wouldn't leave my constricted throat. I jammed my hands into my pockets and clenched them into fists as I headed for the stairs that led outside. I wouldn't—no, couldn't—fail John. He'd put himself on the line so many times for me. He'd more than repaid me for saving his life when we first met and hadn't asked for anything except for a little love in return. I needed to start checking the hotels in town. Cambione had to be set up in another one. Once I'd found him, I would end his wretched existence, save John, and free Marge.

I glanced back to see a tall man in a long coat. He walked with a pace that matched mine but stayed several yards behind me. How long had he been there? He hadn't been at the bar. I must have picked him up somewhere along the way.

John was right.

I always seemed to attract the wrong kind of attention.

33

I sped up my pace and turned the corner. Thanks to John's paranoia we'd met somewhere public, leaving me without my sword again. A dagger rested in a sheath in my boot, covered by my jeans. My jacket concealed the stake on my back hip. I had a couple of Adrian's garlic pellets and some holy water. Not a whole lot to work with. I let out a sigh. I really missed the old days where I could vanquish a demon with a few well-enunciated words. Thanks to the brimstone, that was all but impossible in this city.

I turned a corner, pausing at a newsstand, and then walked in a trot. He'd been joined by a friend. I slipped past a family of five and darted down the stairs into a subway station. The reek of unwashed bodies and old urine surrounded me. My throat closed up, and my heart raced. People huddled at the platform as they waited for the next train. In a panic, they could crush me, and I would have no chance to get away. I doubted anyone would stop my stalkers if they wished to grab me. I needed to get a good look at them and didn't plan on dragging them around the city.

My mouth moved as I counted to ten silently and joined

the crowd. The two men slipped down the stairs and moved to stand behind me at an angle. I glanced at them out of the corner of my eye. One was staring at me. No good. I didn't want to let on I knew they were following me just yet. The train pulled up, and the doors slid open. I followed the crowd in while making sure I would be in the same car as them. They stepped in right before the door closed.

I stared at the floor and let the colors of the people surrounding me wash over. Waves of blue pushed against grays, reds, and orange. I raised my eyes until the men were in my sight. The void around them sucked in the colors from the humans. Shifting shadows obscured their faces and body.

"Esais," I called mentally. *"I have two vampires following me. I could use a little assistance."*

Every minute I waited, my unease grew. He never took this long. I rubbed my closed eyelids. He'd really picked the most inconvenient times to make himself unavailable again. Tres and Adrian were in no condition to help. It looked as though I would have to handle this on my own. Thank God I'd thought to bring a stake. Now to get them somewhere private.

As the train slowed to a stop, I pushed my way past several bodies to the door. It slid open, and I rushed out. With a long breath, I headed to the stairs. The wind hit me full in the face, stinging my nose and cheeks, and I wrapped my jacket tighter around myself as I hurried down the sidewalk. Moments later, the vampires emerged from below. The taller one stuck his hands in his pockets and searched the milling people. Our gazes met, and I turned away, quickening my steps to a light jog.

I scanned the buildings. *There.* The narrow alley across the street would work. I jogged over with my hands jammed in my pockets, kicking aside the bits of trash that rolled in the wind. The sickly sweet tang of garbage hovered in the back of my throat as I came to an L-shape end about twenty feet down. I turned the corner and pulled my knife from my boot and a garlic pellet from my pocket. Footsteps drew closer. A skittering can echoed in the air, followed by the sound of shushing. I counted to ten and tossed the pellet.

"Shit!" one of them yelled.

I pulled my stake out and rushed around the corner at them. The taller one was bent over, heaving, while the other had his back to the wall and was waving his hand in front of his face. I moved to the tall one and slammed my knee into his face. He staggered back. I jammed the stake toward his chest, but he pushed it aside with his arm. The other grabbed me from behind and threw me into the wall. My back exploded in pain, and I tumbled to the ground. The taller vampire pounced. I rolled out of the way and came up in a crouch with my dagger raised. They moved closer cautiously. Strange. Neither seemed willing to pull their guns. Were they actually worried about attracting attention?

The shorter one moved behind the dumpster and shoved it toward me. It came flying at me with the screech of metal against concrete. I dove to the side and right into the tall vampire. He wrapped his arms around me and pulled me against his chest. I struggled against him as my feet lifted off the ground, my breath coming in ragged gasps. He sank his fangs in my neck, and I screamed. A burning sensation raced through my veins and my head began to spin. A chill crept though my skin and down my bones. I had to get free, but I couldn't get my arms to move.

"Hey, lay off man. They said not to hurt her too much," the shorter one said. "Ms. Benson's gonna be pissed if you eat her."

The taller one pulled away with a satisfied gulp. Now that his teeth were out of me, the chill receded and feeling returned to my fingers. I flipped the knife around in my hand

and buried it in his arm. He screamed, and his grip loosened enough for me to squirm out. I landed on my feet, spun around, and jammed the stake into his heart. The vampire vanished into fading shadow and cold. I turned and hopped away before the shorter one could attack. Not that I needed to worry. His mouth hung agape in surprise at the death of his partner. His eyes narrowed, and he hissed at me, baring his fangs.

I snorted. "Really? You're going the cliché route now?"

His sneer turned into a grin as he glanced behind me. I spun, but I was too late. A giant meaty hand encircled my arm. He loomed over me, thicker than both the tall vampire and short vampire put together. He wasn't fat though, it was all hard muscle and a barrel chest. His grin spread across his craggy face.

"She's a fighter, eh?" He didn't take his eyes off of me.

"She just killed Charlie," the short one said with a whine to his tone.

"He was sloppy."

I brought my knife up to stab him in his eye. He caught my arm and twisted. A snap resounded through the alley, followed by my scream as a sharp pain reverberated up and down my arm. He swung me around and sent me stumbling into the brick building. My now broken arm slammed into the wall and sent a shot of white hot anguish throbbing through me. I panted, swallowing the rising nausea. The walking mountain approached me with a swagger. No man should be that big.

The world went grey, and I gasped when I saw the true form. There should have been a shadow, a thing with no soul, but there wasn't. Instead, a giant, green gorilla approached me, using his elongated arms to propel him forward. I was up against a demon possessed vampire. This night just couldn't get any better.

I ducked from his grab and danced around him. No way in all Seven Thrones of Hell would I let him trap me with my back against the wall. I swallowed hard and forced the pain into a tiny part in the back of my mind. I had to somehow get in close enough to stake him while avoiding those giant arms.

The short vampire hovered in my peripheral, trying to get a good shot in. I stepped back to the intersection so I could have a good view of both. The giant roared and charged me. I ducked, but the other one leapt in my path and tackled my legs. My hands scraped against the concrete, and the stake slipped from my grasp. The force jarred my broken arm, sending rivulets of agony through it. The demon stopped from a full run, grabbed me by my hair, and slammed my face into the concrete.

White light burst in my eyes. I groaned and brought my hand to the place where he had me. I tried to pry his fingers apart, but his grip was like an iron vise. I jerked my head forward, and a sting spread across the back of my head as some of my hair was ripped out. It still wasn't enough. He had too much.

"You're only hurtin' yourself, girlie," he said.

He slammed me against the ground again. Blood welled up in the cuts the street left on my forehead. My nose broke under the pressure. I panted and pulled harder at my hair. I had to get away. I couldn't be trapped. Trapped meant a continuous death, lost in darkness and cold.

He sighed and yanked me toward him. I slammed into the back of his chest, sandwiched by his huge bicep. One hand came over my mouth and nose, blocking all air. I slammed my fists against him, ignoring the agony to my broken arm. My eyes fluttered, and a floating sensation came over me.

My body went limp, and I fell into oblivion.

❧ 34 ❧

Pain pulled me from the depths of unconsciousness. It came to me even before the light. My arm throbbed in a constant ebb and flow, eliciting a groan from my lips. I blinked at the grey steel ceiling that greeted me. That wasn't right. I should have been dead. Instead, I lay in a barren prison with my right arm held to my chest in a sling.

I sat up, scanning my surroundings. The walls of the gray room were as bare as the metal slab I lay upon. Chains jangled as I moved, and a cold weight shifted on my wrist, keeping me trapped within a few feet from the wall. The rough material of the white gown I'd been dressed in rubbed against my skin and looked more like a sack than an actual gown. My head and neck were bandaged. Whoever my captors were, they wanted me in good condition. My laugh bounced off the walls of my prison. Who was I kidding? I knew full well who had me.

As if on cue, the door slid open, and two large men in charcoal gray suits stepped in. They moved to each side of the door and pressed their backs to the wall. Raina's heels clacked against the floor as she walked inside. She stopped a few feet from me and crossed her arms, her gaze traveling over me with a cold inspection.

"You don't look like much," she said. "It's hard to believe that you're some bogeyman of demons."

"It helps to look inconsequential." My hoarse voice betrayed the confidence I was trying to convey.

I glanced at the door. Maybe I could break my thumb, slip the cuffs, and make a run for it. No, it would never work.

She gave a sharp bark of a laugh. "Well, we'll see about that. I have a few questions, and you are going to answer them."

"Am I?"

She waved her hand, and her goon on the right moved forward. He drove his fist into my solar plexus. I crumpled on the metal bed with my good arm wrapping around my stomach. My shoulder screamed, but it was nothing compared to the wave of sickness and woe that arose in my abdomen. I gasped, choking on my own saliva. So, this was how things were going to be.

"Now, how do you know Adrian Van Helsing?" Raina asked.

I coughed. "I don't."

The goon yanked me up into a sitting position by my shoulders and kept me in a vise like grip. Raina stepped in front of me. Her hand gripped my chin and she dragged my gaze to her. Her eyes were a pale green, like frost on leaves.

"I can make you beg for death," she said.

I gave a hoarse laugh. "You're too late for that threat."

A cruel smile formed on her lips. Her nails dragged across my cheek, leaving four wet gaps in my flesh. She turned from me. "Restrain her to the table and bring me my tools."

The goon slammed me on the table hard enough that my head bounced, sending waves of dizziness. He pulled leather straps from the bottom of the slab and pulled them across my chest, waist, and legs. My arms were forced above my head, sending screaming agony through my broken bones. Beads of sweat formed on my forehead as I struggled against my bonds. Raina loomed over me and pressed me down against the table with one hand on my chest. Light from the ceiling reflected off something metal in her hand.

"So, once again, tell me of your relationship to Adrian Van Helsing."

"What is your relationship with him?" I asked. "You seem a bit obsessed."

A sharp sting began on my collarbone and traveled down my chest. My body became a conduit of pain. Tears pricked my eyes, and Raina blurred to an indistinct form above me. My throat went dry as the present meshed with the past. The lights dimmed to a soft yellow, and I could almost smell the mix of candle wax and piss. The figure above me spoke in harsh syllables, always with their questions. The church had claimed I'd killed my own husband and child.

"I'm not a heretic," I whispered.

"No, no. I need you to focus."

Cold water splashed on my face, and I gasped, fighting against my restraints. Raina held a jug in her hand as she scowled down at me. I lay back with a cough and closed my eyes. I needed to send my mind someplace different. If I didn't, I wouldn't survive this.

"Where is Adrian?" she asked.

I breathed in, counting to ten, and breathed out. I conjured the sound of the sea in my ears. I could see the diamonds in the night sky as I stood with my feet buried in the sand. The waves crashed against the shore with a hiss, and the wind carried the salty mist against my face. I hummed a tune while I spun in circles and danced across the beach. I stumbled as my body was wracked with a heaving cough and blood sprayed across the white sand, only to be consumed by the ocean.

"What are you doing?" a man's voice asked from somewhere in the distance.

"She is proving difficult." Raina's voice brought me back to the metal room and my pain.

I moaned and squinted at the figure in the doorway. Faust had his hands in his pockets with a frown on his face.

"Perhaps you should take a break," he said.

"I haven't gotten the information I need," Raina said. "All this is doing is making me hungry."

"I don't see why you chose this. So much blood is bound to tempt you."

"I enjoy it that way." She brought the knife to her lips.

I turned my head as another fit of coughing wracked my body. Liquid invaded my lungs, sending small bubbles up to burst against my lips. Every breath was a struggle, and the world slipped out of focus again.

"Damn, it looks like I may have cut too deep," Raina's voice echoed.

"Enough for today," Faust said. "You can start again fresh tomorrow."

The last notes of his voice drifted away and were replaced by a loud buzzing. Everything blended together as the few colors in the room faded to white.

❦   35   ❦

The waves rock the sail boat as I lay on the deck, soaking up the sun. The warm rays kiss my upraised face, and I smile. The skirt of my long dress flutters in the strong wind. A woman's husky chuckle tickles at my ears. I blink in the brightness, trying to focus on the figure that has invaded my private world.

She leans against the bow of the boat with her golden skin glittering in the sunlight. This isn't a metaphor. Her skin is actually golden. Her night black hair caresses her shoulders and hips, amplifying her naked glory. A small chain of purple stones hangs about her waist. She smiled at me with ~~the~~ perfect pouty lips and my own mouth opened in a pant as heat sweeps through me in places the sun can't touch. I sit up, running a hand down my neck and collar bone.

She holds a hand out with the palm upraised. "Come to me, my daughter. You have suffered long enough."

I stand, take two steps toward her, and stop as a chill wind passes over me. I glance up at the sparkling stars. When did it become night? Sirius winks at me from her position in the cosmos. The female before me frowns, and heavy clouds roll in, covering the glittering jewels of the night. The boat rocks as the waves pick up.

"Careful," she says. "There is a storm coming."

Lightning illuminates the black clouds rolling overhead, and the boat heaves to and fro. I grab the side to catch my balance.

"How many more storms do you want to endure?" she asks. "Come to me. Mother will protect you."

Her hand remains outstretched before me. It would be so easy just to agree. How warm her embrace must be. I could stay wrapped in her arms forever. Her purple eyes hold a promise of all I lost. I could have thousands of children to replace my Marco. Men would adore me, turning their eyes from all others.

And you would be just like Allegra.

The thought kills all the remaining heat in my body. No. I wouldn't become what I hated most. I take another step back so that my legs press against the gunwales of the boat. She lowers her hand with a long sigh.

"Why must you be so stubborn, Daughter?" she asks.

I stare down at the churning depths of the sea before meeting her gaze. "I'm not your daughter."

I leap over and let the icy water drag me under.

⁂

I gasped awake and stared at the gray ceiling above me as I tried to catch my first few breaths. The coppery stink of blood filled the air. Naamah had visited me, which meant I must have died again. Though Allegra was the demon to curse me, Naamah was the one who constantly tempted me with her honeyed lies. With each death, it grew a little harder to resist her. Someday, I wouldn't have the strength to do so. I swallowed hard and tried to focus, but my head kept swimming. I drifted into unconsciousness.

Someone was standing over me. I moved my arm to reach for my sword, but something impeded my movement. That's right. I was trapped on this metal table. They must have come back with more questions. I blinked up at the figure and found Faust instead of Raina. He ran a finger down the side of my cheek, and I resisted the urge to shudder in revulsion.

"You still twitch in your sleep. I take it your dreams haven't gotten any better," he said softly.

"What the hell do you know about my dreams?" I glared at him. Who did this demon think he was?

He chuckled.

"I know more about you than you think." He shook his head. "You have really caused a lot of trouble, dear girl. Destroying our warehouses, and our supply. To say Raina is livid is a massive understatement."

I stared at him for several moments. "What? You're expecting an apology or something, hellspawn?"

"Oh no. I'd never expect that. I should have been more cautious when I saw you at the conference." He rubbed a lock of my hair between two fingers. "No matter. We'll just make more, after we kill your friends."

I stiffened. "I'd like to see you try."

"Unfortunately, you won't be here to do so. You see, I contacted Allegra. She's just dazzled to know that you're all wrapped up and ready to be delivered for Naamah."

A chill ran through me. Oh, *Dio*. As much as I wanted to find Allegra, this was not the condition I wanted to be in. God only knew what she would have in store for me. Allegra would make Raina's little interrogation seem like child's play, and she would do it just for the pleasure of breaking me.

Faust patted me on the cheek. "I'm sure we'll get to know each other even more intimately in the future." He walked to the door. "Get some rest. You're going to need it."

I strained against my bonds, but they held tight. The ache in my now healed arm reared up, and I fell back against the table. It was no good. I was trapped. I breathed in and out and calmed my mind. Panic wasn't going to do me any better than it had when they started the torture.

"Esais, I need you," I called out mentally.

Nothing.

I swallowed at the sick feeling in the pit of my stomach. Had they already gotten to them? No, they wouldn't have questioned me so hard. So, where was Esais? Maybe Raina had something that prevented telepathic communication. They had no way of knowing about Esais's gift, though. I would just have to keep trying.

"And if you can't reach him?" A small thought floated up. *"Allegra will come and not even death can save you."*

My mouth went dry. It had been a good long run. Who did I think I was to actually try and win against an entire Throne? As much as I focused on Allegra, Naamah was the power that backed her. If only I'd been able to kill Allegra. She was the conduit for this curse keeping me here.

The door slid open. I stiffened, waiting to see who it was this time. My jaw dropped. It wasn't Raina with more pain or Allegra with her own brand of torture. It was the sweetest face I'd ever seen....

Adrian's.

❧ 36 ❧

Adrian walked to the table and his lips pressed together in a thin line as his gaze ran over me. "You look like hell."

I glared at him. "Less gawking and more helping please."

He unbuckled me from the table. "Can you walk?"

I pushed myself into a sitting position with a groan. I could see why he asked. The entire front of the gown was now red. The blood had darkened and left a sticky congealed mess that caused the fabric to cling to my chest. His frown deepened as he stepped closer and placed a hand on my shoulder. Concern coming from Adrian? I had to look horrible.

"It looks worse than it is," I said. "I'm glad I actually reached Esais. I thought something might have happened when I didn't get a response."

Adrian frowned. "Esais didn't tell me you were here."

"But how?"

"You've been gone for two days, ever since running out on Jonah's meeting," he said.

My hoarse laugh echoed off the walls. "I guess you can really lose track of time in here."

"I accessed Acesco's systems and found a reference to you." He turned to the door, clasping his hands behind his back. "I came to free you."

"Alone? Are you insane?" I stood, took a few steps, and the room spun a little. I leaned back on the table with a pant. "She knows about you."

"I expected her to figure things out eventually. Besides, no one should be left to monsters. Please tell me you're not going to need a shoulder to lean on."

I locked a steely gaze with him and took a few steady steps. "I think I can manage. Just needed to adjust for a moment."

"Good. We need to get out of here."

"Wait. Both Raina and Faust are here. We can't pass this chance up."

Adrian raised the eyebrow above his good eye. "How are we going to do anything? We don't even know if they are still here."

"If we leave now, we may never get a better chance. Once they find out what you did, Raina's going to send whatever legions she has after you and your brothers." Not to mention Faust and Allegra will be after me.

He sighed. "We are in the center of their compound. Just the two of us would be suicide. I don't have enough nanites to bring this building down, and you are missing your favorite weapon."

I narrowed my eyes, my voice dropping in temperature. "I've fought in worse conditions. Alone. Besides, Faust hasn't used brimstone. I can banish him."

It wouldn't solve my problem, but it could delay it long enough so that I could prepare. "What do you have with you?"

"Two holy water grenades, ten of the garlic bombs, three stakes, and my guns," he said.

"The one that can kill demons?"

"As well as one I've modified to shoot silver jacketed bullets with hard wood cores."

I chuckled. "One of the old ones from World War II? I'd heard rumors about that."

A ghost of a smile appeared on his face. "Something like that. That still leaves you without a weapon."

"Give me some of the garlic bombs and the demon gun."

"You're not that good of a shot."

I squinted at him. "I can hit occasionally."

He stared at me, his debate not evident on his face. "Not happening. That is insane. First rule of hunting vampires: attack them when they're weak."

"Are you here at night?" I looked at the doorway, but only saw the opposite white wall, lit by electricity.

He snorted. "Of course not."

He spread his arms and pointed to the navy blue jumpsuit underneath the jacket with the name-tag of Stan. "Nobody questions the new maintenance guy."

He knelt beside a large metal toolbox I hadn't seen before, opened it, and pulled out a rolled up piece of cloth. I grabbed it out of the air and it unfolded into another blue jumpsuit.

"You could have just handed it to me," I said.

"Put it on. I swiped it from the janitor's closet for you."

I slipped into it, turning my back to Adrian as I dressed. He held out a wet towel and a ball cap. Good point. I probably looked like a bloody mess. I wiped my face off as best I could and hid my hair under the hat.

"Where are we, and how far do we need to go?" I asked.

"Underground," he said. "We need to get to the first floor and out the back entrance."

"You are giving me some sort of weapon right? I'm not just going to hang in the back and hope no one notices me."

He sighed and handed me one of the holy water canisters, a couple of the garlic bombs, and a stake. "Try to make it last."

"That will depend on how many guards there are."

"Look, it's in the day. We're going to have more trouble with the human authorities if we get caught. I don't think Raina wants her little setup exposed."

"If you say so." I waved my hand to the door. "Lead the way."

The hallway was narrow. I swallowed hard and kept my gaze on Adrian's back. Fluorescent lights shone from the ceiling and reflected off the eggshell-white walls. We passed several unmarked doors before turning to the right. I clenched my fist and wiped the sweat from my brow. Just a little farther and we would be free. When I saw the figure standing at the elevator, my heart thudded and sank down to my ankles. He took up most of the width of the hall. Adrian came to a stop, and his hand hovered over his guns. The hulking monster grinned down at both of us, flashing a fang. It was the same vampire from the alley.

"Interesting," Adrian said. "Your size won't save you."

"He's possessed," I said.

"And that makes any difference?"

The demonic vampire gave a roar and charged us. He hit Adrian with the back of his hand and sent him flying into the wall. Adrian's guns skittered across the floor as he landed on the ground. I tried to duck out of reach, but the demon's hand tangled in my hair. My forehead met the wall and white pain burst behind my eyes. The room spun, and I pressed my hands against the wall to keep myself upright. The demon's grating laugh rattled around in my ears. It changed to an angry roar of pain as the hall filled with white mist. Adrian must have thrown one of the grenades. The demon shoved past me in his haste to get out of the holy mist. I stumbled, tripped, and toppled onto Adrian. He gave an annoyed sigh, pushed me off of him, and stood up.

"Find my guns." He sprinted down the hall after the demon.

Adrian reached the edge of the mist and stopped. A few feet from him, a door stood open. A large arm, red with sizzling blisters, reached out from the doorway, grabbed Adrian by his throat, and yanked him into the darkened room. I scanned the hall, my breath coming in short pants. Where the hell had his guns gone? There. A small black square in the corner. I rushed to it and scooped the revolver up. It was plain with no tube. This had to be the one that shot the special cartridges. Damn, where was the other gun? I would probably need both to kill the demon. The second gun lay near the doors of the elevator.

Adrian gave a strangled cry from the room. I scrambled to the other gun and opened the cylinder of the first one. The cartridges scattered across the floor. I unloaded the second gun and grabbed several of the silvery cartridges. *"Please let this work."* Adrian told me the symbol wasn't created until the gun was fired. The gas from the tube created enough heat to stamp it into the bullet. I was on my feet and down the hall in a matter of seconds. I leaned against the wall and peered into the room.

The demon had Adrian pressed against the wall by his neck. Adrian's face was turning blue as the demon squeezed harder. I held my breath as I crept behind him. I pressed the gun to his back and pulled the trigger. Black wisps of shadow wafted from the neat hole in his back. The demon stiffened and turned to me with a look of shock on his paper-white face. He burst into a cloud of shadow that dissipated on the air. Adrian dropped to the ground, gasping and holding his throat. I knelt beside him.

"Can you speak?" "*Please speak.*" I had no idea how to fix a crushed windpipe.

His voice was hoarse. "Help me up. We need to go."

He groaned and clutched his side as I helped him up. I gave a low laugh as we hobbled to the elevator with his arm around my shoulder. We stopped to pick up his gun and several of the cartridges. We didn't know how many more we would have to face to make our escape. I pressed the button and took a deep breath and focused on Adrian reloading his guns with a quick ease. I could do this. The doors opened, and I gulped in a huge breath before stepping in.

"Which way?" My voice was at a higher pitch than normal.

"Up two floors. We're leaving through the parking garage."

Adrian groaned when I jerked both of us out into the garage. He waved to our right in a half-hearted hand gesture. I scanned the rows of cars for any sign of movement. The yellow light from the ceiling cast eerie reflections over the shiny chrome and glass surrounding us. Our footsteps echoed against the concrete walls.

"Not far now," Adrian said. "To the left, at the end of the row."

Car doors slammed near us, and I stiffened. The next voice froze the blood in my veins.

"Just the man I wanted to see. It looks like you were right about her being the perfect bait." Raina's shrill words surrounded us.

Faust stepped away from the car he'd gotten out of and into the light. "Don't scurry away just yet, little mice."

Without wasting time thinking, I ripped the pin from the holy water grenade and flung the canister toward them. Adrian pulled away from me and tossed one of his garlic bombs. We escaped in a hobbled sprint to hide between two parked cars. I peered past the metal bars that ran horizontal and separated this level from the lower one. It was a short drop. I glanced at Adrian and tilted my head. Could he handle it? He gave a soft snort, crawled under the bars, and dropped down. He didn't make a sound despite the fact it had to hurt. With a wince for him, I followed his example to land with a small thud beside him and into an immediate crouch. We darted between the cars until we were a small distance away from our escape point.

"Well," I whispered. "We're as far down as we can go unless you want to make a break for the elevator again."

Please say no.

He shook his head. "She'll have guards all over the place. That building is a trap."

He peered up at the slanted drive that led to the next level. "We need the van."

"I could cause a distraction and you could run for it."

He gave a hoarse laugh. "I'm not that quick. Let's reverse that plan. You get the van."

I blinked at him. "You're joking. I have no idea how to drive."

"You've been in enough cars to at least get the basics right?"

I gave a hesitant shrug. "I guess."

"Good. Then listen closely. Right pedal for gas, left for the brakes. Turn the wheel in the direction you want to turn, otherwise keep it straight. And please, try not to hit anything. You only have to go a few feet."

"Are you sure you can distract them?"

He smiled coldly. "I'm just going to talk. She likes to talk."

I shook my head. Well, she had talked a bit when torturing me. I'd stopped listening. I squeezed his hand and crawled to the front of the car. The smell of motor oil clung to the back of my throat. I pressed against the rail and slid past the front of the bumper. The sound of high heels echoing became louder. I froze behind the bumper and ducked my head.

"There's no point in hiding. You have nowhere to run," Raina called. "Besides, I'm sure we can have a civil conversation."

"I see you made the wrong choice," Adrian's voice came from farther back than I'd left him. Had he moved already?

She laughed. "As opposed to going to prison? I saw what happened when you opposed Durnovo. Besides, he offered me ultimate power."

"Prison is better than becoming the abomination you are. You already had power and you still let him seduce you, fuck you, turn you into a monster, and you're still his obedient, little bitch. How's that ultimate power working out for you?"

I blew a silent whistle. So, Adrian's plan of distraction was to drive her into a rage? I peered around the car. She glared into the distance with her fists clenched. It seemed to be working. She hadn't even looked in my direction. I moved past a few more cars until I got to a point I could climb up.

"You know nothing about us." She gave an angry growl that changed to a chuckle. "Still an asshole, I see."

"Coming from a bitch like you, that's a compliment."

"You'll see how much of a bitch I can be. I have special plans for you. I plan on taking the amount of loss you caused me out on your hide."

He laughed. "You have more to worry about besides me."

"Oh, I've heard of your little family. Imagine the Van Helsings are actually vampire hunters. I suppose you'll tell me Dracula is real, too."

"He's just a myth," Adrian said.

"Well, your family isn't that impressive."

"We'll see. You may be surprised."

I slid under the bars and crawled between two cars on the next level. Hopefully he could keep her bickering until I brought the van around. He had to have more weapons there, though unfortunately, my sword was still at the offices. Footsteps sounded near me, and I pressed my back against the car. I peeked through the windows. Two of Raina's thugs walked in my direction. They blocked the way between me and the van. I pulled out one of the garlic bombs and a stake. If I snuck past them, they would still hear the van coming. It was best to take them out now.

I tossed the bomb, and a yellow cloud covered the area. I leapt out and jammed the stake into the back of the first vampire. The body folded in on itself until nothing remained but escaping shadows. The other turned my direction and pulled out a gun. I ducked under his arm before he could point it at me, got in really close, and shoved the stake in his chest. The gun clattered to the ground as he dissolved. I picked it up. My armory was running low. I could use the extra firepower. I closed my eyes, rubbed my temples, and let my breath out slowly, willing the pain to leave with it. It worked for three seconds before the throbbing began anew. *Dio,* let there be pain medication in Adrian's van as well as weapons. The shadows flickered overhead and the level darkened to dusky gray. That was weird. The vampires didn't have their powers in the day.

Faust's chuckle washed over me. "Raina's a special girl. Very few like her are able to survive vampirism."

Only a few feet away, he leaned against the front bumper with his arms crossed and a smirk on his face. My pace slowed and died. I pulled the demon killer gun from under my jacket and held it behind me.

Faust waved to the van. "Is this yours? You won't need it."

I raised the gun and fired off several shots in quick succession. The grin on his face disappeared, and he jumped to the side. The bullets pierced the grill with one shattering the right headlight.

"You really should put that away. You'll hurt someone." He ducked behind one of the cars.

"That's the plan," I said.

I leapt on the hood of one of the cars, the metal whining under me, and pointed the pistol at Faust. The light above me fizzled into blackness with a small buzz. As Faust's laugh filled my ears, I gripped my gun tighter and squinted. The darkness receded to a muted gray world as a small pop bloomed in my head. Faust's glowing crimson eyes stared at me from behind his true face, the comedy and tragedy mask. I pulled the trigger.

The heavy duty light fixture above him crashed down

onto his head. With a shout of pain, he fell. I'd hit him! Well, indirectly. He woozily crab crawled away until his back was against the rails. I rushed over and leapt on him. He gave a groan as I landed on his chest. I pressed the gun to his head.

"Looks like this is goodbye," I said.

A shout echoed from the lower level. Faust turned his head to peer below us. The shadowy form of Raina towered over Adrian on his knees with her fingers pressed into his head. The vibrancy of his yellow and green aura leeching away into a dull cloud. My heart pounded in my throat and reverberated in my ears.

"How many bullets do you have left?" Faust asked. "I doubt enough for both of us."

He was right. I'd used several already on the vampire and at Faust himself. If I didn't do something, she was going to kill Adrian. But what would I have left for Faust?

"His life or mine?" Faust's grin widened. "We both know what choice you'll make. We'll see each other again, Gabriella."

If I couldn't kill him, well, there were other ways. I aimed the gun at Raina and began chanting the words to banish his ass back to hell. Faust's eyes widened. He shook his head and a light flared in his eyes before his body went limp. Damn, he'd escaped. I pulled the trigger. The bullet missed Raina's chest and caught her in the shoulder. She staggered back, and her arms dropped. That was all Adrian needed. He lunged forward and pressed his own gun to her chest. His shot, which boomed through the garage, didn't miss her heart. She gave a shudder with a surprised gasp and the darkness dissipated. There was something almost romantic about the way she disintegrated in his arms. I shook my head. Sometimes, I'm too morbid.

"Are you all right?" I called out to him.

"Just get the van."

I climbed into the driver's seat, pushed the key in the ignition, and started the van. I stared at the gages in the glass panel. John had once tried to teach me how to drive. One bent bumper and a scarred tree later, he'd given up. Still, I remembered a little of his advice. I jammed my foot on the left pedal and switched the gear to the D. I lifted my foot and the van rolled forward. My stomach did a small flip. I spun the wheel and the van shifted and turned. So far, so good. I rolled along at a crawl down to the next level where Adrian waited at the end. I slammed my foot down on the brake and the van jerked to the stop, jostling me forward.

Adrian walked to the driver's side and opened the door. "Move over."

I climbed over to the passenger seat and relinquished the power to him. I let out a long breath and rolled down the window. My body itched to be out of this metal death trap, but that wasn't happening for now. Adrian raced through the rest of the garage and sped up as we approached the exit. I gripped the armrest and covered my face as we crashed through the little wooden obstacle blocking us from freedom. The guard in his shack ran out, but he was too late. Adrian had already merged with the other traffic on the street. It was over.

❧ 38 ☙

We dumped the van a few blocks away. I huddled next to Adrian, trying to keep my head up as we walked down the street. Adrian's face was locked in a blank look, but his ragged breathing betrayed how much he struggled against the pain in his ribs.

"Lucy, can you hear me?" He stared straight ahead as he spoke. "I found Gabby. I need you to pick us up."

He stopped and leaned against a brick wall. "On Fifth and 186th. We'll be waiting."

I scanned the sidewalk. A man in a pale gray suit passed us with a cell phone to his ear. I sighed. The vampires had taken mine along with everything else I had on me. Thank god that I'd left my sword at the office when I'd gone to see John. Adrian leaned against a concrete pot that held a small tree. Little flecks of snow hung on the bare branches.

"Why didn't you call her in for back up earlier?" I asked.

He sighed. "It would have taken her a while to get to the building, and I for one didn't want to wait in a cell like yours."

I nodded. "I prefer the cold to a cage as well."

He snorted.

"Raina dispersed. Faust has escaped. That leaves Cambione," I said.

"Faust is the one who started this," Adrian said.

"Ah, but his plans are ruined. He's going to have to start all over again and we can be waiting when he rears his head. Unless you think he'll go back to Acesco, or Erebus."

Adrian shook his head. "Perhaps. It depends on how much the CEO wants this wonder drug as opposed to how much Faust has screwed him."

I chuckled. "Is he that big of a badass?"

"He's a corporate boogeyman," Adrian said. "Being a vampire is the least of his powers."

"Let's hope that Faust didn't have a chance to show how good his drug was. Maybe he'll be dealt with by your business leech." I stared down at the pavement and lowered my voice. "Raina was a nephilim, wasn't she?"

"Mmm."

"How long have you known about them?"

"We were on the same project together. Raina claimed she wanted to study them and learn more. I didn't find out about her secret until later." He shook his head with a small laugh. "Of course it wasn't the only secret she was keeping."

"What else?"

"Her vampire lover, Durnovo. Thanks to him I ended up in prison."

"So, now that she's dead, you're looking for a way to go after him?"

He stared at the passing traffic and his jaw tightened. "Let's worry about things here and now, like is there any aspirin around here?"

I shuffled to the newsstand close by and bought two packets from the huddled man behind the counter. Adrian downed one pack dry in one gulp. Mine acted stubborn and took several swallows to get them down, leaving a bitter taste behind. I pressed close to his side, grateful for the warmth that radiated from him as the cold seeped through my pores and settled in my bones. My eyes fluttered, and I leaned against the post. A car pulled to the curb, and a window rolled down to show Lucy peering at us from the driver's seat. I let out a long breath of relief. I helped Adrian into the passenger seat. I climbed in the backseat, and Lucy pulled away.

"What in the bloody Thrones of Hell happened to the two of you?" she asked.

"Vampires," I said.

"Demons," Adrian said.

"Well, I hope they're dust in the wind."

"Not all," I said and laid my head back against the seat.

Lucy moved through the traffic and spun a U-turn. She had us back at the offices within ten minutes. Tres hurried around his desk and helped Adrian onto one of the examination tables. Adrian leaned forward with a groan and struggled to remove his jacket and shirt with Tres's assistance.

"I hope whatever it was, it was worth it," Tres said as he pressed his good hand on Adrian's abdomen.

"Well, they no longer have the formula to make more brimstone-based drugs," Adrian said.

"That is excellent news," Jonah said from the door. He moved to stand beside my table. "Lucy informed me that you may need assistance."

Tres gave him a weary smile. "I could use an extra hand."

I snorted as he turned back to examining Adrian. Jonah looked at me with a raised eyebrow. I sighed and began the long story of my nights.

"Hold still," Tres snapped at Adrian. "You don't know how hard this is with a broken arm."

"Physician, heal thyself," Adrian said.

Tres glared at him. "You don't think I've tried?"

"He's right," I said. "You really need to figure out why you can't."

"Well, it's not happening right now," Tres said. "So, shut up so I can deal with you, then I'm going to lie down. This is exhausting."

I frowned. "That's new. I thought you had more of an itch to hurt people."

Jonah gave a choking cough beside me, and I gave him a look. "That's how he described it."

Tres snorted. "Those weren't my words, but it's still there along with this deep feeling of exhaustion."

"We really need to learn more about your abilities," I said and looked at Adrian. "All of yours."

Adrian closed his eyes and lay back. "Just get it over with."

Tres leaned over his brother and closed his eyes. The bruising around Adrian's throat faded, leaving only pink healthy skin behind. The shadows that had hovered under his eyes disappeared. He sat up with a sigh and nodded.

"Do me a favor." Tres turned his gaze to me. "Try to stay out of trouble. I don't have enough energy to keep this up. If demons come knocking, send Lucy or something. At least she heals herself."

Speak of the devil, and she should appear. Lucy knocked on the doorway. "Gabby, you need to take this phone call. John has been calling a lot. He sounds desperate."

I hopped off the table. "Why didn't you say something?"

"You were busy," Lucy said.

I rushed to the next office and picked up the phone. "John? What's wrong?"

"He's after me," John's voice crackled through static. "Every time I think I've lost him, he's there again."

"Who's after you?" I asked.

"Cambione, Gabby. I can't run much more."

"Where are you?"

"Central Park. Please come. I need you now."

"I'm coming." I hung up the phone and spun around to find Lucy behind me.

"You really aren't going to listen to Tres," she said.

"Sorry, demons don't stop just because he needs a nap. I won't let them get John."

I pushed past her and headed up to the fourth floor. The pressure in my chest weighed on my lungs and heart. So, was this Faust's revenge? He was sending one of his pieces after my lover. I stopped and closed my eyes as my throat tightened. It didn't matter if he did. I would save John. I just had to hurry. My sword lay on the bench, next to my bag, just where I'd left it. Lucy stepped into the room with her arms crossed.

"Well, you are going to take *part* of Tres's advice." She held up the keys. "I'm not letting you go alone."

Lucy parked her car off of 72nd street. I pushed open the door and bolted out of the car before she even got her seatbelt off. She called after me as I rushed down the trail toward the Strawberry Fields Memorial, but her words were mere murmurs against the blood pounding through my ears.

"Please let me be in time," I chanted in my head.

I stopped at the memorial and caught my breath, resting my hands on my knees. The concreted disc with the word *Imagine* that served as a monument to John Lennon had been cleared of snow. The area was strangely empty of people, even for winter. He said he'd be waiting here. My heart squeezed in my chest, and my stomach tightened. A man's scream echoed from the copse of trees. I took off in that direction.

Branches scraped against my face and caught in my hair and against my jacket. I ignored them and kept going. I burst into a small clearing and stopped. Cambione had John on his knees. The demon had his hand around his neck as he stared into his eyes. He glanced in my direction, smiled, and twisted his arm in a quick motion. A snap echoed through the air.

The sound sent a jolt that tore through my chest and pierced my heart. I'd been too late. A pale light rose from John's blank eyes and filled Cambione's. He inhaled deeply and smiled back at me.

A buzzing filled my ears and the world around us became distorted. All that was clear was the demon in front of me. The demon that needed to feel the sting of my blade over and over before he met oblivion. I didn't even realize I had drawn my sword, but it was in my hand as I rushed at him. He dodged to the side with a laugh as I sliced at his chest.

"You'll have to be a little faster than that, Gabriella," he said.

I couldn't form words, so I gave a rage-filled scream and rushed him again. My sword met only air. I spun around with a pant, but he had disappeared. His laughter filled the clearing.

"I thought you were this fearsome demon slayer. You look pretty pathetic here." His voice echoed around me. "Come and see if you can find me."

White mist slithered in from the trees and surrounded me, so thick I could barely see a few feet in front of me. I tightened my grip on my sword and moved forward, scanning as I went. The bastard still had to be around here. It didn't matter what tricks he had. I'd find him and make him bleed for what he'd done. A silhouette undulated to my left. I spun and lashed my sundang out to cut it down. The blade sliced through the mist and nothing else. I gave a growl and moved forward as Cambione's laugh pounded in my ears. There. A figure stood in the mist in front of me. I sprinted, leapt, and tackled him to the ground. I pressed my sword across his throat and froze.

Lucy stared up at me with wide eyes. The clouds above us broke and the sun peeked through. The mist vanished. It didn't just dissipate—it disappeared in an instant, leaving us alone with the dead trees and John. I turned back to his body. His face was turned to the side, and he stared off at nothing. He'd fallen at an odd angle with one arm trapped behind his back. I knelt beside him, straightened his limbs, and placed his hands on his chest. I gripped the sleeves of his sports jacket, and I swallowed hard. Tears burned my eyes and threatened to spill from the corners. There were too many. They trailed down my cheeks as I bowed my head. I gulped back the sob rising in my chest.

"Give him eternal rest, O Lord, and may Your light shine upon him forever," I whispered in Italian.

Lucy grabbed my shoulders and pulled at me. "We have to go. We don't want anyone to find us here."

I held on tighter. This would be the last time I'd see his face. I'd never hear his laugh again or feel his fingers on my skin. Why hadn't I been more patient with him? He'd begged for my help, and I had failed him. I'd always had more important things to worry about.

Lucy half-carried, half-dragged me to where her car was parked. I stared at the steel-gray clouds and prayed the rain would start pouring from the sky. My prayers went unanswered. I sat stiffly in the seat of the car, blind to the world passing by the window. The sorrow I'd swallowed churned in my stomach and turned into a boiling heat. Someone would pay for this.

"Not today," Lucy said. "You are in no shape mentally to handle the demon."

I gripped the handle of the door. "We can't just let him get away."

"He won't get away, dearie. But you need to sleep and to mourn. Otherwise, you'll be running on rage, and you'll make mistakes like you did with Allegra."

I gritted my teeth. It wasn't that I hadn't tried to kill Allegra multiple times, even without my sword. Somehow, she'd known I was there and had always laid a trap for me. I'd thought having Dimitri there would help, but that had proven futile. The results had been the same, except that Dimitri had nearly been killed. I seemed to get the people I cared about hurt or killed while the monster got away. Not this time. The monster would pay for his sins. I'd see to it personally. I would do it alone, so this time, if I failed, I would be the only one to die. Lucy was right, though. I couldn't go after him now. I'd proven myself unfit in the clearing.

As we sat in more traffic, the burning knot in the pit of my stomach unfurled. It traveled up and constricted my chest, pressing until I released the first sob. I leaned against the headrest of the backseat and cried until all that remained was exhaustion. Lucy remained silent, but her arms were comforting as she led me to my apartment.

"Do you want me to stay with you?" Lucy asked.

I shook my head.

She left. I curled up with a pillow clutched in my arms. There, I found that I did have more tears to shed. They continued until I fell asleep.

🙆 40 🙆

The stench of burnt flesh pervades through the room, sinking into the wood floor and walls. It stains the house with the tragedy that happened mere moments ago. I sink before the fireplace and shift through the smoldering cinders, unmindful of my own hands burning. The pain cannot be greater than that in my heart. I pull the tiny body to me as a new set of tears wash down my cheeks. My poor Marco. He'd only just seen his first year. I would never see his first steps, watch him grow tall, or find a good wife.

His body crumples to ash in my arms and I'm left to clutch my chest. Sobs strangle my throat and create a vise in my chest. What had I done? I'd meant to protect my husband. Instead, the demon sought her revenge by destroying everything I held dear. I crawl to Dario, ignoring the ever growing pool of blood that surrounds his body. I take a shuddering breath as I avoid the gaping hole in his chest. His head is turned from me with a lock of dark hair splayed across one cheek.

I caress his cheek and pull his face towards mine. I gasp and the world grows arctic. John Roda, not my husband, stares back at me.

I woke in a darkened room with a hoarse wail. I clutched the pillow tighter and buried my face in it. Once again, I'd failed to keep my lover safe. Another demon had taken someone dear to me. I would never have a chance to rectify things between us. I sat up. Maybe I still could. I grabbed my house phone and called Lucy.

"How are you feeling?" she asked.

"Better," I said. "But I need a favor. Can you meet me at the Lexington Hotel on 5th street with your séance materials?"

Lucy met me in the lobby of the hotel. She was dressed in jeans and had a black duffel bag slung over her shoulder. She studied me for several moments with a concerned expression. I gave her my best smile to show her I was all right.

"Ciao," I said, crossing my arms around me.

She rested a hand on my arm. "Hello, dearie. Are you sure you want to do this? His soul might have already moved on."

I took a deep breath. "I need to do this. I need closure."

She nodded. "How are we getting in?"

"We need a key."

"He didn't give you one?"

"I didn't visit often." My voice shook. I never had time. There had always been the demons and the brimstone to worry about. John, once again, became secondary.

She looked over at the clerk and back to me. A mischievous smile lit on her lips. "I'll handle it."

A few minutes later, she came back with the key. She waved it and headed for the elevator.

"Nothing a little money, flirting, and maybe a flash of tittie won't get you," she said.

"What if he'd been homosexual?"

"Then there would have been more money."

The elevator ride was thankfully short, and we got off on the third floor. Lucy slid the key card in the slot and the door opened with a click. I held it open to let her enter first. I took a deep breath and let it out in a slow release before I entered. The maid had been there during the day. Both beds were made and his laptop and briefcase were set on the desk. The police must not have found him yet. I swallowed hard, but it did nothing to alleviate the bad taste in my mouth. I'd had to abandon him there. Police questions would have been too inconvenient. I couldn't even show him the respect of a vigil or burial.

"Let's get on with this," I said.

We pulled the small dining table to the middle of the room. Lucy drew a circle with chalk around it while I moved the chairs. She pulled out candles, a knife, and a large metal mirror. I raised an eyebrow.

"What? I'm setting the mood and the mirror will help me see the other side better," she said. "Not all of us have your gift. I'm surprised you're not doing this yourself."

"I can see spirits, not hear or speak to them. Besides, do you know how hard it is to call a spirit to possess you and try to have a conversation with it?"

"Hmm."

I sat down and watched as she powered the circle. There was a difference in vibration once the circle closed. The air smelled cleaner and lighter. Lucy sat across from me, closed her eyes, and took several deep breaths. She pricked her finger with the knife. Three drops hit the surface with a small splat.

"O ye spirit of John Roda, ye I conjure by the Power,

Knowledge, Wisdom, and Virtue of the spirit of God, and by the Holy name of God, Eheieh, which is the root, trunk, source, and origin of all other Divine names," Lucy said.

I stared down at the mirror even though I wouldn't be able to see anything. It was sympathetic magic more than anything else. It allowed Lucy to focus enough to connect to the Eclipse. What she would see would be in her mind.

"I conjure thee, and I powerfully urge ye, O spirit, in whichever part of the Eclipse ye may be, that ye shall be unable to remain in any other part of the Universe, or any pleasant place that may attract ye, but that ye come promptly to accomplish our desire, and all things that we demand from your obedience."

Lucy's shoulder's jerked and her head fell forward, her pigtails brushing against her cheeks. A shudder passed through her body and her hand tightened on her knife.

I frowned. This wasn't right.

"Lucy?" I asked. "John?"

She gave a small whimper, and her head lifted. She looked in my direction with wide eyes but they seemed to stare past me and a million miles away. Her hand patted the table until it found mine. I tried to pull back, but she held on tight. She jabbed the point of my finger with the knife.

"Ow, Lucy, what the hell are you doing?"

She pulled my hand forward and let my blood drip on the mirror. "O Adonai, most holy, most righteous, most almighty God, who sees all, grant Gabriella the ability to see what vision I see until this ritual be complete."

I threw my head back as my mind was filled with images.

I climb out of a car and slam the door behind me. I slip my hands in my pockets and walk towards a two story warehouse. I look up at the sky and the constellation as a feeling of satisfaction fills me. I'd gained more power. I was so much closer to being the First. I run a hand through my hair and inspect my face in the reflective glass window of the warehouse. Cambione's face. I gasped. *I, no Cambione, pauses and looks around. A sense of being watched fills me. Someone is riding me.*

The sound of breaking glass filled the room. I stared up at the ceiling of John's hotel room and panted. Lucy held the handle of the knife over the shattered mirror.

"What was that?" I asked.

"When I tried to call John, I got the demon instead." Lucy pulled a marijuana cigarette out of her pocket with shaky hands. "I'm damn lucky it didn't notice me at first. Otherwise, you'd probably be talking to it face to face right now."

The nauseous feeling in my stomach grew as I glanced at the bed. It couldn't be. But I knew who had the answers. I snatched the cigarette out of her mouth before she lit it.

"Hey! I need that for my nerves."

"No time. Call the others. We need to catch Cambione before he moves again."

"And how are we supposed to find him?"

I close my eyes, picturing the night's sky from Cambione's view. "The stars will guide us."

❧ 42 ❧

The clouds broke, and I could see the small patch of stars that weren't eaten away by the city lights. Before me was the warehouse from the vision I had through Cambione's eyes. If I stepped two feet to the right, I would be in the exact position as he was. A car engine rumbled through the night as it drew closer. I ducked behind Lucy's car as lights flashed in our direction. She crouched next to me, her gaze steady in the approaching vehicle. The car drew near, its silver sheen reflecting in the lone lamp from the warehouse.

"That's Tres's car." Lucy stood.

I pulled myself up and grumbled. "They couldn't think of anything less conspicuous to bring?"

"Adrian's van is gone. Besides, does it matter?"

No, I supposed it didn't. I wasn't planning on stealth. Tonight we were going to end it. I turned back to the warehouse with my eyes narrowed. Doors slammed and footsteps approached. The air grew warmer as I was surrounded by my allies. Everyone was here, including Esais and Viktor. Even

Jonah had put on his work clothes and pulled out his cane sword.

"So, this is it?" Marge asked. "Doesn't look like much."

"It never does," I said.

The building was two stories and a muted gray brick that matched its siblings that lined the street. A lone lamp hung over the concrete steps that led up to the front door, but light shone through the dingy windows of the first floor.

"What's the plan? More sneaking?" Marge asked.

"I'm going through the front door," I said.

Marge grinned at me and nodded her head. "Finally."

"Are you insane?" Adrian asked.

Esais frowned. "I'm not sure if you're emotionally stable enough to do this."

I pulled out my sundang. "Trust me. I'm a master at aiming my anger in the right direction."

"That's what I'm worried about," Esais said.

Adrian shook his head. "You are going to be a liability to us."

Esais sighed. "Maybe it's best if you stay behind."

I clenched the sundang's hilt and gritted my teeth. Stay behind? And let Cambione get away again? No way in hell was I letting that happen. If it wasn't for Lucy and I, we wouldn't even know his location.

Lucy put her hand on my shoulder. "I have her back. I don't have to worry about it as much."

The back of my neck grew hot at the thought of any of them having to look after me. I was older than everyone combined and had been through more death and demons than anyone should have to. Jonah cleared his throat and I raised my gaze to meet his.

"Please," he said. "It would do our hearts some good to not see you die tonight."

I sighed and nodded.

"So are we going?" Marge said.

"There are two doors and the loading docks," I said. "We need all the exits covered. Lucy and I will take the front."

"Viktor and I will take the loading dock." Esais turned to his boyfriend. "Do you think you can keep them locked down?"

Viktor smirked. "Easily."

"I'm taking the back then," Marge said. "But I'm not staying there. I'm finding Cambione."

"I will cover the back door," Jonah said. "They shall not get past me."

Adrian pulled out a stack of holy water grenades and held some to Tres. "We can toss these through the windows."

"And back up who needs help." Tres took two of the grenades.

"Good," I said. "We use that as our signal."

We snuck to the door as the others crept to their positions. The sound of shattering glass filled the night followed by several inhuman yowls. My boot slammed into the handle. It caved under the assault with the sound of splintering wood and groaning metal. I pushed Lucy through the door and stepped up so we stood side by side. A bajang rushed us with wild eyes intent on the open doorway. Lucy stepped forward and rammed her punch dagger into the demon's stomach. Her second blade punctured the soft section under the creature's chin. I turned at movement behind me and found Tres in the doorway. Perfect. With Tres covering the door and Lucy occupied, I could sneak off to find Cambione.

"Make sure nothing gets out!" I yelled to Tres before heading into the mist.

Tres called after me but he stayed where he was. I stepped over a puddle of metallic liquid, most likely once one of the oily demons. Shouts echoed throughout the warehouse along with the blast of gunfire. A hand wrapped around my arm and jerked me back.

"You're not getting away that easily, dearie," Lucy shouted over the clamor.

I shook loose and pushed onward. I was going to kill Cambione with or without Lucy at my back. Another bajang stumbled into my path and I lashed out in an arc, slicing her from hip to shoulder in a diagonal cut. She fell with a choking gurgle, but I didn't stop moving. A brown haired figure hunched over a table, choking or shuddering. My heart sped up. Esais? He spun around and screamed at me wordlessly. His face was streaked in red blisters and blood streamed from the corners of his eyes. Right, not Esais, demon. I slashed him in his midsection. He crumpled to the ground, clutching his abdomen.

Jonah's shout reverberated from our right, causing Lucy's eyes to widen and her lips press into a thin line. She raced in his direction and, with a long sigh, I followed. He hunched down, clutching his shoulder with a cane sword grasped in his hand and three demons towering over him. Lucy rushed forward and buried one of her blades deep in the back of the middle bajang. The hellcat howled and swung around with her claws aimed at Lucy's face. Jonah's usually stoic look disappeared into a scowl and he jammed his sword to the hilt between the bajang's shoulder blades. The creature gave a gasping mewl as she collapsed.

Platinum blond flashed to my left. Cambione raced up the stairs to the second floor, his face in ruins and panic in his steps. Marge followed after him with a grin on her face. Hell, she wasn't going to kill him alone. I glanced back at Lucy and Jonah who now stood back to back as they fought off their two remaining demons. They could handle it. I sprinted towards the stairs after Cambione and Marge.

A rainbow slick tentacle glittered in the lights as it

wrapped around my wrist and yanked me off of my feet. I gripped my sword tighter as I was dragged across the floor with the concrete scraping against my hands and arms. The orang attached to the tentacle leaned over me with its face rippling like a pool with a stone dropped in it. I rolled to the side, cut through the bond holding me, and hopped to my feet. I took one of the holy water grenades from my belt and lobbed it at the demon's feet. As it gave a high pitched gargle and went into spasms, I raced toward the stairs. The longer these nobody demons delayed me the more I lost my chance of killing Cambione myself and avenging John.

The clang of metal echoed as I sprinted up the stairs to the row of offices overlooking the bottom of the warehouse. Cambione yanked the door open and ran inside one of the center ones with Marge right behind him. She stopped in the doorway and swayed back and forth. I came behind her and shook her shoulder. Her eyes widened and her cream complexion paled as she whimpered.

"Snap out of it, Marge." I gave her a small push so I could step inside the office. "He'll get away if you fall for his tricks."

I gritted my teeth with a muttered curse at the empty office and the open adjoining doors on both the right and the left. He could have gone either way. I turned back to Marge, who stood with her arms wrapped around herself and trembled. Sweat beaded on her forehead and she gave shallow pants and stared at some point just past my shoulders. I didn't have time for this. With a sigh that overshadowed the gunfire below, I stepped forward and made a shallow cut on Marge's arm. She blinked and jerked her arm to her chest as she gave a small hiss and stepped back.

"Fuck," she muttered.

"Glad to see you're with me again." I flicked the tip of my blade toward the ground. "Thought I'd lost you to Cambione's dream world."

She glared as she stepped up beside me. "Aren't you supposed to be with your babysitter?"

"She's lousy at her job," I said. "Come on before we lose him."

"Fine. I'll double back to the stairs and make sure he doesn't get away." She rushed out the door and down the walkway.

"Works for me," I said to the empty air and headed through the left door. I dashed through two offices with their chairs and desks passing in a blur and burst through the door of the last one on the row. Cambione turned with his hand on the door leading to the walkway and he smirked at me. Cheeky bastard wouldn't be smug when I was through with him. I stepped forward and blinked as a violet light flashed before my eyes.

John reached toward me. "Gabby."

I shuddered. No this wasn't real. My arm dropped to my side and my sword hung loosely in my fingertips. The light brightened, and I stood in front of his bed in the hotel. He leaned back against the pillows and laughed up at me.

"Are you planning on killing me?" he asked.

I looked down at the sundang and furrowed my brows. Why did I have it out again?

He held his hand out. "Come here."

I took a step forward and stopped with the shake of my head. Something wasn't right here. John shouldn't be lying in bed with that sexy smile on his face. My heart twisted in my chest as tears burned my eyes. John had died and no tricks from the hellspawn responsible would change that. I took a step forward and slashed at the bed with a low growl. The vision shattered in a thousand sparks of violet. Cambione's eyes widened as his leer vanished.

"Your lies can't fool me," I said in a cold, soft voice.

He chuckled. "Actually, they've been fooling you since the beginning. You're just too blind to see it. Your precious John was a part of me long before I took his essence."

A chill crept up my spine. "What?"

Cambione took the opportunity my momentary confusion caused and lunged at me with a small knife aimed at my stomach. I batted it away with the back of my empty hand and it left a gash on the upper side right below my wrist. I spun and attempted to disembowel him with a swift slash. He ducked to the side and buried the knife in the back of my calf. A sharp burning sensation spread through my leg followed by numbness and I fell to my knees. Cambione rushed to the door with a loud laugh. It crashed open, slamming him in the face before he touched the handle. He fell back and hit the ground with a groan.

Marge loomed in the doorway, panting with her eyes wide and a twisted grin on her face. "You forgot about me, jackass."

She tramped forward and slammed her foot in his midsection. His breath left his body in a whoosh and he gripped his abdomen. With gritted teeth, I pulled the knife from my leg and rose to my feet. Marge pushed Cambione on his back and stomped down on his chest.

"That's for those stupid dreams," she yelled.

His breath wheezed as he laughed. "Even if you kill me, neither of you will be free."

"No," I said. "But it's so satisfying."

My sundang swung down on his neck and severed his head from his body. His eyes blazed violet brightly for an instant before the light vanished. I let out a long shuddering breath as my throat tightened and willed the ache in my chest to ease. This wasn't the time for tears. Besides, I didn't want to hear Marge's mouth on it. I wiped the blood from my sword, ripped a part of my shirt, and bandaged my leg. I limped down the stairs without another look at my fallen enemy.

"Are we clear?" I asked through the comms.

"Just taking care of the remainders," Lucy said. "Where the hell did you run off to?"

"To finish things," I said.

I hobbled to the table I'd come across during the chaos of battle. Many of the bottles and beakers had been shattered, their liquid running together in multicolored pools. A suitcase of plastic bags filled with yellow powder was sprawled across the floor with some of the plastic broken and powder spewing out.

Adrian walked up behind me. "I will handle this."

"Your way is better than fire I suppose." I said. "I leave this to your capable hands."

Lucy put an arm around me. "I'll drive you home."

I shook my head and pulled away. "I'll be fine. You should stay here with your family. They might need help."

I walked out of the doors and into the cold and wandered the night until I found myself at the frozen lake John had taken me to. With a sharp intake of breath, I eased down on the pier and gazed up at the stars. Cambione's words replayed in my head, filling my stomach with a queasy flutter. It had to be a lie. He'd wanted to throw me off my game so he could escape, like Faust managed to.

I pulled my good leg to my chest and wrapped my arms around my knee as the tears began to fall, leaving arctic trails down my cheeks. Vengeance wouldn't bring John back to me. He'd risked his life many times to help stop demons and had died for it in the end. I stared up at the twinkling lights in the vast blackness and gave a long sigh. Cambione was dead, brimstone had been stopped in both its forms, and fewer demons roamed the Earth. Those thoughts warmed the ice in my heart.

Faust leaned over, clutching the rail on the subway as the body he wore was caught in the throes of a hacking cough. He pressed his forehead against the window and breathed in a shuddering breath once it was over. He wanted to blame the human body he inhabited, but that would be a lie, and Faust knew about lies very well.

No, a piece of him was missing. Destroyed by that damn woman. It had been a substantial amount since Cambione had been working on collecting as much of Faust as he could. Now it was just gone. The hole it left in his essence burned and at the same time felt cold and empty.

He needed to get somewhere safe and recuperate. The Thrones were out of the question. His many enemies would jump on the chance to attack him while he was this vulnerable. He couldn't show Naamah his weakness, either. She would consider this a failure and might very well throw him to the others, or come up with a worse punishment. That left hiding in the mortal world. This body was suitable enough, but he sure as hell wasn't staying here with that demon slaying bitch and her group. Maybe somewhere warm, like the Caribbean.

The subway car came to a stop. Faust followed the herd out and climbed up the stairs to the airport. He got within a hundred feet and froze. Sweat beaded down his forehead and he swallowed hard. If he went any farther, that would be the end of him. He could feel the ward in every part of his being, keeping him trapped in this frozen wasteland. Someone didn't want the demons leaving this city.

Who, though? Gabriella? No, he should have had her twisted around enough that she wouldn't have thought of this. Besides, this wasn't her style of binding. It felt more . . . holy.

Faust cursed under his breath as he backed down the stairs to the subway. There were other options. Whoever this was couldn't have blocked every escape. He would find a way out of New York and rest before returning to give Gabriella a special reward.

The End

Ready for the next book in the Van Helsing Organization?
Purchase The Omega Effect now!

Thank you so much for taking this journey with Gabby and me. I cannot express how much I appreciate that you decided to pick this book up and read it! And now, you are reading this as well.

Brimstone, as I lovingly call this book, actually started out as what will be the third book, Omega Effect. When I finished the first draft, I found that I had created two main stories and I had to split them. So, A Dose of Brimstone was born. Of course, after I finished and published Brimstone, Ive taken a long break from the series. This year will be the year for the Van Helsing Organization. My goal is to have the entire series released by the end of the year.

In this book, Gabby lost another lover, but she was left with a lot of unanswered questions about John. Many of these questions will be answered in book three, The Omega Effect. Book three should be released in May of this year. So, be sure to keep an eye for it. You can actually do this via several ways.

The best way to keep up with news is by joining my newsletter, the Van Helsing Organization. When you join, you as will receive Midnight Magic for free. This is a collection of short stories, including Flower of Hell, which features Gabby's first hunt with Dimitri.

Sign up for my Newsletter.

You can join my reader group. This is also a great place to talk with other fans of the series. It's very small now, but I'm hoping it will grow like an avalanche.

Join Noree Cosper's Myth Maniacs.

If you enjoyed this book, please consider giving it a review. Your kind words and encouragement help motivate me to write more. Reviews and word of mouth is some of the best ways for other readers to find my work.

One again, I want to give special thanks to my husband Jayson. You are my rock. I also want to thank my Andrew, Chad, JD, Matt, and Jericho for the inspirations of the characters. Thanks to all of the fans of this book who have stuck with me over the years. I love you! I want to thank Rebecca Frank for her awesome job on my covers!

And finally, thank you to all my readers. Without you, I'd be nowhere.

Yours in books,
Noree Cosper

ABOUT THE AUTHOR

Noree Cosper is a USA Today bestselling author. She loves writing about magic in the modern world, and while growing up in Texas she constantly searched for mystical elements in the mundane.

She buried her nose in both fiction and books about Wicca, religion, and mythology every day becoming an adventure as she joined a group of role players acting out her fantasies of vampires, demons, and monsters living among us.

Noree grew but never left her love for fantasy and horror. Her dreams pushed her and her hand itched to write the visions she saw. So, with her fingers on the keys, she did what her heart had been telling her to do since childhood. She wrote.

Her first published novel, A Prescription for Possession, was awarded the B.R.A.G. Medallion from IndieBRAG as well as Reader's Choice Award for Horror from the Blogger Book Fair.

Noree lives with her husband and two adorable cats, Mab and Nyx.

Visit Noree Cosper's Website